PRETEND YOU LOVE ME

A NOVEL BY
JULIE ANNE PETERS

Megan Tingley Books
LITTLE, BROWN AND COMPANY
New York   Boston

ALSO BY JULIE ANNE PETERS:

Between Mom and Jo
Define "Normal"
grl2grl
Keeping You a Secret
Luna
She Loves You, She Loves You Not . . .

Copyright © 2005 by Julie Anne Peters
Questions for Discussion Copyright © 2007 by Little, Brown and Company

Little, Brown and Company

Hachette Book Group
237 Park Avenue, New York, NY 10017
Visit our website at www.lb-teens.com

Little, Brown and Company is a division of Hachette Book Group, Inc.
The Little, Brown name and logo are trademarks of Hachette Book Group, Inc.

The publisher is not responsible for websites (or their content) that are not owned by the publisher.

First Paperback Edition: April 2007
Originally published in hardcover by Little, Brown and Company as *Far from Xanadu*.

The characters and events portrayed in this book are fictitious. Any similarity to real persons, living or dead, is coincidental and not intended by the author.

Library of Congress Cataloging-in-Publication Data

Peters, Julie Anne.
  [Far from Xanadu]
  Pretend you love me / Julie Anne Peters.
    p. cm.
  Previously published in 2005 under title: Far from Xanadu.
  Summary: In a small Kansas town, sixteen-year-old Mary-Elizabeth "Mike" Szabo tries to come to terms with her father's suicide and her own homosexuality.
  ISBN 978-0-316-12741-7 (pbk.)
  [1. Self-perception — Fiction. 2. Family problems — Fiction. 3. Lesbians — Fiction. 4. Homosexuality — Fiction. 5. Interpersonal relations — Fiction. 6. Grief — Fiction. 7. Suicide — Fiction. 8. Kansas — Fiction.] I. Title.
  PZ7.P44158Pr 2011
  [Fic]—dc22

                                                                 2011009254

ISBN 978-0-316-12741-7

10 9 8 7 6 5 4 3 2

RRD-C

Printed in the United States of America

A long overdue acknowledgment of support, encouragement, and love to Wendy Schmalz. The kind of literary agent a writer only dreams of.

Chapter One

After my dad's suicide, the town council decided to remove the bottom portion of the ladder from the Coalton water tower. Like that was going to keep me down. We pooled our savings, me and Jamie, and bought a thirty-two-foot extension ladder at Hank's Hardware. In the long prairie grass around the tower, we could keep it hidden so no one would ever know.

Who were we kidding? This was Coalton. Everyone knew everything.

The sky was already pinking up and I was going to miss the whole show if I didn't hurry. I dragged the extension over and clanged it against the remaining rungs, then clambered up to the landing. The sun was peeking over the horizon as the gate screeked open to the walkaround. It was chilly. I could see my breath. I'd pulled a pair of Dad's sweats on over my boxers, but now wished I'd dug out a flannel shirt from the laundry. His ribbed undershirt was flimsy.

I sat on the metal platform and dangled my feet over the rim. Resting my forehead against the railing, I thought, Oh man. The colors —

rose and amber, indigo, orange-streaked clouds. Dad said angels painted the sky at dawn and dusk. Dad was a liar, but I could almost believe him on that one. The magnificence, the majesty, the sheer magnitude of sky was beyond human dimension. Beyond understanding, expression. It was bigger than life. Bigger than death.

Only one thing could be better than a sunrise in Coalton — sharing it with the person you loved.

Someday . . .

Someday . . .

When I got home the house was quiet. Good. They were both still in bed. Maybe I could get out of here without an encounter of the ugly kind.

I changed into a clean muscle tee, but decided to wear the boxers to school. They looked cool. I threw on a hooded sweatshirt, since it'd be late by the time I got home tonight. "Morning, morning, morning." I performed my morning ritual — finger kissing all my nudie posters: Evangelina, Beemer Babe, the Maserati girl.

Down the dim hallway I heard Ma's radio click on full blast to a morning call-in show. I hustled to the kitchen to make a power shake and bail.

Two raw eggs, a scoopful of protein powder, water from the tap. I covered my plastic glass with a palm and shook it. As I swigged down the chalky goop, I lifted a shock absorber off the top of Darryl's stack of car zines and did a set of curls. My upper arm strength wasn't where it should be. The game with Deighton yesterday I underthrew to second and T.C. had to dig the ball out of the dirt. Inexcusable. I made a mental note to add another set of tricep extensions to my circuit. Another rep of lat pulls.

In my reflection off the grimy back door, I flexed. The sleeve of my sweatshirt bulged. Nice definition, if I did say so myself.

Darryl slimed into a chair at the dinette. On his way he'd snagged a can of Dinty Moore beef stew off the counter and popped the pull top, managing to slop half of it down his bare chest. Disgusting. I didn't claim him as a brother.

"I'm taking the truck today," I said.

"Fuck you are." He slurped right out of the can.

I considered crushing his skull with the shock absorber. Then figured his thick head might actually absorb the shock. "I need it for work. Everett wants me to run a load of feed up to the Tillson ranch near Ladder Creek."

"Use the Merc's flatbed." Darryl swiped the back of his hand across his mouth.

"Everett needs it for hauling portable stalls."

"Tough titties. Last time you made a delivery the inside of the truck reeked of sheep shit for a week."

"This is only grain. Milo and horse feed."

"No," Darryl said. He picked up his pack of Marlboros off the table and shook one out. "I need wheels today."

"For what? So you can joyride all over the county and take potshots at prairie dogs?"

"You been touching base with my secretary again?" Darryl smirked. He lit up a smoke.

The café doors to the kitchen crashed open and Darryl and I jumped.

Ma thundered into the room. She nearly wrenched off the loose handle as she yanked open the refrigerator. The door wouldn't swing all the way with her between it and the counter. I noticed she had on the same outfit she'd worn all week — a sleeveless gray shift that clung to her breasts and belly. Argyle knee socks bunched at the ankles. Her hair hadn't been combed or washed in, like, a month. She smelled worse than she looked.

"No milk," she stated flatly, releasing the handle so the door shut on its own.

"I'll go get you some," Darryl and I said together. Our eyes met briefly. He added, "I'm heading over to the Suprette, anyway. I got a job interview there this morning."

"What!" I screeched.

They both twisted their heads at the echo in the room. Did Ma focus? Did she actually see me? The momentary flicker of recognition died as she snatched a bag of powdered donuts off the top of the fridge and trundled back to her bedroom.

Ugliness, I thought. Too much ugliness in my life.

"I'll drop you at school if you want," Darryl said, sucking on his Marlboro.

I glared at him. "You're looking for a job? What about the job you've got?"

He exhaled smoke through his nose.

"*My* job. The one you stole from me." The one I'd be doing now if I didn't have to haul sheep shit in the truck.

"Mike, I keep telling you. It's not my fault —"

I slammed out the back door, seething to myself. Hating him. Hating both of them for crapping out my day.

<hr>

Coalton High was my refuge. Not that I loved school or anything; it was just a place to go. I took the back way, through the Ledbetters' woodpile and behind the propane tanks at the Co-op. It was still only six blocks. I hit the front door as the warning bell rang for first hour.

Mrs. Stargell glanced up from roll call as I sauntered in. "Mike," she said.

"Miz S," I replied.

"Glad you could join us."

"It was on my way."

She stifled a grin, unsuccessfully.

Ida Stargell had to be a hundred years old, easy. She'd been teaching at Coalton High since the Jurassic Period. No kidding. Dad said he'd had her in high school for English, Math, and Biology — the only three A's he'd ever gotten. I was trying to beat his record by taking her for Lit and Bio in tenth grade last year, then Creative Writing and Geometry this year.

Geometry class was crammed. At Coalton High that meant fourteen seats were filled. Well, two desks were empty today. Shawnee Miller had been rushed to the hospital in Garden City on Tuesday after her appendix burst in gym. And Bailey McCall was out helping with the spring calving. So, twelve seats full. I should get an A in math for that calculation alone.

I liked Mrs. Stargell. Everybody did. Not only for her generosity in grading; she cared about us. Too much sometimes. If you were out sick for more than a day, she'd call or stop by your house in the evening. Two years ago she was stopping by to see me and Darryl a lot. She'd bring us casseroles and Jell-O molds, which Ma snarfed down like a sow in heat.

Miz S began writing a theorem on the board when a figure filled the open doorway. The pencil I'd been gnawing on clattered to the floor. This . . . this girl appeared. She was the most beautiful creature in the world.

She stood beside the metal cart of textbooks inside the door, eyes darting around the room. People stared. No one spoke. Who could? She pursed her lips and tapped her foot as Mrs. Stargell continued to write.

"Um, hello?" the girl finally said. She had this low, sultry voice.

Miz S flinched. "Oh. I didn't see you there. Come in."

The girl pranced across the room and handed Mrs. Stargell a slip of paper. Then she headed down the aisle toward me.

Toward me!

I scrambled to stand and offer her my seat, but she slid into Bailey McCall's desk in front of me. She sat up straight.

"Class, we have a new student," Miz S announced. "I'd like you to welcome . . ." She glanced at the sheet of paper in her hands. Squinting, she removed her bifocals and let them dangle between her boobs on her neck chain. "Is it . . . Xanadu?"

"Wonders never cease," the girl said under her breath. "She can read."

Her long, dark hair flipped over the back of the seat and onto my desk. I had the strongest urge to touch it, stroke it. The color was . . . otherworldly. Like roasted mahogany. Like Cherry Coke.

Miz S said, "Come up here and introduce yourself."

The girl — Xanadu? — swiveled in her seat to face me and said, "Didn't she just do that?" Loud enough for the three or four people around us to hear. No one reacted.

I might've smiled. I was still speechless.

"Come on. Don't be shy," Miz S urged.

The girl ignored her. "Is she serious?" Blinking at me. She had these huge, expressive eyes.

"'Fraid so," I managed to croak. And shiny white skin, like porcelain china cups. Her eyes were an unusual color, gray-blue, rimmed with lots of eyeliner and eye shadow. That gorgeous brownish-maroonish hair.

Mrs. Stargell set her piece of chalk in the blackboard tray and brushed her fingers on her flowered dress. "Xanadu, please. Come up here. We won't bite."

She should speak for herself, I thought.

"Shit," Xanadu hissed. Even that didn't evoke a response from the people around us. They just gawked at her. She stood noisily and clomped up the aisle. She was tall, taller than me. Which was no genetic feat, considering I'm probably the shortest person in school. But she was statuesque. At least five ten. A faint scent of perfume settled around Bailey's desk. What was that fragrance? The junk Jamie slathered on after getting stoned? I floated in her fumes.

"Tell us a little bit about yourself," Miz S said, snaking an arm around Xanadu's waist. Xanadu, aka the goddess, had on tight low-rider jeans with a form-fitting, see-through, black lace top. So fine. So very, very fine.

"Like what?" She crossed her arms in front of her, looking embarrassed, self-conscious. Her top rode up a little and my eyes fixed on her belly-button ring.

"Xanadu. That's an interesting name." Miz S's eyes glazed over. She peered off into the middle distance and cleared her throat.

Uh-oh, I thought. Here it comes.

"In Xanadu did Kubla Khan
A stately pleasure-dome decree:
Where Alph, the sacred river, ran
Through caverns measureless to man
Down to a sunless sea."

Miz S paused. "I forget the rest. Do you know it?" she asked Xanadu.

"Know what?" Xanadu said flatly.

Miz S opened her mouth, then shut it. She asked, "Were your parents great lovers of Samuel Taylor Coleridge?"

Xanadu stared into Mrs. Stargell's wrinkly face. "Nooo," she drew out the word, "my 'rents were lovers of float. They were meth-heads, obviously amped up on jack when they had me."

During the stunned silence even the dust motes fainted over dead. Xanadu's gaze cruised around the room at all the bulging eyeballs. Was I the only one who saw it? The slight sucking in of her lips? The teasing eyes? I burst into laughter.

Her eyes met mine and she cracked a smile.

The shock on Mrs. Stargell's face didn't help me sober up. She withdrew her hand from Xanadu's waist like human contact with this foreign body might be hazardous to one's health.

No one else was laughing. Why not? They had to have figured it out by now.

"Thank you, Xanadu." Mrs. Stargell's voice chilled. "You may return to your seat."

Xanadu clomped back to Bailey's desk. Flopping down with a huff, she swiveled around again and said, "Is she for real? God help us."

I figured God was doing His part for me today.

After class, as I was exchanging my math book for my cleats, that same dusky perfume bit my nose. I wheeled around.

"Hi," she said, hugging her books to her chest. Her very fine chest. "I just made that up about my parents, like on the spur of the moment. Can you believe it? I freak under pressure. My parents are so totally straight; they'd die if people thought they were meth-heads. God. I can't believe I actually said that out loud. Can you?"

"No," I admitted.

She smiled. My insides melted.

"Apparently no one else got that I was just blowing her off. Nobody even laughed."

A couple of people passed us in the hall and glanced back over their shoulders, checking her out. I couldn't blame them. We'd never experienced anything like Xanadu at Coalton High.

"I wasn't serious," she said. "Did people think I was serious?" She peered after them, curling a lip.

"No," I said. "They knew. We're not as dumb as we look."

Her eyes swept the floor. "I didn't mean that."

My face burned. "No. Me neither. I knew you knew." Had I offended her? Hurt her feelings?

She raised her eyes to mine and we melded together. I could feel it. Her chest heaved and she expelled an audible sigh. "God." She lowered her chin to her chest. "I am so lost here. So out of my realm."

I'll help you find your realm, I thought. I'll ride you to the castle on a tall white steed and slay every dragon in your path.

"I guess you know my name." She tilted her head up and crossed her eyes at me. "I'm sure the whole school does by now. What's yours?"

"Mike." I cleared my windpipe.

"Mike." She bumped my shoulder with hers. Coy. Flirty. God, give me strength. It was suddenly a hundred and ten degrees in here.

"'Scuse me," I stammered. Setting my cleats back on the shelf, I pulled my sweatshirt over my head and hung it on the hook in my locker. When I turned back, she was staring at me. And not at my face.

"Sorry," she said, her jaw slack. "I . . . I thought you were a guy."

"Yeah." I tried to smile, but the smile twisted, like my stomach. "I, uh, get that a lot."

Chapter Two

I stood at the pulldown station, balancing the handlebar at crotch height, studying myself in the wall-to-wall mirrors. Mike Szabo, I thought, you are one ugly girl. If I had to be born a girl, why couldn't I at least have been a regular girl? Attracted to guys, like every other girl in the world?

"It's all yours, Mike." Armie sat up, straddling the flat bench. He swabbed his dripping neck and chest with a towel, then caught his own reflection in the mirror and sucked in his gut. The hair on his back was all matted with sweat — gag — and the bench was slimy now. Darryl accused me once of wanting to be a guy. He was wrong. Guys physically repulsed me. Maybe when I was younger I wished I was a guy, but I got over it.

Armie said, "Is the bench press next on your circuit?"

"Yeah."

He bunched the towel around his neck and crouched to replace the plates. "How much you lifting?"

"Eighty," I told him.

"With reps?" He whistled. "That's about your limit, I'd say."

So he thought. I hadn't reached my limit.

"Baby, the sky's the limit," Dad's voice sounded in my head.

Shut up. Is that what you were reaching for when you jumped?

"I'm only loading sixty for you," Armie said.

Damn him. I lay prone on the bench, my knees bent, feet flat on the floor. My fingers curled over the dumbbell, caressing it. I loved the smooth feel of the metal, the cool slickness in my palms. I spread my hands apart, deltoid distance, the bar directly over my chest. Armie fastened the second collar and stood. "I'll spot you," he said.

"Not necessary." I could press sixty in my sleep.

He spotted me anyway.

I concentrated. Converted the solid steel plates into bone and muscle. Mine. I closed my eyes and pictured her, Xanadu. She hadn't run from me, exactly. More like took off fast when she figured me out.

Up and off the rack. Damn, she was beautiful.

Inhale. Down. I wanted her.

Exhale. Up. She'd never be mine.

Inhale. Down. Why not?

"Slower," Armie said. "Make each rep count."

Focus. Concentrate. Exhale. Up, up, and hold. If I believed it, I could have it.

Dad again. "Believe it, baby. Believe it and it's yours."

Stop it. Down. Stop talking to me. My muscles contracted, quivered. Block it out, Mike. You're strong. Feel the power. Let it grow, radiate. Exhale. Up, up, and up.

"Anything is possible."

Shut up, Dad.

"Anything."

You're a liar. Remember?

Armie reracked me.

"Hey —" I was on the verge of my adrenaline high.

"You're shaking," Armie said. "Take a break." The phone rang and Armie headed toward the office. Over his shoulder, he added, "Do some curls."

I waited until he was out of view and pressed another set. I needed my high.

As I was toweling off the bench for the next person, Armie reappeared. Swinging a clump of keys on a shoestring around and around his wrist, he looked at me and shook his head.

"What?"

"You're the best advertisement I got for this place," he said.

I exaggerated a smile. He was right about that. I struck a pose like Mr. Universe, which made Armie laugh. He ruffled my hair and headed over to the Nautilus.

After Armie blew out his knee playing football at K State, he found his way back to Coalton. Guys like him always did. Townies. People with deep roots. His family had been here longer than mine, lucky for me. Lucky for all us jocks. Armie'd bought up the old VFW building at the end of Main and remodeled it into a weight room on one side and tanning salon on the other. The gym was totally equipped: a multi-station machine, Nautilus, flat and incline benches, squat rack, barbells, dumbbells, a treadmill, couple of stationary bikes. He called it Armie's Hut. It'd always be the VFW to us. When you're used to something, it's hard to change your way of thinking.

Dad and Armie were old drinking buddies from way back. Dad had bailed Armie out of the drunk tank more than once, so I guess Armie felt indebted when he'd offered to waive my membership fee. I told him forget it. I'd pay my way.

I took a quick shower, then poked my head into the salon, thinking I'd catch Jamie in the tanning bed. It was open and empty. Renata Pastore, Armie's live-in girlfriend, was cleaning out the spigot on the espresso machine. "Hey, Renata," I called to her.

She whirled around. "Oh hey, Mike." She smiled, her head tilting at an odd angle. I knew what was coming. "How's your Ma?"

"Doin' good," I lied. "You seen Jamie?"

"Not yet. That cheerleader jamboree was today."

It should've been over by now. That was the reason I was here instead of softball practice. The visiting squads were hogging the field.

"We're sure having a gorgeous spring, aren't we?" Renata said, rinsing out her dishrag. "It's warm for April, though. Bet we're in for a long, hot summer."

"Probably." When wasn't it long and hot in Coalton?

Renata had on a tie-dyed psychedelic skirt with an embroidered peasant blouse. Jamie called her a throwback to the sixties. Renata's sister, Deb, who was in my class, was sort of retro too, except I think it wasn't by choice. She mostly wore Renata's hand-me-downs. My eyes strayed to the watch on my wrist — Dad's old Timex. Crap. If I didn't haul ass, I was going to be late for work.

Thompson's Feed, Seed, and Mercantile was a historic landmark in Wallace County. A couple of years ago lightning had struck the original structure and burned it to the ground. Everett Thompson, the proprietor (as he liked to call himself), managed to salvage one charred beam, which he extended vertically from the roof with the new Mercantile sign. You couldn't miss it from the highway, not after he attached the rotating pig on top.

The pig lit up at night. You could see it clear from Goodland. The town council had been after Everett for years to take down that beam with the turning pig. Coalton was more than a pig on a spit.

Everett met me at the open barn door in back. "Mike, where ya been?" He didn't give me a chance to answer. "I need you to take this order up to the Davenport place. You know where it is?"

"Out by the main power line past Blaylock's Dairy."

Everett nodded as he rubbernecked around me into the gravel parking lot.

"Darryl needed the truck." I answered his unspoken question. Fire me, I prayed. Fire me. Set me free. Give me an excuse to kick Darryl's ass for losing the family business.

Out the side of his mouth, Everett spit a stream of chew. "Think you can handle the flatbed? I gotta stick around here for an order of well pumps and troughs coming in from Dallas."

"Sure, no problem." Okay, that'd be fun. I'd ridden along with Everett's son, Junior, enough times on delivery runs to see how all the gears worked. If June could drive the flatbed, there was no reason I couldn't.

"Here's the order." From his apron pocket, Everett pulled out a crumpled piece of paper and handed it to me.

I scanned the list. A pallet of horse feed, bottle of dewormer, two bags of dog chow. Everett's handwriting was all spidery from his Parkinson's.

"Faye specifically wants the Profile Horse Feed and not the Purina. She says Purina gives her mares the bloats."

"Got it." I started for the feed aisle.

"If you need help loading the truck —"

"Got it," I said over my shoulder, flexing my biceps.

Everett chuckled and shuffled off. He was a good guy, but I still hated this job. I never thought I'd be working at the Merc. Never thought I'd need a job. I had a job. A career. A purpose in life. But that was gone now. All of it. Thanks, Dad. You knew Darryl couldn't be trusted.

The keys to the flatbed were in the ignition. I backed up to the rear of the Merc, maneuvering as close as I could to the pallets of feed. At least it's physical labor, I thought as I tossed up the first bag of Profile. And I got to work outside, stocking feed and garden supplies. It wasn't what I loved to do; wasn't what I thought I'd be doing the rest of my life. It wasn't what I was born to. If I had to work, though, this job was better than the Dairy Delite or the Suprette, where most people ended up. I could never work at the Dairy Delite. Couldn't bring myself to wear that candy striper shirt with the cow on the breast pocket. Jamie loved it, but that was Jamie.

My muscle tee was soaked clear through by the time I finished loading the flatbed. I would've liked to stop by home and change — make myself more presentable — but it was getting on to dusk already and I'd only sweat out again unloading at the Davenports'.

The Davenports'. I hadn't been out there since the summer before sixth grade. Dad and I had been contracted to plumb their new barn — install a toilet and utility sink, an outdoor shower for cleanup. That was before Mr. Davenport — Leland — fell off the roof and broke his back. I remember Ma had baked a rhubarb pie for me to take to Faye. Wow, that was a long lost memory. Back when Ma was a functioning, productive human being.

The dogs met me at the gate. Bean and Howdy. They were looking older, grayer. Bean was hobbling around like he had arthritis.

"Hey, guys," I greeted them from the cab. "Stay back." I inched up the gravel entrance to the farmhouse. The Davenports probably owned the majority of sections south of town, but since they were getting up in years, they leased the land to commercial farmers. Most everyone around Coalton grew wheat or milo for feed. Farther east were the stink holes, the cattle lots, and pig farms.

I jumped down from the cab. The dogs sniffed my crotch.

"Bean, Howdy, get down," Faye hollered from the house. The screen door slammed behind her. "Hello, Mike." She clip-clopped down the porch steps in her rubber clogs. There was this painting from ninth grade Art Appreciation called *American Gothic*. That's what Faye and Leland Davenport reminded me of, those two stoic farmers. Except more human.

"How nice to see you again." Faye wiped her hands on her apron, then gave me a hug. "How's your mother?"

"Doin' good," I lied.

"Leland's down at the horse pens, if you want to take that feed around." Faye pointed past the big barn. I shielded my eyes at the sun glinting off the metal roof. For some reason, my focus fell to the hammock in Faye's yard, strung between two cottonwoods. Specifically, the person in it who was sleeping with a pair of earphones on.

My heart shattered my rib cage. The sound of cracking bone must've carried because her eyes opened and she swiveled her head around.

Xanadu struggled to sit up. She clawed off the earphones, swung her legs over the hammock, and smiled. At me. Or was that my imagination running wild? Because it was running wild all over the place.

Slipping into sandals, she floated across the greening lawn. She was wearing shorts. Short shorts almost invisible under an oversized tee. Which my X-ray vision might've been trying to see through because it was obvious she wasn't wearing a bra. A twinge of electricity surged between my legs.

When she got to where I was, she shoved her CD player under the waistband of her shorts and said, "Hi, Mike. Wow, I'm glad you're here. I was just about to die of terminal boredom. Let's see if I did." She slapped her cheek. "Not yet. I still have feeling on one side." She grinned. I laughed. My heart pounded like a well drill.

Without her clunky shoes, she wasn't that much taller than me. Four, five inches.

"I see you've met my grandniece," Faye said.

"Uh, yes, ma'am. I've had the pleasure."

Xanadu snorted. "What are you doing out here in the boonies?" She crossed her arms loosely over her chest. Maybe because my eyes were glued to it. "Besides rescuing me?" she added.

I looked from her to Faye. Faye smiled thinly. "I'm delivering your order from the Merc," I said. "Well, not *your* order." My mouth was dry as chicken scratch. Xanadu was still grinning at me. It was making me light-headed. Get a grip, Mike. I stumbled to the rear of the flatbed to retrieve Faye's dog food.

"Why don't you ride out with Mike and give her a hand unloading?" I heard Faye say.

I peered around the truck. Xanadu curled a lip at Faye, like, Are you serious?

Hefting a bag of dog chow onto my shoulder, I said, "That's okay. I can handle it." I headed toward the house. "Where do you want this, Miz Davenport?"

"Just inside the door'll be fine," she answered. "Thank you, Mike."

I opened the screen and dumped the bags on the floor next to the dog bowls. The house still smelled of meatloaf and baked potato from dinner. My mouth watered. I couldn't have come an hour earlier and been invited, could I? I hadn't eaten since my PowerBar on the way to Armie's.

Xanadu was leaning against the truck hood, fiddling with her CD player, when I got back. She and Faye had obviously had words. Faye did not look happy. "It'll be easiest to go back to the road and come in behind the horse corrals," Faye told me.

"Okay." I climbed into the cab. The passenger door squeaked open and Xanadu hoisted herself up onto the cracked leather seat. "I'll ride along, at least, to keep you company."

Be still my heart, I thought.

She added under her breath, "Maybe you could drop me off in Siberia. It can't be that far from here."

Faye must've heard because she scorched Xanadu with a look. "This *is* your Siberia, Missy," she snarled. "It may be your last stop anywhere."

Xanadu's eyes slit and shot a firebolt. Faye matched her glare with equal heat.

Holy shit. I booked it out of there before the truck burst into flames.

Chapter Three

As I circled back onto the road, Xanadu cranked down her window. The wind caught her hair, blowing up streams of red ribbons around her face. She was breathtaking. I almost drove into a ditch. At the last minute, I swerved to the center of the straightaway, hoping she hadn't noticed my temporary lapse of control.

"How can you stand it?" She turned to face me.

I knew what she meant. The silence. The slowness of life. "You get used to it," I said.

She averted her eyes to gaze out on the wheat fields. "I'd kill myself first."

My breath caught. She didn't know what she was saying. It was just an expression. We reached the turnoff at the back of the property and I pulled onto it, lungs screaming for relief. I calmed myself, tried to. Let out air.

Driving between two corrals, I stopped next to a double-wide horse trailer and saw Leland Davenport wander out of the covered stalls. He removed his Stetson and swiped his gritty face with a forearm.

"Hi there, Mike. Oh good, you brought the feed." He slid his hat back on. "I heard you were working at the Merc. Why don't you back her up to the gate here, if you can get in close." There was a feed bin behind him, alongside a cone-shaped storage shed.

I cranked the flatbed ninety degrees and let Leland direct me in, even though it wasn't necessary. I could've done it. When he began to unload the feed, I jumped out and said, "Know what? I can get this. It's what I get paid for."

He eyed the pallet, then scanned me up and down. I knew what he was thinking: You're too small; it's too much for one person. He hadn't seen me in action. I yanked out the work gloves from my back pocket and put them on. I might've nudged him gently out of my way.

"Hi, Uncle Lee." Xanadu appeared at my side. Her bare arm grazed mine and spiked my heart rate.

Leland reached over and gave her a tweak on the nose. I launched myself onto the truck bed, wondering if the tingling under my skin was a permanent condition. I hoped so. They both watched me heft one bag off the pallet and onto my shoulder, then jump down and lug it into the storage shed. Xanadu said, "Okay, major guilt trip. I can help with this."

Leland cuffed her chin and headed back into the stalls.

Xanadu said, "Why don't you hand the bags to me and I'll stack them in the garage, or whatever it's called."

I smiled to myself. This should be good. Looping a leg up onto the flatbed, I scrambled back onboard. I lifted a bag of feed off the pallet and passed it down to her. She caught it between her arms and proceeded to collapse in the dirt.

It was hard suppressing laughter, but I managed, sort of.

"Jesus." She staggered away from the bag, straightening up. "How much do these things weigh?"

"Fifty pounds," I told her.

She arched her eyebrows. "They didn't look that heavy when you were doing it."

"I have a better idea." I leaped off the truck. "You slide them to the edge and I'll haul them in."

"Help me up." She extended a hand.

I grasped it. Long, slender fingers. That electric charge surged through me again. Xanadu clambered onto the bed and stood for a moment, surveying the pallet. "I can do this," she said, sounding determined. She tucked her hair into the back of her shirt and got to work.

We finished the job in fifteen or twenty minutes. By then Xanadu was looking withered and I was soaked with sweat. She sank to the end of the truck bed and slumped forward. I hopped up next to her.

Why'd I do that? I had to reek. Wiping the rivulet of sweat running down my ear with the bottom of my muscle shirt, I snuck a sniff under my pit. Whoa. Kill a moose.

"You're strong."

I turned. She was eyeing me, my arms. "You must work out."

"A little. At the gym." A little? I was obsessed. Now I knew why. Unconsciously — or consciously — I flexed my bicep.

"There's a gym in this podunk town?"

"At the VFW, next to the tanning salon."

"Tanning salon? What is it, like a chaise lounge under a lightbulb?" I smiled.

She closed her eyes. "I'm sorry. I didn't mean that. I'm just —" She expelled a long breath.

"It's a real tanning salon," I told her. "Well, there's only the one tanning bed and my friend Jamie's usually in it. But I can get you in for free." Why'd I say that? It'd be taking advantage of Armie. Taking him up on his offer.

"That's okay," Xanadu said. "I'm not into melanoma."

That was the truth. Her skin was white as summer clouds.

"What's your real name?" she asked.

I felt as if someone had sucker-punched me. Why'd she have to ask? I didn't want to say. I hated my name. On my eighteenth birthday, I was legally changing it.

"Come on." She pressed against me with her shoulder. "I won't tell."

She had to know how funny *that* was. This was Coalton. Her elbow nudged mine and stayed touching. Why was she always touching me? Not that I didn't like it; she was driving me crazy. I exhaled a long breath. "Mary-Elizabeth," I mumbled. "If you ever call me that, I'll kill you." The moment I said it, I wished I could take it back. I'd never hurt her.

She laughed. "You should have *my* name. Xanadu. How stupid. Call me Xana, by the way."

No, I didn't think I would. She was Xanadu. Exotic, enchanted, poetic.

"God," she went on. "I wish my parents *were* crackheads or something; at least I'd have an excuse why they did this to me. To me and my sister both. Know what her name is?"

I shook my head.

"Babylon."

Did I snort?

"Yeah." She grinned. "So Mary-Elizabeth is, like, ordinary, normal."

Not to me. "I just don't like it," I said. "It isn't me."

She met my eyes and nodded. "I get that. I so get that." She held my attention. Vibes passed between us. Something. Intense. We both looked down. I saw her eyes skim my bicep, my forearm, settle on my hand. My filthy work glove. I pulled it off, along with the other, and stuffed them both in my back pocket. Xanadu's gaze gravitated to my Timex. "Seven thirty-eight," she said. "Let's see, I've only been here three days, four hours, and thirty-eight minutes, and already I regret my decision to come."

My heart sank. I wanted her here. I needed her here.

Looking off into the wheat fields, she added, "I just needed to get my head straight, you know? See if being away for a while would make things better. I was going to blow off the rest of the school year, but it's so freaking boring out here, I figured I might as well go. Hook up with some people, maybe. I don't know."

Hook up with me, I thought.

"You're probably wondering why I'm here, right?" She spread her hands out beside her and clutched the edge of the truck bed. She had delicate hands, girl hands.

"Right," I said. I didn't really care why. Just stay.

"My parents gave me an ultimatum. I could either exile myself at Aunt Faye and Uncle Lee's in Kansas or enter this diversion program in Englewood. I've known a couple of people who did the program and they say it's like a prison. Worse than a prison. You can't leave your house at night or call your friends. I mean, what choice did I have?" She reached behind her with one hand and lifted her hair out of her shirt, letting it cascade over her shoulders.

I had no idea what she was talking about. But I wanted her to keep talking, keep playing with her hair. "Where's Englewood?" I asked.

She blinked at me. "Denver. The suburbs. I mean, I understand where my parents are coming from. I was definitely headed for trouble. It wasn't my fault, though, or even my choice. Okay, maybe it was my choice." She glanced away. "*And* my fault. What choice do you have, though, when everyone does it? E, I mean. Or worse. And if they're not doing drugs, they're getting stoned. I hate smoking pot; it makes me sleepy and gives me a headache. Does it do that to you?"

I was so enthralled in watching her body language, the way her lips moved, her eyebrows danced, her eyes expressed every word, that I'd tuned out the content. I suddenly noticed the quiet, her staring at me. "Huh?" I said.

"Oh, never mind." She shook her head. "You're so removed from the real world, you've probably never even gotten stoned."

"Yeah, I have," I said. "Once. With Jamie." Once was enough.

"Who's she?" Xanadu asked. She wiggled her eyebrows. "Your girl-friend?"

I choked. "Not hardly."

Xanadu leaned back, propping herself on her elbows. She raised one leg, the one closest to me, and bent it so that her knee was eye level with my face. Her legs were unbelievably long. And smooth. She must shave, I thought. Well, duh. Most girls shaved. Femme girls.

"The ecstasy was bad. I admit that. But everybody does it. That or dust. But dust'll mess you. You don't want to do dust. You have to do E, though. I didn't think it was dangerous or anything. Not until . . ." Her voice changed. "Until . . ."

I twisted my head around to look at her.

She swallowed hard and met my eyes. "Until Tiffany died."

"What?" I shot up straight and whirled on my butt. "Someone died?"

"God." Xanadu's head lolled back. She closed her eyes and released a thin, shallow breath.

"What happened?" I asked.

Through the globs of mascara, a tear glistened on her eyelashes. She hunched forward in a ball, clutching both knees to her chest and rocking a little. "I didn't know her that well," she said. "Tiffany. She was a senior. It was her birthday party at her house, her eighteenth birthday. Her parents weren't even there. Okay, that doesn't matter. Even if there are adults around, someone always manages to sneak in a bag of E and sell it. Maybe it was a bad batch or something. I don't know. Tiffany took too many. Who knows? She just passed out in the bathroom and everyone was too scared to call 911. Someone should have called, you know? They waited an hour. A whole fucking hour." Xanadu exhaled a long breath. "By the time the paramedics arrived, she was already in a coma."

I was trying to absorb all this. Tiffany, ecstasy, coma.

"I can't believe she died." Resting her cheek on her kneecap, Xanadu picked up a chunk of horse chow and flung it off the side. "None of us could. I mean, God. I've never known anyone who died. Have you?"

My stomach clenched.

"You have?" She lifted her head and looked at me, through me.

"A couple of people," I said.

"It's freaky, isn't it? It makes you realize, you could be next. That it could happen anytime, anywhere. Without warning."

No warning.

"Mom and Dad got all I-don't-know-you-anymore, how-could-you-do-this-to-us?" Xanadu mocked in a sing-songy voice. "I don't know how they even found out I was at the party. Or who told them I was doing E. Mom went ballistic, of course. She was ready to turn me over to the authorities and, like, have them put me in lockdown. Whatever." Xanadu released her legs and stretched them out in front of her. "She always overreacts. Is your mom like that?"

I let out a laugh.

"What?"

"Nothing." I hunched forward.

"Come on. I just revealed my whole life to you."

She was right. I never talked about my stuff. Who cared? "I'd be happy if my mom *could* react," I muttered.

Xanadu's eyes widened. "What do you mean?"

Why'd I say that? I couldn't do this. Not yet. "Forget it." My eyes raked the ground and I twisted away from her.

Xanadu said, "I'm sorry. I talk too much."

In my peripheral vision, I saw her gaze out across the fields into the deepening sky.

"No," I said. "It's just, I don't want to go there. I'm sorry."

She nodded. "That's fine. You don't have to. You don't even know me; why should you trust me? It's strange, but I already trust you. It usually takes me a long time with new people. There's something about you, though. You're so . . . open."

Me? I wished I could be. I wanted to be. She trusted me. I felt honored.

We watched the sky together. After a minute Xanadu said, "They were right. Mom and Dad. I was on the road to ruin, in Dad's words. With the drugs, though, yeah. I mean, I didn't do that much, but my grades were shitty and I was ditching a lot. I was in trouble already. Then . . . Tiffany." Xanadu blinked to me. "I'm sorry. I keep telling you all this."

"It's okay. It's good." Get it out, I thought. "So you came here," I said.

"Yeah. Like I had a choice." She let out a bitter-sounding laugh and nudged me again with her elbow. "I definitely needed a change of scenery. I wasn't exactly prepared for *this*." She swept her arm out to the side, as if indicating the entire planet. Another planet, which, I suppose, Coalton had to seem to her.

Leland trudged out of the barn, humped over, obviously in pain. "You two still here?" He arched his back and grabbed his spine.

"We finished the unloading," I told him, in case he thought I was slacking off.

He eyed the storage shed, the neatly stacked bags of feed. "Nice job. Thanks." He smiled at me, at Xanadu. His eyes warmed to her. "Well, I'm all done in, girls." He smacked his dusty hat against his leg. "Headin' back to the house. You coming, Xana?"

She ran a fingernail over a freckle on her leg. She had exactly fourteen freckles, that I could count. "I'll get a ride back with Mike, if that's okay."

Please let it be okay, I prayed.

"Fine by me," Leland said. "Stop by the house on your way, Mike, so the missus can write Everett a check."

"Will do."

He puttered off in his boat-sized Buick. The hearse, Jamie called it. A cloud of dust billowed across the road in his wake. "I can't believe I'm doing this," Xanadu said. "I am so *not* Rebecca of Sunnybrook Farm." She tilted her head at me and grinned. "Neither are you."

She got that right. "Since I'm a townie, I wouldn't qualify anyway." Her smile widened. She had perfect teeth, white and straight.

The sun was beginning to descend behind her, illuminating the sky in a color wash of gold and orange and peach. "So, okay," she said. "I'm stating the obvious here, but you're gay, right? Is this like your total butch look?" She passed a hand down my body.

All my muscles seized at once. I felt the blood drain from my face.

"God." Xanadu covered her mouth with her hands. "Oh God. I'm sorry, Mike. I didn't mean . . ." She reached over to touch my leg, but retracted her hand. "I have a big mouth. You can't shut me up. Someone should wire my jaw shut or better yet, remove the language chip from my brain. I didn't say that, okay?"

I flexed my quads. I could move, at least. Run if I had to.

"I know a few gay people back home," she kept on. "It's no big deal. Not to me. But maybe here . . . I'm sorry. I'll shut up. I won't tell anyone."

My eyes rose to fix on hers.

"So, um, listen." She flipped her hair. "Change of subject. What does one do on a Friday night in Cans Ass, USA?"

I swallowed the lump in my throat. She knew gay people. Guys or girls? How well did she know them? What did she think of me really? I think she liked me. Forcing a light tone, I said, "Usually we hang out at the Dairy Delite and chug-a-lug Mr. Mistees."

Xanadu frowned. Then she burst into laughter.

Jokes, I thought. She likes to laugh. "Or we drag Main, which takes about ten seconds. Sometimes we run the service road on both sides of the tracks and pitch cow pies in each other's windows."

Xanadu laughed louder. I smiled, and wished it was a joke.

She slugged me on the arm. The sun grew to a huge red orb and set the world on fire. Xanadu gasped. "Wow," she breathed. "I've never seen anything like *that* before."

I felt proud, as if the beauty of nature originated here. A Coalton creation. A reason for her to stay.

There were no words. Speaking would've spoiled it. We sat on the flatbed watching the sun sink slowly off the horizon and vanish into space. I wanted so much to put my arm around her, have her lay her head on my shoulder.

"What's the best time you've ever had in Coalton, Kansas?" Xanadu asked quietly.

"I'll have to think on that," I answered. I didn't have to think at all. Sitting here on a flatbed truck sharing a sunset with the most beautiful girl in the world? It doesn't get any better than this.

Chapter Four

I snuck into Ma's room a little after midnight. Her radio had clicked off an hour or so ago and she was propped against the headboard, mouth agape, breathing labored. Both pillows were crushed under her neck to keep her head up. It was the only position she could lie in anymore without suffocating herself.

I tiptoed past her fleshy mound and over to the double dresser. What I wanted was in the bottom drawer. I'd seen it there on Tuesday when I'd come in to get more undershirts and boxers. Ma had fallen asleep in front of the TV that night, giving me extra time to snoop.

I knelt in front of the dresser and lifted the brass handle. I pulled gently. Crap. The drawer was stuck. I gave it a tug. Nothing. I wedged my palm onto the edge of the frame and tugged harder. The drawer popped open and all the contents shifted, clinking and clanking around. I braced, holding my breath.

Why? It's not like she'd yell at me. She didn't speak to me. And it wasn't like his stuff didn't belong to me.

There was a lot of junk in this drawer. Five or six softballs rolling around, Dad's mitt. All my team pictures. His stat book on me. I wouldn't touch that. Presents I'd made him for birthdays and Father's Days. I didn't know he kept all this.

There it was — the lighter. The one with DMS engraved in the chrome. I snatched it up and flipped open the lid. I held it to my nose and inhaled. The smell of lighter fluid; the scent of him. I closed my eyes. Dad.

"Baby, don't play with Daddy's lighter." He'd taken it away from me when I was little. "Here, I'll show you how it works." He popped the cap and his thumb flicked the spark wheel. Licks of flame. Orange, yellow, blue. I reached for it. "No, Mike. Hot. Don't touch. I don't want it to hurt you." He closed the lid. "Nothing's ever going to hurt my baby. Not if I can help it."

My breath came out in short spurts. I thumbed the cap shut and clenched the lighter in a tight fist.

I felt eyes on me, watching.

I turned. Her eyelids fluttered. Was she awake? Aware? She gulped in an ugly snore and every pound of flesh on her shuddered.

A chill made me shudder.

How? How could he have ever loved her?

Jamie called me first thing Saturday morning. "Today's the day, huh?"

"Yep."

"Two years. Hard to believe. You going to River View?"

"I guess."

"Want me to come?"

Did I? Yes. No. This was something I had to do alone. "Not necessary. But thanks."

"Give Luigi my love. Or whatever."

Whatever, I repeated to myself.

"See you at the game. Oh, did I mention I made up a new cheer for you?"

"Jamie," I threatened, "don't you dare embarrass me at the game."

"Me? When have I ever embarrassed you?"

The phone buzzed in my ear. Damn Jamie. I downed the rest of my power shake and tossed a frozen bottle of water into my duffel. The game was in Garden City, a doubleheader, so I wouldn't get back before two or three this afternoon. I considered snitching one of Mom's frozen hoagies but didn't want her to starve to death. Heaven forbid she'd miss a meal.

The back screen door rattled and a kid's voice called in, "Pig slop for the big fat elephant."

I crashed out to see who the mouth was. Too late. He'd cut across our yard and was halfway down the block. Probably one of the Tanner boys. They were all brats. Two boxes of groceries teetered on the edge of the crumbling back porch. How long had they been here? A little kid couldn't have carried them.

Great. Now she was having it delivered. Why didn't we just insert a feeding tube in her stomach? Tie on a feedbag? I don't know why I was being so hateful today. Two years. Get over it.

I dug through the boxes: Banquet frozen dinners and Toaster Strudels and pies and doughnuts and greasy chicken from the deli. I'd be happy to do the shopping if she'd only ask.

Oh yeah. I forgot. I didn't exist for her.

I hauled the boxes inside and started unloading, making as much racket as I could. Where was Darryl? In bed probably. He and his stock jocks had had a big Friday night dragging Main. On cue, Darryl padded into the kitchen. His gut hung over the waistband of his sloppy jeans. "Food," he intoned. Snatching the Hostess box out of my hand, he ripped the tab open and popped a Donette into his mouth.

"You could at least help put these away," I said.

"What do you think I'm doing?" He popped another Donette and smirked. His gnarly tufts of hair resembled the Ledbetters' Persian cat that had to get shaved last summer. It had an abscess on its butt. Darryl was the abscess, his bald spot the butt. If he looked this way at twenty-four, he was going to be completely bald by thirty. Same as Dad.

I edged around him with a stack of frozen pies and crammed them into the freezer. "I'm taking the truck today," I informed him. "I have a game in Garden City and I'm stopping by River View first."

There was a long moment of silence, static in the air. If Darryl was going to fight about this —

"What time?" he asked.

"What time what?"

"What time are you leaving?"

"Why? You planning on coming?"

Darryl relieved me of the gallon jug of milk. "Maybe."

"To River View?"

He cut me a death look. He'd never go there. "To your game." He uncorked the plastic plug on the milk and glugged straight from the bottle.

I said flatly, "You're coming to my game. Let me guess. You're bringing Ma too. A show of family. Oh wow. I'm all choked up. I'll save seats for you guys. Wait. I'd have to save the whole cheering section for her."

Darryl just looked at me. I reciprocated the gesture. His eyes drifted down to my body, swept me head to foot. "You know, you look more like a guy every day," he said.

"Thank you." I elbowed past him.

"That crap you drink. What's in it? Steroids?"

"Get real," I muttered.

"You get real. I mean it, Mike. You're getting too . . ."

I whirled on him.

"Hard," he finished.

I smiled. Hard. Just what I wanted to be. Inside and out.

"You could, at the minimum, shave your pits."

"Why? So you can glue the hair on your head?"

No response. Okay, it wasn't that funny.

I kicked the second box over to him. "You finish this. I have to go."

I helped myself to a hoagie from the top of the box. I'd earned it. Dropping the sandwich into my duffel, I double-checked my gear: cleats, batting gloves, a Tampax. I hoped to God I wouldn't need it halfway through the game. Shouldering the duffel, I held a palm out to Darryl. "Keys?"

He dug into his jeans pocket. Then teased me with the keys so I had to grab for them. Butthead.

"Be back by three." He trailed me to the screen door. "Me and Gordo are heading up to Oberlin to see his cousin about this funny car a guy wants to sell. We might go in on it together."

Like I cared. Gordo was a gonad. All Darryl's friends were. "Where are you getting the money for that?"

"It's coming out of your inheritance," he said.

That did it. "You're not missing work, are you? Or didn't you get the job at the Suprette? I can't imagine them not being impressed by your vast on-the-job experience in plumbing and heating. Your managerial expertise. The last two years you spent running the family business into the ground."

Darryl came after me with a fist, but I slammed out the door. Even if he could catch me, which I doubted, he couldn't hurt me. No more than he already had.

At the outskirts of town, I made a pit stop at Nel's Tavern. As usual, Nel was on the phone behind the bar. She waved me in.

I slid onto a bar stool to wait. There was a clump of old timers at the end of the bar — truckers, railroad engineers, drunks. They barely glanced my way. Nel never refused to sell to me, and she probably should have. More than once I'd bought a quart bottle of Old Milwaukee and taken it home instead of to River View.

"How's your ma?" Nel asked, hanging up.

I hated lying to Nel. She'd always been good to me and Darryl. "You know. The same."

Nel sighed. She reached across the bar to cradle my chin, but I pulled back. Not today. I couldn't handle her kindness today. Hers or anyone else's.

"The usual?" she asked.

I nodded. She packaged the beer and rang up my sale. I handed her a ten and she counted out change. As I grabbed the paper bag by the neck of the bottle, Nel held on and said, "Tell your ma I'll try to stop by to see her soon."

Like me and Ma talked. "Okay." I separated from Nel and swiveled off my stool.

"She's been through a lot, Mike," Nel said at my back.

We've all been through a lot, okay? You don't see me giving up on life, do you? I didn't say it. I didn't dare. Instead, I stiff-armed through the door, thinking this beer might not make it to River View.

"Hey, watch it," someone barked in my ear. "What's your rush?"

I'd almost mowed Miss Millie down in the doorway. "I'm sorry, Miss Millie." I reached out to steady her. "You okay?"

She blinked at me, her rheumy eyes sloshing around in loose eye sockets.

I reeled back. The odor emanating from her set off my gag reflex.

"Two years." Her face flooded with recognition. "Two years today," she said, aiming a limp finger at my face.

Great. If Miss Millie remembered, the whole town did.

There was no river in River View, no river anywhere in Coalton. The streambed that ran along the south side of town had been dry as a cracker barrel as long I'd lived here. Which was forever. I guess it was supposed to sound serene: River View. View of the river. What view? Floating corpses?

I pulled up alongside the row of junipers that had been planted on Arbor Day last year as a wind break. Waste of money. Once the wind began to blow on the Kansas plain there wasn't any living thing that could break it. I grabbed the beer and took off in search of Dad.

He was in the same place. Duh. What did I expect, that'd he get up and leave? He lay between Darryl Michael Szabo II — Grandpa — and Camilia Lynn Szabo. INFANT, the headstone read. Sister. My sister.

"Hey, Pops." I curled cross-legged in front of his headstone, setting the beer beside me for the moment. Propping my elbows on my spread-apart knees and lacing all ten fingers together, I rested my cheeks on my knuckles and asked, "How's it going?"

Just once I'd like to hear his voice. In my ears, not my head. I couldn't remember the last thing he'd said out loud to me. It wasn't, "Goodbye." It wasn't, "Have a nice life without me." I squeezed my eyes shut. A breeze prickled my skin and I shivered in my sleeveless uniform. The wind rustled the trees. Was that him? I'd take it as a sign. I'd take anything.

I opened my eyes and tried to feel his presence, his warmth surrounding me. His strong arms around me. "Jamie says hi." I plucked a few blades of grass and tossed them aside. "Dad, guess what? I met someone." I smiled at his imagined surprise. "Well, yeah she's pretty. Think I'd pick a dog? Actually, she's bee-oo-tiful." He'd laugh to hear me imitate him. He used to say the exact same thing about cars and women: "Ooh, baby. She's bee-oo-tiful."

"Xanadu. That's her name. Cool, huh? You'd like her, Dad. Except, she's a talker. Man, can she talk. I know you always say when people talk too much there's something they're not telling you. Usually, the truth. I don't get that with her. She's totally honest. I wish you could meet her, Dad. You'd see. I wish —"

The words stuck in my throat. I fought them down. Wishing, hoping. It was destructive. "Doesn't matter. She'd never be interested in me. What?" I paused. Unfurling my legs, I bent forward and put my ear to the ground. "Anything's possible? Yeah, you would say that."

I straightened to sit up. "I do think she likes me. She isn't repulsed, let's put it that way."

A prairie dog chirruped a few feet away. The colony was growing larger. Last time I was here, on Christmas day, there were half as many mounds. I'd counted. Twenty-five. I'd thought it was a sign. Twenty-five, December twenty-fifth. Weak. I watched as the prairie dog sat up on its haunches and barked a warning. "Don't worry," I told him. "I won't be here long."

"So, anyway," I said to Dad, "things are about the same. Darryl's a wastoid. But you knew that. What else is new?" We miss you, I wanted to say.

I couldn't say it. I wasn't sure Darryl *did* miss Dad. They were always hacking on each other. Especially the last year. Darryl and his cars. Dad and his drinking. Dad telling Darryl to get off his butt and get a job. Right, Dad. Talk about wishful thinking. Darryl was a slacker. Dad knew that. He reminded Darryl often enough. Darryl probably praised the Lord the day Dad offed himself.

My stomach knotted. Two years today. I removed the bottle of beer from the paper bag and unscrewed the lid. "To celebrate your anniversary." I saluted him with the bottle. "Here's to ya, Pops. Cheers." I scrambled to my feet. Ceremoniously, I sprinkled the beer all up and down his grave. "One for the road," I told him. "Drink up."

Did he laugh? Did his hearty boom echo across the open cemetery?

Did I feel him take me in his arms and smother me in a hug? Then smell his stinking boozy breath all over my face. God. I hated him.

No, I didn't. I loved him.

I hated him.

I loved him.

I lingered another minute until all the foam was gone, swallowed up by earth, guzzled in the ground by him. Absently, my hand ran along the curve of his marble headstone. Too big, too expensive. They didn't have to buy a headstone this ornate. They didn't have to buy one at all. I read the engraving aloud, "Darryl Michael Szabo, the Third." He never went by Darryl. "Here come the Mikes," people would say. "Mike and Mike Junior." Or as Jamie called me, "Miss Junior Mike."

People. They were still talking about it. Two years. They couldn't let it go.

I touched my baby sister's headstone too. She'd only lived five days. I couldn't remember how she died, or why. Not for the first time, I wondered if life would've been different with three of us, a younger sister. If Camilia would've looked like me. Hopefully not. If Mom would've loved her, the way she did Darryl.

Never me.

Back to Dad. He loved me. He loved me more than anyone in the world.

"Rest in peace, Pops." I broke the bottle across his headstone. "If you can."

Chapter Five

*T*he team was in the outfield warming up when I finally found Cleaver Field. You could get lost in the maze of streets and avenues and courts and drives in Garden City. Coalton was easy. First Street through Tenth, east to west, square grid. We only had the one stoplight at the west end of town as you came off Highway 40.

I parked the truck in the paved lot behind the dugout. Which was an actual dugout, rather than a lean-to aluminum shell like we had. As I started toward the field, I remembered this wasn't Coalton and returned to remove the keys from the ignition. I noticed then how the insignia on the side panel of the truck was fading. Szabo Plumbing and Heating. Italics underneath: The Name You Know and Trust. The name was running a little low on trust these days. I rubbed off the grime around Szabo. The least Darryl could do was keep the truck clean. Out of respect, if not for Dad, then for the family name. The business.

What business? I asked myself. The business was in the toilet.

"Mike, there you are. I thought you weren't going to make it." Coach

Kinneson scribbled a hurried note on her clipboard as I rounded the dugout.

"I made it," I told her. "I've never missed a game in my life." If she didn't know that by now . . . A ball came whizzing in from the field and my hand shot up in reflex to cup it.

"Just seein' if you showed up to play," T.C. called to me, grinning.

I sidearmed a stinger back to her. "There's your answer."

"Five minutes," the ump hollered from behind home plate.

Garden City was already through with warm-ups and they looked good. Prepared. At least prepped-out in their flashy new yellow-and-brown uniforms. BUFFS, their uniforms read on front. Short for Buffalos. Who'd want to be called buffalos? Big, lumbering animals. Every player's last name was appliquéd on the back. Shoes to match. La di da. Coalton Cougars wore your basic black-and-gold jerseys with ironed-on numbers. So what? I loved my uniform, the feel of it, the way the stretchy fabric fit nice and tight around my quads. My cleats were getting a little stretched and holey, but they'd last another season — I hoped. I couldn't see dropping a hundred bucks on new cleats if I was only going to be wearing them one more year.

I gathered my team together in front of the dugout. "Huddle up, ladies." We jammed into a closed circle and put our arms around each others' shoulders. "What do we know about buffalos? They're hairy and they smell bad."

Everyone snorted.

"They almost went extinct," T.C. chimed in.

"Right," I said. "Let's finish the job." We stacked hands. "Go Cougars!"

It looked like most of Coalton had driven down to watch us play. Which wasn't unusual. Didn't matter if we had a winning season or not, girls' fastpitch always attracted a crowd.

For some reason Coach Kinneson put me first in the batting order. I would've asked her strategy, but was afraid she didn't have one. She'd only volunteered to fill in while our real coach, Coach Archuleta, was in St. Louis helping his mother through hip replacement surgery. He was planning to be gone for a couple of weeks — five or six games — but his mother wasn't recuperating as fast as he'd hoped and we were stuck with Coach Kinneson. Supposedly, she'd coached a junior rec league somewhere in Pennsylvania. A league with lower standards, obviously.

As I took my practice swings in the warm-up circle, I heard Jamie start a chant: "Sza-bo. Mighty Mike. Sza-bo . . ."

The audience picked it up: "Sza-bo. Mighty Mike. Sza-bo . . ."

Shit. I shot eye daggers at Jamie. Like the rest of the squad, Jamie was dressed in the official CHS cheerleading uniform, only instead of a short skirt he wore skintight short shorts. You could see everything. I kept telling him he should wear a cup. He did a split jump in the air and landed it splayed on the ground. Ow. That had to hurt.

Jamie finger-waved to me. I pretended not to know him.

On the first pitch I hit a solid double. Could have been a triple, or a homer. Next up I'd adjust to this pitcher. She was new, a freshman. Fast, but she telegraphed with her eyes where she was going to place the ball. I read the catcher's signals. Same as last year. Not smart. I had a good memory.

T.C. advanced me to third with a sacrifice fly and I stole home on a wild pitch. We scored two more runs in the first inning.

Amy Babcock was the best pitcher Coalton had ever had. Unfortunately, Amy graduated last year and her sister Gina was our starter now. Gina wasn't Amy. Her first three pitches scudded off the plate. She was rushing it. I rose from my crouch behind home base and signaled her to slow down, take a deep breath. On her next pitch, the ball hit the strike zone, at least, but the Buffs batter connected and tripled to left.

Gina looked shaken.

I called time and loped to the mound. "Forget it," I told her. "She got lucky."

"Yeah, right. That was my best pitch."

"Gina . . ."

"I know. I'm sorry." She shook her head at the ground.

I smacked the ball down hard in her glove. "You got the whole game, girl. Show 'em what you're made of." If not steel, I thought, aluminum foil. Don't crumple.

The next pitch was a rocket, in there for a strike. Atta girl, I sent Gina a nod of encouragement. The Buffs batter popped the next pitch high in the air over my head and I threw off my catcher's mask to snag it. Easy out.

Their third batter singled up the middle, then made the mistake of trying to steal second. Guess she hadn't heard — no one steals on Mike Szabo. My bullet smoked her so bad, she'd be embarrassed to show her face in Garden City again.

After the first inning jitters, we settled into our game.

Bottom of the last inning, it was Cougars nine, Buffs eight. Two outs. Gina had hung in there. She was getting tired, though, a little wild. Garden City's power hitter was up next. Lacey Hidalgo. I'd been hot for Lacey since Little League, not that she knew it. She pumped twice and took her stance at the plate. "Nice ass," I said under my breath.

"What?" She turned as the ball whizzed by.

"Stee-rike one," the ump called.

Lacey slit eyes at me. I grinned behind my mask. Signaled Gina, inside corner. Lacey's weakness. I don't know if the ball got away from Gina or her arm gave out, but the pitch sailed. Lacey's bat caught the ball high and ripped it.

T.C. sprang like a cat toward second base and nicked the ball with her glove, but it dropped behind her and rolled into the outfield. I groaned inwardly. The runner on second tagged up and sprinted to third. Then T.C. mishandled the ball and the runner got waved home.

"Throw it, T.C.," I hollered.

T.C. whirled. I kept my focus on the base runner. As she went into her slide, kicking up a cloud of dirt, the ball smacked into my out-stretched glove. Perfect throw. I brought my glove down hard on the runner's ankle an inch away from the plate.

"Out!" The ump punched the air.

I said to the runner, "Gee, sorry. Didn't mean to soil your new unie."

She nailed me with a death look.

I loved this game. I don't remember when I started playing softball. Probably the day I was born. Dad said I had a sixth sense about the game, that I could size up a hitter with one swing of her bat. An accurate assessment, if I do say so myself. I was built to be a catcher. Strong leg muscles, center of gravity low to the ground. Speedy too. I could fly. I had to improve on timing, though, and upper body strength to turn those doubles into homers.

For the limited time left I had to play, that is.

"T.C." I caught her arm on the way into the dugout to gear up for the second game of the night. "Dead-on throw, girl."

T.C. beamed. "It was, wasn't it?"

We knocked fists.

In a doubleheader you can't let the first loss affect you, but the Buffs did just that. By the end of the fourth inning it was clear they'd checked out. We routed them twelve-zip.

Most of the people who'd driven down from Coalton made a point of coming by to high-five, or say, "Good game, Mike." They congratulated the other girls too. It wasn't like I was a one-man team. Maybe I did bring in the majority of our runs, but I didn't win the games singlehandedly. That's the thing about softball; it's a team sport. No one player can determine the outcome.

As I was removing my knee pads, I saw Coach Kinneson over by the backstop, jabbering away with a couple of suits, gesturing at me. What were guys in suits doing here? It made me feel uncomfortable. Guilty. Like I was wanted by the FBI or something.

Jamie flounced up beside me. "Kicked their asses, Szabo." He held up a palm to high-five me. When I went to slap his hand, he jerked it away and jutted his hip into mine. God. He was so queer.

Kimberleigh Rasmussen, head cheerleader, bounded up behind Jamie and poked him in the ribs. He yelped and slapped her away. "Hi, Mike," she said. "Awesome games. You busted butt."

"Thanks," I said.

"Jamie, we're going to the A&W in Garden City," Kimberleigh told him. "You want to come?" The rest of the squad was piling into Kimberleigh's SUV in the parking lot and hollering for Jamie. "You too, Mike," she added.

"No thanks," I said. "I gotta get back." I didn't really; just didn't feel much like partying today. The end of every game was a letdown. But especially this year. One less game to play. Counting down.

Jamie looked from Kimberleigh to me. "I've got to get back too," he said. Shocking the hell out of me. Why would he choose me over "his girls," as he referred to the squad?

Oh. I got it. "Go," I told him. "I don't need your pity party."

He looked at me funny. "If anyone's throwing a party, *you* weren't invited."

I sneered at him. He pressed his cheeks together and pooched his lips.

Kimberleigh gawked at us like she didn't know what the hell was going on. Me and Jamie did seem to have a language all our own. Jamie said, "I'm scheduled to work at two, okaaay?" he drew out the word. Waggling a finger at Kimberleigh, he added, "Don't you girls do anything I wouldn't do."

Kimberleigh said, "What would that be?"

Jamie smiled. "Good point. Don't get caught."

She pinched his arm and he yowled. He was eating up this cheer-leading crap. How he ever got voted onto the squad is a mystery. His tryout cheer in front of the whole school went:

"Strawberry shortcake

Banana split

We think your team plays like —"

It must've been a joke to vote for Jamie. Maybe not. He was popular. Class clown. Athletic, though. Into gymnastics. He was fun to be around, even if he was the world's queerest queer. People seemed to get past it. Jamie was just Jamie. He'd always been this way.

"Hey, you all right?"

I blinked back to the moment. "Yeah, why?"

He stared into my eyes the way he does, like he's trying to see down to my soul. Sorry, closed for repairs. Jamie said, "Let's climb the water tower tomorrow and work on our bods. It's perfect weather for sunbathing. Not so hot we French-fry our fannies."

"Sounds good."

"Eleven o'clock." Jamie ground a stiff index finger into my bicep. "Don't be late."

"You're the one who's always late." I slapped him away.

He clucked his tongue. "I operate on gay time. Oops, forgot." He snapped his fingers in front of my face. "So do you."

I clubbed his hand down. "I have to get my gear."

"Meet you at the truck," he said.

Coach Kinneson clomped into the dugout as I was guzzling the last of my ice water. I was starving, eyeing that hoagie in my bag. I should've eaten on the way down. "Great game, Mike," she said. "Both of them. You're amazing."

I might've blushed. She was always doing that, singling me out. It was embarrassing.

"Thanks," I mumbled, adding as an afterthought, "You too."

She gave a short laugh. "What do I do except make sure we have enough players on the field? Six, right?"

I smiled. She knew her limitations, anyway.

"I talked to Mr. Archuleta yesterday and he said his mother is better. They're planning to bring her home from the hospital tomorrow.

If he can get a nurse to come in for home visits, he'll be back next week."

"Yeah?" My hopes soared. I suppressed my urge to jump up and holler, "All right!" I don't know why the news excited me. We were holding steady in the standings, despite Coach Kinneson. Oh, that was mean. She was doing the best she could. She was new to the team, new to Coalton. Most of us had been playing together long enough that the game was second nature by now. We knew the teams, the competition. Winning was simply a matter of confidence and execution.

"Listen, Mike." Coach Kinneson sat beside me on the bench as I switched out my cleats for my grungy Nikes. "I want to talk to you about your future."

"What future?"

She cast me a weird look, like I should know. "We need time to sit down and discuss it," she said. "At length."

What length? My future was predetermined. I'd be shoveling pig slop at the Merc till I died.

"Do you think you could stop by my office on Monday?" She started jamming bats into the golf bag she used for hauling equipment.

Coach Kinneson also happened to be the new principal of Coalton High. I squatted to help her as a little quiver of fear shot up my spine. She'd only been at CHS three months and already she had a rep as a hardass. You didn't go to Dr. Kinneson's office unless you were in deep shit. People would wonder what I'd done.

"Mike?"

You also didn't argue with the principal. "Sure," I said. "No problem."

"Come during your homeroom. I'll make time for you." She squeezed my shoulder on her way out. Pivoting back, she added, "I can see it now." Arcing her hand in front of her face, Dr. Kinneson quoted an invisible headline, "Hometown Girl Makes the Grade."

What grade? The only grade I knew for sure was Miz S's A in Geometry. Had Dr. Kinneson been talking to my teachers? Is that what this was about? What'd I do? I did enough to get by. More than enough.

Jamie was sprawled on the hood of my truck, pumping his pompoms at people as they drove off. He had a future — in the hospitality industry.

"Get in," I ordered him. He scooted off the front of the truck and jumped in the passenger side. We slammed our doors in unison. As I followed the stream of cars heading back to Coalton, Jamie cranked up the radio. On I-83, I accelerated to the speed limit. There was no limit for Mike Szabo. Not today. I was feeling good. Forget Dad, the anniversary. Forget the future. We'd won both games, the sky was blue, the wheat was green. Toby Keith came on the radio and Jamie cranked up the volume. We had hand gestures for this song. Pointing at each other, poking our chests, we sang along with Toby at the top of our lungs: "I wanna talk about *me*, I wanna talk about *I*. I wanna talk about number one, old my, me my . . ."

I dropped Jamie off at the Dairy Delite. There was an hour to kill before my wastoid of a brother needed the truck, so I figured I'd swing by the Merc, see if Everett could use me. I wasn't scheduled to work, but I could always use the money. Especially if Darryl was out spending Dad's social security on stock cars.

I slowed at the stoplight. Idled the engine. It wasn't a conscious decision, almost as if my brain shifted gears and took me along for the ride. I turned in the opposite direction of the Merc, toward the main power line, heading straight for Xanadu.

Chapter Six

Xanadu came tearing out of the house and sprinting across the yard as if she'd been anticipating my arrival. "Thank God you're here," she said. "I've been calling you all morning to get out here and save me. Where've you been?"

"I had a game," I told her. How'd she get my number? How else? From the tri-county phone book.

"What do you mean, a game? What kind of game?" She flipped her hair over her shoulder, then lifted it in the back and let it fall.

"Softball," I replied, wishing I could touch it. Run my fingers through it.

Her eyes scanned me up and down. I knew what she was thinking: Coalton's a bush league.

Maybe we were. Maybe we weren't.

"Are you any good?" she asked.

I shrugged. "We're okay. We usually go to quarterfinals." In case she didn't know what that was, I added, "The state tourney."

"Not the team." She gave my shoe a little kick. "You."

Me? My foot tingled. "I made first team All-State two years running."
Did she smile? Did she realize what a big deal that was? To me, anyway. My time was running out. "Come on, let's go." She grabbed my jersey front and yanked me toward the driver's side door. I stumbled at the unexpected move, the strength and force of her.

Faye appeared on the porch and Xanadu called back, "Mike and I are going to town, Aunt Faye. That okay with you?"

Going to town. I liked the sound of that.

"I finished unloading the dishwasher and folding the tea towels like you asked." Xanadu crossed her eyes at me, adding in a mutter, "Six hundred fucking tea towels. Who uses tea towels, anyway?"

I waved a greeting at Faye. Please, I prayed, let it be okay.

Xanadu didn't wait for Faye to answer. She climbed in on my side and slid across the front seat. My duffel was in the way so she tossed it into the back, then kicked off her sandals and curled one leg underneath her, fanning her hair out over her shoulders.

I don't remember starting the truck.

"Hold on a minute," Faye called.

"Shit," Xanadu hissed under her breath. "Just go."

I turned off the ignition.

"Dammit."

"Sorry," I said. I felt I should respect Faye's wishes. This was her house.

Faye disappeared inside the mudroom and I said, "She probably forgot about those other hundred tea towels in the cellar."

Xanadu snorted.

I hoped I was forgiven.

A moment later Faye came back out balancing two pies, one in each hand. She handed them to me through the open window. Yes! I was famished. From her apron pocket, Faye removed a jar of jam and offered it to me. "I bought a bushel more strawberries at the market than I needed. Take these to your mother. You and Darryl enjoy them too."

"Thanks," I said, setting the pies beside me on the seat, then changing my mind and transferring them to the back. We didn't need anything between us. The pie plates fit perfectly inside two toilet seat rims behind me. I slid the jam in the front pocket of my duffel.

Faye peered around me at Xanadu. "Be back by dark."

Xanadu expelled an audible sigh.

Faye added, "You'll want to be here when your probation officer calls."

My head whipped around.

Xanadu snarled, "Let's go." She folded her arms. "Oh wait. I need my purse." She pulled up the door lever and leaped out the passenger side. Eyeing Faye across me, she added, "I keep my drugs in it. In case you were checking." Xanadu left the door swinging free and dashed toward the house.

"I think that was a joke," I said to Faye.

She didn't smile. I kept my eyes on the screen door, willing Xanadu to reappear — now. Faye remarked, "She's a piece of work, isn't she?"

Work of art, I thought. What could I say? Our opinions differed.

Xanadu returned, sliding in beside me and slamming the door.

"Okay, I'm ready. Let's fly."

I revved up the truck again and shifted into gear. Faye's eyes stayed on my face as I circled the drive. What? Did she think I wouldn't get Xanadu home before dark? I'd get her home.

Once on the road Xanadu wrinkled her nose at the radio. "I hate country," she said. She fiddled with the knob to find another station.

"Good luck," I replied through the static. On a good day we could get two FM stations out of Goodland. Both country. "You can listen to the farm report on AM," I told her.

Xanadu widened her eyes at me, then laughed. I felt the heat rise between my legs. Her eyes looked brighter today. Clearer. Cleaner. She wasn't wearing all that gunk. Not that it mattered how she expressed herself, but she was a natural beauty. She didn't need enhancements. She punched off the radio and leaned her head against the seat back. "Thank you for coming," she said, closing her eyes. "Thankyouthankyouthankyou."

I felt your need, I almost whispered. The pull of you.

"I don't care where we go, I just need to get the hell out of here for a while."

I didn't care where we went either. I just wanted to spend every waking moment with her.

We tooled down the rutted road at a leisurely sixty-five mph. I figured she was a girl who liked speed. She flung an arm out the window to catch the breeze and parted her lips, seeming blissful and at peace. I was right.

"What was the score?" Her voice rose over the wind.

"What?"

She'd turned her head. "Of your game."

"Oh. Nine to eight, first game. We won. Twelve-zip, second game."

"Ouch. Your twelve?"

I nodded.

Her eyes fixed on my biceps. "All-State, huh? I guess that's a big deal around here, huh?"

Was she being sarcastic? "It's big," I said flatly.

She lowered her eyes. "I'm sorry, Mike. I don't mean to . . . you know. Demean your life." She pressed the button on the glove box and it popped open.

I panicked. What was in there? Dad's hip flask? Jamie's grass? Once I found a package of condoms, obviously Darryl's. Made me wonder what he really did on his road trips to Goodland.

She didn't rummage through the crap, just shut the flap and said, "I know you think I'm this rich city bitch who has no appreciation for the joys of boonie living."

I smiled. "No. I don't think that."

"What *do* you think of me?" She paused for a second before adding, "Don't answer that."

I almost blurted the truth, that I thought she was perfect in every way. "I . . . I think you're cool," I said.

A joyful smile lit up her face. I'd made her happy. I pledged to make her happy every day in every way.

We were nearing the stoplight and I was racking my brain about what to do in town. She'd want to have fun, but what was fun for her? We didn't have a movie theater. No clubs. Just the Lucky Strike Lanes. I'm sure.

Xanadu said, "I didn't mean to lie to you before, Mike. About what happened to Tiffany. It's just, I didn't know how you'd react when I told you I killed someone."

My foot slammed on the brake. "What!"

"And now I know," she added coolly.

The light was green so I pulled ahead into the empty lot at the grain elevators. People shouldn't joke about death. Not even her. "That whole ecstasy thing, that girl dying, that was just a story you made up?"

Xanadu frowned. "No. Of course not. It happened. The only difference . . ." She paused. "The truth is . . ." She let out a ragged breath. "The truth is, I'm the one who sold Tiffany the E."

My eyes might've bugged out of my head.

"Yeah," Xanadu said. "I was her dealer."

"Jesus."

She lowered her head, then covered her face with her hands. "I know. It was bad. I got charged with possession. And, um, distribution of a controlled substance." She uncovered her face, but kept her head down. "I've got a police record now. And I'm expelled from school. Thank God they tried me in juvenile court or I could've gone to jail."

"Jesus," I said again.

"I know." She met my eyes. "But I spent forty-five days in detention and paid a thousand-dollar fine and did sixty hours of community service to repay Tiffany's family." Xanadu repeated, "Repay her family. Like I could ever do that." Her eyes welled with tears. "I never lied about it in court. I never blamed anyone. Tiffany's death was all my fault and I'll have to live with that for the rest of my life. I have to live with it. Every. Fucking. Day." She buried her face in her hands again and started to cry.

"Hey." I reached over to touch her arm or something. Make contact. "Hey." It was all I could think to say.

Xanadu sniffled and swiped her nose with her forearm. "What do you think of me now?" she said.

"I think you're b —" I almost said it. Because she was, beautiful. She'd made a mistake. She admitted it. She'd paid for it. She was still paying. We've all been there. "I think you're brave," I told her.

"What?" She blinked and her eyes grew wide. "Really?"

"Yeah. For telling the truth. For owning up to it. That had to be hard."

"It was. God, Mike. It was so hard." With her palms, she blotted her tears and smiled tentatively at me. I smiled back. My hand was on the cushion and she reached over and covered it with hers. "You're great." Her fingers curled under my palm. "You know that? You get me."

Heat surged through my body. Yeah, I got her.

Xanadu added, "You won't tell anyone, will you?"

"No. Of course not."

"I came here to get away. From everybody. Everything. I'm still on probation, but Dad arranged for me to stay with Aunt Faye and Uncle Lee. He thought maybe if I got a fresh start . . ." She swallowed hard. "I can't believe you're okay with this. It's like . . . you don't even care."

I cared. I cared about her and what she was going through.

"I'm glad I found you," she said quietly, increasing the grip on my hand. "After it happened, after I got charged, everyone turned against me, all my friends. Even my best friend dumped me. God." Her eyes welled again. "I really need a friend."

I needed more than a friend. I needed her to stay like this forever, stay close, hold my hand, trust me. I threaded my fingers through hers and pulled her hand closer.

She straightened in her seat. "Come on," she said, giving my fingers a final squeeze, then releasing them, and me. "Let's go have some fun."

She was a girl, right? Girls liked to shop. The best clothes shopping in Coalton was at the Merc. Everett stocked a decent selection of jeans and tees and long skirts and coats. There was this black canvas Carhartt jacket I'd been drooling over since last winter.

I couldn't picture Xanadu in any of those clothes, though. They were hick duds.

What else? Food? Eating topped *my* list of enjoyable activities. I was a girl, to some degree. Everyone liked to eat. I decided on the Dairy Delite. There was no other choice, really.

The Dairy D looked deserted. Jamie must've been in the john. At the takeout counter, I called, "Hello. Anybody home?" Jamie shot to his feet. He'd been crouching on the floor in front of the frozen custard machine, dispensing a stream of chocolate soft-serve directly into his mouth. I sighed at Xanadu. "Meet Jamie. Jamie, Xanadu."

Jamie looked from me to her. A grin spread across his face, ear to earringed ear. "So you're the infamous Xanadu." He leaned across the counter and waggled a finger in her face. "I heard about you, girl."

A look of terror streaked through her eyes.

"Not from me," I said quickly.

"You're the talk of Coalton," Jamie said. "Meth-heads. God. I would've loved to have been there to see Glinda's face when you said that."

"Glinda?" Xanadu asked me.

"Mrs. Stargell," I explained. "It isn't her real name."

Xanadu's brow furrowed.

"Jamie makes up names for people."

"Not true." He shook his head from side to side. "I give identity to one's inner being. I visualize their essence."

I rolled my eyes. "Ask him what he calls his mother."

Xanadu arched eyebrows at Jamie.

"Elle s'appelle Geneviève," he said with a fake French accent. So queer.

Xanadu laughed. She was indulging him. Not a good idea. "Make up a name for me," she told him.

"Honey," he said, "your essence has already been identified and personified by your name."

That was true. She was the embodiment of poetry.

Jamie slapped the countertop. "What can I get you, girls? The special today is the chili cheese dog, but I don't recommend it. The buns are hard as day-old dicks and the hamburger was looking a little E. coli, if you know what I mean. The curly fries are hot and fresh cuz I just made a new batch. Well, half a batch now." He tilted his head. "We're running low on custard too, don't ask me why." He stuck an index finger into his right dimple and twisted it.

Xanadu laughed again. "You," she said, pointing to him. "Both of you are going to save my life."

Ditto, I thought.

Jamie quipped, "We're out of Life Savers. We have gobs of sprinkles for sundaes, though." His tongue, I saw, was a hideous shade of green and pink and orange. "Oh hey, Mike. Kung Pao called over a few minutes ago."

"Shit." I glanced at my watch. Twenty after three. "Listen, I've got to go drop the truck off for Darryl. Take care of Xanadu, will you? I'll be right back."

Jamie eyed the length of her. "I'm not sure what to do, seeing as how I'm not that kind of boy."

I shot him a silent warning: Shut it off.

She made some remark I didn't hear as I tore to the truck. Jamie had her laughing, anyway.

I parked at the curb and honked, left the keys in the ignition, then sprinted the eight blocks back to the Dairy D. Xanadu had ordered onion rings and a Mr. Mistee, and was sitting across from Jamie at the outdoor picnic table. He'd fixed us our usual — a raspberry Mistee and an order of curly fries to share.

"What do you do around here for fun?" Xanadu asked him as I eased in beside her.

"You mean instead of this?" He lassoed a curly fry in the air.

She sipped on her Mistee. Sitting so close to her, the charged air between us made the hair on my arms stand up.

Jamie tapped his chin. "Let's see. Mike is into Internet porn."

I lunged across the table and slugged him in the chest.

"Hey, owie." He rubbed his pec. "Don't damage the merch."

"You were damaged from birth," I muttered.

"You're the one with hormone deficiency."

Xanadu laughed. "You are both so gay —" She stopped. She swiveled to face me. "I didn't say that."

Jamie said, "Use it or lose it." He flapped a limp wrist at her.

I hated when he got this way. All show-offy, exhibitionist. He validated the stereotype. He played to it. Exhaling an irritated breath, I scooted out the end of the bench and said, "Anyone else want ketchup?"

Jamie raised his hand. "I do. I do."

I bent his hand back until cartilage crunched.

On my way to the gallon jug out front, I heard Xanadu say to Jamie, "Um, is it okay to talk about it?"

"About what?" Jamie said. "Us being gay? It's not like it's a secret. Look at me. Am I flaming, or what?"

Xanadu said, "I didn't notice."

They both cracked up.

As I scooted back in with a pee cup of ketchup, Xanadu smiled at me. I melted. She said, "So, the two of you . . ."

"Coalton's token ten percent of the population," Jamie answered. He swirled a curly fry in the ketchup, adding, "One fag and one dyke. You couldn't order it up any more predictable than that."

I glared at him. "Cram it."

"Oh, excuse me. Mike doesn't like to admit she's," he cupped a hand to his mouth and mock-whispered to Xanadu, "queer."

"I don't like labels," I snapped. "Especially that one."

Xanadu turned toward me and held my eyes. "I know what you mean. God, how I know what you mean." She gave me a long, knowing look. "I respect that, Mike. I really do."

Heat fried my face. She got it. She understood me perfectly. Vice versa. We had a connection.

Jamie took a sip of Mistee and said, "Did you get to River View?"

My eye daggers sliced through his heart.

"Sorry." He blanched. "I'm sorry."

I thought, Broadcast it to the world, why don't you?

"What's River View?" Xanadu asked.

Jamie answered quickly, "The big party scene outside of town. It's where us townies go to shoot up and perform degrading acts of sex and civil disobedience."

Xanadu's eyebrows lifted. "When can we leave?" She grinned. "Just kidding." She helped herself to a curly fry. "I don't do drugs and I'm giving up sex."

"Forever?" Jamie and I said together. We cut each other a glance.

Xanadu shrugged. "Guys blow."

Jamie said, "Which ones? Could you get me their numbers?"

Xanadu must've kicked him under the table because he yelped and grabbed his shin. My Mr. Mistee ran dry so I sighted a rim shot to the trash can. *Whoosh.* Two points.

"Really. Where do you guys party? What do you do here? It's so boring I just want to strip naked and go running through the cornfields."

Jamie's eyes bulged. "Could I sell tickets to that?"

I clicked a tongue at him. That was a joke. I'd buy up all the tickets, though. "Wheat," I said.

"What?" Xanadu blinked at me.

"Nothing," I mumbled. It's wheat, not corn.

She opened her purse and fished around for something. A poison dart for Jamie, I hoped. He opened his mouth to humiliate me again, but got distracted by a black Ford pickup veering into the parking cove and grinding to a halt on the gravel. "Great. Talk about guys who blow," Jamie said under his breath. He sighed heavily and stood.

"Who is it?" Xanadu pulled out her shades and reclasped her purse.

Both truck doors slammed in unison. Xanadu's jaw dropped. "Oh my God." She clenched my arm. "Who is *that*?"

I shielded my eyes against the blinding sun. You couldn't mistake those two silhouettes. "Which one?" I said.

"The one with the hat."

They both had Stetsons. "Beau and Bailey McCall," I told her. Maybe she meant Bailey, since Beau was carrying his hat. "Beau is Jamie's wet dream."

Xanadu's head spun in Jamie's direction, but he'd already skittered back inside. Beau raked a hand through his mop of curly brown hair and eased his Stet back onto his head. Xanadu watched as they neared us. She pressed a palm to her heart. "My God," she breathed. "They're divine. Bailey's the taller one?"

I hadn't noticed before, but I guess he was a couple of inches taller than Beau. They were both over six feet. "Yeah."

As they passed our table, they acknowledged me — us — with identical hitches of their chins. Like Bailey, like Beau. It was sort of a running joke. Jamie ran with it.

"Hey," I said in greeting. Xanadu seemed dumbstruck, frozen in the lips-parted position. She slid her shades down the bridge of her nose and peered over the rim, sexily.

At the takeout window they both ordered burgers and Cokes. "Would you like fries with that?" Jamie asked Beau. "They're on the house."

Jamie, I admonished silently. Nothing was on the house here. He had to pay for everything he ate, which pretty much meant he volunteered his time. Why was he always doing that for Beau? Giving it away? He came off so desperate.

Xanadu scooted out the end of the bench and moved around the table to sit opposite me. Why? To get a better view? "I didn't see them at school," she said in a lowered voice across the tabletop. "And believe me, I checked out everyone."

I thought back. "They've been gone a couple of days. Helping with calving." At least, Bailey had. Like Bailey, like Beau, I assumed.

"Where?" Xanadu asked.

"Where what?"

She let out a little huff. "Where do they live?"

"Oh. Out by you," I answered. "Near your aunt and uncle. You just continue on the county road a couple of miles until you see the big windmill. You'll smell it first. Their feedlot."

"No shit?"

I laughed. Was that a joke?

Xanadu's lips twitched up at the ends. "I might have to take up cattle rustling."

Slaughtering, I almost corrected her.

We watched as they pumped mustard and ketchup and spooned relish onto their burgers. Xanadu stared so hard at Bailey's back it made him turn around. "Oh my God, he's looking at me." She hid her face behind her purse. "I didn't even put on makeup today."

You don't need it, I wanted to say. You're beautiful the way you are. Besides, he can't see your eyes.

She asked, "Does he have a girlfriend?"

"Who?"

She cocked her head at me like, Hel-loo?

"Bailey? How should I know?" It came out harsher than I meant.

"I thought everyone knew everything in Coalton."

When they cared, I thought.

"Is he still looking?" Xanadu sneaked a peek over her purse.

"No, he's inhaling his burger." I looped a leg over the bench and stood up. "I better get you home before dark." Thank you, Faye. Thank you, God, for rotation of the earth and making the sunset arrive at this time.

Xanadu exhaled an irritated breath. She pushed out the end of her bench and paused for a moment, studying Bailey. Looking breath-taking backlit by the rosy sun. Then she turned and accompanied me to the truck.

The truck.

Xanadu must've realized it the same moment I did. There was no truck. We both skidded to a stop in the gravel. She removed her shades and dropped them into her purse, then said, "I think I know where I can get a ride. Is there a restroom in this place? I have to put on makeup."

My heart sank. "Knock on the back door. Jamie'll let you use the one inside."

She reversed direction and walked toward the Dairy D. Halfway there, she turned and called to me, "I'll let you know how it goes."

Chapter Seven

I couldn't sleep. Couldn't stop thinking about Xanadu. Dad's lighter was under my pillow. I felt around for it in the dark. I flipped the cap and filled my nose with the oily smell of butane. "If you dream it, you can be it." Dad. He was talking about softball, about being picked for All-State, playing competitive, playing college ball. About making a career of it, going pro. When was that?

Didn't matter. My dream wasn't about softball. I wanted her. She wasn't a dream. She was here, now. Dreaming doesn't get you anything, Dad. You have to do more than want it so bad it hurts. You have to take action.

I shut the lighter and focused on my clock across the room. 3:46. Sunday morning. If I added more definition to my arms, or my quads, where she could see. . . . There wasn't much I could do about my height. I could wear my cowboy boots. They'd add an inch or two.

The VFW didn't open until noon, but Armie said I could use the resistance equipment any time I wanted. He may not have meant four AM. So he shouldn't have given me a key.

It was quiet in Coalton. So quiet you could feel the silence like a blanket wrapped around you.

I warmed up with side, tricep, and quad stretches, then ran through a couple of sets of curls, pulldowns, leg presses. I benched a hundred. My muscles were spazzing bad, but I power-crunched till it hurt.

My mood lifted, my outlook. I felt more in control. Nothing had happened between her and Bailey. What could happen on a ride home?

I locked the VFW door and started back. People who weren't in church, or had gone to an early service, were already sitting out on their front porches, drinking coffee and reading the *Tri-County Gazette*. "Morning, Mike." From the ratty old sofa in front of his trailer, Mayor Ledbetter waved to me. "It's a warm 'un already, isn't it? Hot for April."

"Sure is," I called back.

"Cougars are looking mean."

I flexed a bicep at him.

He flexed one back. "Marie and I don't miss a game." Marie was the Missus Mayor, as per Jamie.

The Coalton neighborhood was alternating blocks of houses and trailers, as if in the old days people who arrived here couldn't decide whether to stay or move on. Szabos stayed. Our family had been here for three generations now, four counting me and Darryl. Great-Grandpa Darryl was a gunslinger with Wild Bill Hickok, according to Dad. He'd told us all these stories when we were kids about how famous, or infamous, our relatives had been. It was b.s. We were plumbers.

I turned the corner on eighth and the Cadillac parked in our driveway made me grind to a halt. Crap. Pastor Glenn from United Methodist. Why did he keep coming here? He had to park with his butt end in the street because Darryl's auto carcasses were clogging the driveway. Darryl claimed that once he got them fixed up and running, he'd either sell them or race the cars himself on the circuit. Sure, Darryl. Big dreams. Darryl never finished anything he started. Most of his junk heaps had been propped up so long on cinder blocks there was bindweed choking the carburetors.

I eased open the back screen and tiptoed into the kitchen. Pastor Glenn was in the living room with Ma. Like always, he was reading the Bible and she was weeping. Sometimes he'd recite his Sunday sermon, since Ma was too fat to go to church. She'd sob through that too.

Ma'd always been heavy. She stayed indoors, in hiding. Which was fine with me. I didn't need all the kids in school making fun of her. After Dad died Ma got worse about going out in public. Eating too. I bet she weighed close to five hundred pounds now. And she hadn't left the house in a year. Not to go to church. Not to shop. Not to step outside for a breath of fresh air.

Unfortunately, the only way to my bedroom was past Ma and Pastor Glenn. He glanced up from his reading. "Hello, Mike." He grinned. He had a gap between his two front teeth that made him look like a big kid.

"How's it goin'?" I said.

"Every day is a blessing. Thank you for asking. We miss you at church."

I forced a grim smile. "I'll try to get there next week." That was a lie, and he knew it. I'd stopped going to church after Dad died. Too many sad eyes. Too many prayers said for me and Ma and Darryl.

I took a shower. While I was soaping up, I could feel Pastor Glenn in the other room. It creeped me out. A memory seeped into my mind. The last time we all went to church. The Szabos, five of us, along with half the town. It was Camilia's baptism. I was, what? Seven, eight? Ma had handed the baby to Pastor Glenn, then sat on a folding chair. She couldn't stand too long, even then. I remember, she started bawling. Tears trickling out the sides of her eyes and streaming down her blotchy face. Dad had handed her a handkerchief and patted her shoulder. He wasn't crying. He never cried. He was strong. He was holding my hand, smiling down on me.

Why was Ma crying? It was a happy occasion. Did she know then that Camilia was going to die?

What? That thought brought me up short. I blinked soap out of my eyes and rinsed off my face.

Camilia died the next day. Ma couldn't have known. Not the way she reacted when it happened.

But how did Camilia die? As hard as I racked my brain, I couldn't remember. It wasn't violent, I don't think. I'd remember that.

By the time I was done and dressed, Pastor Glenn had gone. Thank God. Ma was back in her room, doing whatever it was she did in there thirty-six hours a day. Consume pies by the box load, then ask the Lord's forgiveness for gluttony. Darryl'd been up. He'd left the milk out to sour. I fixed myself a power shake and took my glass out back. On the porch stoop, I drank and tried not to think about stuff. About how it might've gone with Xanadu and Bailey.

When I got to the water tower at quarter to eleven, the ladder was already propped up against the side. I freaked. What if some dumb kid had climbed to the top and did a copycat? This town couldn't take another death. They couldn't afford it. Dad's suicide had cost everyone, not only in terms of burial costs. I scaled the ladder as fast as I could.

The dumb kid turned out to be Jamie. He was greased from head to toe with baby oil. Somehow he'd managed to cart up a chaise lounge and cooler, in addition to his boom box and beach bag.

"What's that?" I said, noting with disgust what he was wearing. Or wasn't wearing.

"Like it?" He snapped the strap on his thong. "I bought these on eBay. One for each day of the week. Want to see where it says 'Sunday'?"

I ignored him as I spread out my towel. The metal walkaround was already generating visible heat waves. I pulled my undershirt over my head. All I had to wear were my sports bra and boxers, since my swimming suit was way too small. I'd bulked up a little over the summer — okay, a lot. But it wasn't worth buying a new suit. I hadn't been to the town pool for two years, and might never go again. Dad and I had installed the pump and filtration system, and it was just another reminder.

"I thought you'd invite Xanadu," Jamie said. He offered me the baby oil.

I pulled sunblock out of my pack instead. "Why would I do that?" I asked, squeezing a blob of cream into my hand and smearing my abs.

"Oh, I don't know. You want to eat her?"

I just looked at him.

He grinned. "It's so obvious, the way you look at her and go into heat."

"Shut up." Was it? Had she noticed? What if she had? I rubbed sunblock over my left shin. "You'd know about dogs in heat."

"Yes, I would." He panted.

"You don't know squat." I retrieved my shades from my pack and slipped them on. "Turn up the radio. I like this song."

"Ooh, yeah, me too."

Jamie sang and I hummed along to Faith Hill's *Breathe*. I closed my eyes, picturing Xanadu in my mind. I wondered what she was doing at this very moment. Running naked through the corn. I chuckled to myself. It's wheat. I should've invited her today. I could've spent the next three hours in rapt fascination as she swabbed her entire body with sunblock. Maybe I could've helped with those hard-to-reach spots.

But she wasn't into tanning.

The song ended and the news came on. Jamie switched off the radio. "She is a babe." He rolled onto his side and propped himself up on an elbow. "What do you know about her?"

All I need to. "She's staying out at the Davenports'. Faye and Leland are her great-aunt and uncle."

"Boring. Tell me something private and personal that she swore you to secrecy never to reveal."

In his dreams. I recapped my sunblock and set the bottle beside me on the towel. Withdrawing an eight-pack of Capri Suns from my pack, I peeled the outer cellophane wrapper and handed a box to Jamie.

"Word of advice, Mike," he said, sticking his straw through the foil on top. "Give it up. Unless you know something I don't, she's straight. You saw her with Bailey. She was all over him like maggots on meat. We shouldn't hold that against her. She was obviously BTW." He sipped noisily.

BTW — born that way. What did he mean, all over him?

I lay back and beckoned the sun. Heat me, give me life. Jamie was exaggerating.

A finger poked my arm and I flinched. "She'll only break your heart," Jamie said.

I twisted his finger, or tried to. It was slimy. "What are you, the voice of experience?"

"Unfortunately, yes." He sighed. He resettled on his chaise and pulled his sunglasses down from atop his head.

He was referring to Beau. Last year and most of this one, that was all he talked about. Beau, Beau, Beau. I wanna blow Beau. Problem was, besides Beau being straight as a rail, he was too polite. Beau'd never tell Jamie to fuck off, like most of the guys had. "You know," I said, "maybe if you didn't act so queer, you'd have a chance with Beau."

Jamie burst into laughter.

What? Was he laughing at me? That pissed me off. "Look, if you're going to give advice, you should be able to take it."

"Mike, Mike, Mike." Jamie shook his head. Sliding his shades back over his spiky bleached hair, he said, "Beau was never a possibility. I knew that. You didn't think I was serious about him, did you?" He batted his eyelashes at me. "Oh my God." Jamie cupped a hand over his mouth. "You did."

Jerk. I'd been so sympathetic too. So concerned when he moped around after school, crying about how he was never going to meet anyone, how he was doomed to become an old maid. An old fag is more like it.

"It's a game," Jamie said. "I play it all the time. Jamie's fantasy dream date. Really, Mike. I thought you knew that."

"It didn't look like a game." How can you manufacture tears?

"Okay, I admit, there was an element of hope."

I knew it.

"But Mike," he reached over and touched me again, "I have a rule with straights — and so should you. Look, but do not touch."

I plucked his greasy fingers off my forearm. "Play by your own rules."

"You still won't admit it, will you?"

I acknowledged I was gay, okay? I just wasn't like him.

"Anyway," he stretched his arms over his head and wriggled his skinny butt down into his chaise. "Beau was yesterday's cock tease. I'm in love with Shane now."

Shane. Jamie's imaginary boyfriend. This guy he'd supposedly met in an online chat room. Jamie'd been bringing up his name for the last month or so, but I'd tuned him out. Next month it'd be someone different.

"He called me last night. From Mississippi."

"Who?"

Jamie turned his head. "Hello? Shane?"

I whipped around and frowned at him. "You're kidding. You mean, like, on the phone?"

"No, from a hog-calling contest. 'Hoo eee, Jam-eee.' Yes, on the phone. From work." Jamie crossed his arms over his chest and sighed. "He's everything I ever dreamed of. And more."

"What did he say?"

"None of your business," Jamie sniped. "It was a very private, very intimate conversation. Maybe if you ask me nice . . ."

This bothered me. Sitting up, I took off my shades and swung around to face Jamie. "You shouldn't have given him your phone number. That scares me."

"Yeah, it scares me too," Jamie admitted. "I've never had anyone actually be interested in me. I have to wonder why."

That wasn't the problem. Jamie was attractive. He was a good guy. Anyone would be lucky to have him for a boyfriend. Although, I couldn't imagine Jamie having a boyfriend. "You're not planning on meeting him, are you?"

Jamie dropped his jaw. "Well, duh. Of course I am."

"Jamie, you can't!" My voice rose an octave. "Come on. You've heard the horror stories about meeting people on the Internet. All the perverts and child molesters. Get real."

"What choice do I have? It's not like we live in San Francisco. You want me to go to Wichita and hang out in the gay bars?"

"No," I said. God, no.

"Then tell me, where are we going to meet people?"

Here, I thought. They'll come here. She's here.

Jamie's head lolled back on the chaise and he closed his eyes. "I don't want to be the oldest living virgin on Earth. Aside from you."

I sneered, which he missed because he was totally out of touch with reality.

"He's calling me again tonight."

"Jamie —"

His voice softened as he added, "I like him, Mike. I really do. We have a lot of the same interests: music, movies, porn stars."

I blew out an irritated breath and put my shades back on. The water tank behind us was reflecting heat like a solar panel. My skin sizzled. I needed to move. Take action. I scrambled to my feet. At the railing, I leaned over to catch a breeze and asked Jamie, "How old is he? Where's he from? What's his family do?"

"You sound like Geneviève. 'James, sweetie, who is this Shane person? Where is he from, honey? How big is his dick?'" He imitated his mother perfectly, except for the last part.

"Well?" I said, turning and extending my arms along the crossbar. "Inquiring minds want to know."

"Okay, Katie Couric. He's from Alabama, and he's got the sexiest southern drawl to prove it. He works in a gas station, but that's just temp. He wants to become a filmmaker. He's twenty-two —"

"Twenty-two!" My voice bounced off the water tank. "He's too old for you."

"No, Mother Superior, he is not. That's only five years' difference. Geneviève and Hakeem are twelve years apart and it works for them. They're celebrating their twentieth anniversary this year." Geneviève and Hakeem. Jamie's parents.

Jamie scrunched up, hugging his knees. "He lives in a small town where there's not much action. None, he says. He's lonely, Mike. Like me. I'm so fucking lonely." Jamie's eyes bore into mine. "And so are you."

I hustled to gather up my gear and shove it in my pack. My towel, sunscreen. "You're a horndog," I told him.

"And you're not?"

I shouldered my pack and headed for the gate.

"You're leaving already? It's barely noon."

Let him wallow in self pity. My life was fine, perfect. So what if I didn't have a girlfriend? That was about to change.

As I stepped onto the top rung of the ladder, I glanced back to find Jamie staring at me. Excavating my soul. I had to admit, he knew me better than anyone. What was it we had between us? An indefinable connection, an understanding. A shared desperation. I don't know. The gay thing.

He was right. I was lonely.

"Just be careful," I said. "Please?"

Jamie nodded. "You too."

⸺⸺

There were five messages on the answering machine. The first was Nel, from the tavern. "Mike, call me as soon as you can. I have a disaster here and I need your help. Let's see, it's twelve-forty. Call me."

What kind of disaster? I wondered.

The second message was from Xanadu. "Oh my God, help me!" she cried. "I'm stuck in a freaking time warp in Sublette, Kansas. Where the hell is Sublette? Isn't that an apartment? You think Coalton's small? Aunt Faye and Uncle Lee dragged me along on their weekly visit to his folks, who are old as Egyptian mummies. Right now Uncle Lee and his dad are in the parlor — yes, the parlor — comparing war injuries. God. Before that, they pulled out these shoe boxes full of old photos for me to see, like I know who Bella and Abel Cleveland are and all their twenty-five-hundred children and grandchildren. They're probably all dead by now —"

Beep. The message timed out. A memory resurfaced. My grandparents. Grandma and Grandpa Szabo. Darryl and I used to go stay at their house in Leoti for two weeks every summer. I loved how we'd dump out Grandma Szabo's hatbox full of black-and-white photos and pass them around. She'd tell us about the people; share the family secrets. She didn't make up stories the way Dad did.

Grandma Szabo. She made me a quilt for my tenth birthday. I loved that quilt; still do.

Beep. "How rude. I'm back. Uncle Lee's mother and Aunt Faye are in the kitchen with the next door neighbor, Elektra. Yes, Jamie. That's her real name. I actually laughed out loud when she said it. Of course, I had to repeat my name three fucking times before she got it. They're comparing recipes for their Jell-O ambrosia. Do you know what's in a Jell-O ambrosia, Mike? Lime Jell-O and coconut; fruit cocktail and cottage cheese. Cottage cheese, in Jell-O. It has to look like someone blew chunks in a cake pan."

I burst into laughter.

Beep.

Jell-O ambrosia. Wow, I hadn't had that since . . . since I stopped going to church. The church ladies used to hold a potluck after the last service. I sort of liked Jell-O ambrosia.

Beep.

"You need to set your machine for longer messages if we're going to be best friends," Xanadu said. My heart leaped. Were we? Going to be best friends? "Anyway," she exhaled loudly, "there's this church-y social thing that I'll no doubt be forced to go to and be paraded around. So glad I wore my black leather S&M bustier and spiked dog collar. When Gramps saw my belly-button ring, he about popped the blood vessels in his one good eye. Did I mention he has a patch?"

I snorted.

She blew out a long breath. "He had to show me the shrapnel scar on his abdomen too. That's when I checked out. I'm holed up in the downstairs bathroom now, which smells like moldy mildew. There's a mousetrap by the sink. You don't think that means —" She screamed.

I laughed so hard, I about peed my pants.

"Okay, false alarm. It was only a cockroach. I'm sorry to bother you with all this, Mike. It's just I'm going psychotic here. Aunt Faye won't let me call my friends at home. . . . My friends, right. Like I even have any. They all turned on me after . . . you know. They made me feel defective. Which, I guess, I am. If, or when, you get back from wherever you are — pitching cow pies — whatever, would you please, *please* call me? My cell number's seven two oh . . ."

I rummaged through Darryl's junk on the counter to find a pencil and paper, and missed the number.

Xanadu's voice on the machine muffled. "I'm down here, Aunt Faye. I'll be right up. No, I just have a touch of diarrhea." More distinctly, she spoke to me. "I am now going to attempt to suck my brain out through my nose with this toilet plunger." There was this weird sound, then the machine clicked.

I replayed the last message to retrieve her cell number. She'd rattled it off so fast, and our machine tape was scratchy, and I had to replay it six times. When I thought I finally had it, I dialed the number, but only got a recorded out-of-service message.

The Davenports were in the phone book. I dialed their number. It rang and rang. Maybe I could drive out to their place. Park and wait. I didn't want Xanadu to think I wouldn't call her at the first possible moment. She needed to hear she wasn't defective.

The phone rang. I lunged for it. "Hello?"

"Mike, thank God you're there. Did you get my message?"

It took me a moment, since I was expecting, hoping, to hear Xanadu's voice again. "I just got home," I told Nel.

"This is a disaster. Both my toilets are overflowing and I can't find the shutoff valve." She sounded frantic. "I don't know if the septic's full or there's something in the line. It shouldn't be full. I had the tank pumped a couple of months ago. I'd call up to Goodland, but they won't come on a Sunday, and even if they did it'd cost me an arm and a leg. Your dad always handled this kind of thing for me. Do you think you could come over and take a look?"

I hesitated.

"Mike?"

"Sure," I said. "I'll be right there." This was Nel. She had an emergency.

"You're an angel." She hung up.

There was a clog in her line somewhere. An easy fix. I'd have to stop by the shop for the snake and pump —

No.

Please no.

Not the shop.

Chapter Eight

My stomach felt queasy as I turned up Main. I could see it from a distance, the front window, Szabo Plumbing and Heating. I'd done the lettering myself in sixth grade. Stick-on letters — big deal. The glass was still cracked from the hailstorm that about demolished the town the day of Dad's funeral. Our roof at home had been pulverized so bad a bunch of shingles had busted loose. Did Darryl fix it? No. Every time it rained the water spots on the ceiling in my room spread like a grease fire. One of these days the whole roof was going to collapse.

This vision materialized in my mind: Me, that day, standing on the porch at home watching the world get ripped apart. Same way my insides felt. Like an idiot I'd rushed out into the mucky backyard to retrieve a handful of hailstones. They were still in the freezer as a memento, I guess. I didn't need any mementos.

I parked in the alley behind the shop and sat for a minute, trying to slow my pounding heart. I swore I wouldn't do this; wouldn't come here. I'd respect his wishes, his decision.

Respect.

He didn't extend it to me. All the times I'd come to work with Dad, come to the shop, we'd make a day of it. A pit stop at the Suprette for a couple of sticky buns and a quart of orange juice. Our favorite breakfast. He'd pour the juice into his coffee mug, then mix it with vodka when he thought I wasn't looking.

I was always looking, Dad.

I turned off the truck. I got out, leaving the keys in the ignition. I could just run in, get what I needed, get out. The back door key was still on the windowsill where it always was. Only over the years it'd been incorporated into a spongy spiderweb. The door still required a good heft of shoulder. Dad vowed he'd fix that loose frame. Someday, he'd said. Someday.

"You ran out of somedays, didn't you, Dad?" I flicked the light switch. Nothing. Of course, the electricity would be off. What was I thinking, that everything was the same?

Some things were. Dad's two oak filing cabinets, *circa* 1940. His steel desk. The stockroom shelves of PVC pipe and copper tubing, bathroom fixtures, valves, vent caps, flare plugs, flex connectors. When I was little and Dad would bring me to work with him, he'd plop me on the braided rug behind his desk and give me boxes of elbows and wyes and flare nuts and male and female adapters and nipples and stub outs and tees and unions and compression caps. I'd play for hours and hours fitting all the parts together, screwing and piecing. Everything fit perfectly. Like life. No leaks.

What was I saying? Life leaked from every loose coupling. There wasn't enough plumber's putty in all the world to keep the life from leaking out of Dad.

Stop it, I admonished myself. He'd made his choice.

That was the part I was having trouble with. His choosing to die.

The building still belonged to us, at least. Great-Grandpa Szabo had built it himself, brick by brick. From the ground up, he'd built our reputation, the family business. He meant for it to stay in the family. Forever. It would have too, if only Dad had trusted me.

Shut up, brain. It's not his fault.

Whose fault is it?

Darryl's, if anyone. He trashed the business.

Breathe in deeply; hold, hold. Don't let it get to you, I told myself. Control. Action. I released my breath, along with the tension in my muscles. In my jaw, my stomach. It's all about control.

Action and control.

Dad's toolbox lay open on his desk. I closed the lid and latched it; noticed a stack of mail in his outbox. For some reason, I riffled through the envelopes: Rural Phone and Electric, Farmer's Insurance, Aquastar Heaters, the Mercantile —

"Dammit, Darryl," I cursed him out loud. "The least you could've done is paid the bills. He trusted you."

He trusted you, Darryl. He trusted you with the business. The least you could've done is cared.

Nel was swabbing the floor when I pushed through the café doors at the tavern. She flung the mop down and rushed over to meet me. To hug me. "Mike, you're a lifesaver," she said.

"I thought I was an angel."

She cupped my chin. "That too. I found the shutoff valve, at least." The hardwood floor was damp and discolored around the booths, and the whole place reeked of sewage. Poor Nel. She'd be bleaching for days. The phone rang and she hustled around the bar to answer it. "You know where everything is in the bathrooms?" She lifted the receiver.

"I'll find it."

"Hello? Oh, Miss Millie. I just wanted to call and tell you I had to close early today. . . ."

Miss Millie. She'd assumed Dad's exalted position of town drunk after he'd relinquished the honor.

Both restrooms had been mopped, but there was still standing water around the toilets. I'd never worked on these particular units. They were ancient even by Coalton standards. In the women's room, I removed the tank lid and examined the ball-cock assembly. Rusty, but intact. Did I smell sewer gas? I followed my nose out the back door to the septic tank. All the other buildings in town had hooked into the main sewer line a few years back. Dad and I had done most of the conversions. Darryl had helped a little, if you want to call it that. "It's not my gig, Dad," I remember him saying. Remember him whining the whole time. Then bailing on us.

He and Dad got into a fight about it later. Darryl hollering he didn't want to be a turd herder.

The septic wasn't full, as Nel suspected, so there had to be blockage in the line. I'd augur it first. Clear the siphon holes in the toilets. If I had to root the main line or dig a trench to cut through the pipe, this could be a mammoth job. I almost hoped it was. Not for Nel. For me.

I loved plumbing. Loved the problem solving, discussing with Dad solutions, how to fix things, connecting the parts, the pieces. I loved new installations, planning the architecture, the piping, soldering, installing the fixtures. I loved every aspect of plumbing. It was in my blood; it ran through my veins.

It took a few tries, first with the snake, then the power snake. Eventually, I twisted through. A huge clot of cloth, like a dishrag, came out attached to the snake blade. Weird. It was in the men's urinal.

I showed it to Nel. She said, "Oh shit. I know whose that is. Charlene and Reese. They stopped by to show me their new baby girl on Saturday. Charlene's in seventh heaven finally having a girl. After those boys of hers . . ." Nel shook her head. So did I. The Tanner boys. Look out, world. "The baby needed changing and Charlene and I were catching up on news, so Reese said he'd do it. That man has the brains of a two-year-old, I swear. That might be giving him too much credit. I can't believe he'd flush a diaper down the toilet."

"Maybe you should have him arrested," I said.

Nel looked at me and burst out laughing. Reese was the town sheriff. Nel laughed and laughed. Her smoker's wheeze degenerated into a coughing fit.

"Do you want me to help clean up?" I asked, rewinding the snake.

"Not necessary. You've done enough. You are an angel."

"I don't mind."

"You go on home."

I didn't want to. I wanted to replumb the whole tavern.

Nel trailed me out to the truck. After I hefted the power snake into the back, I turned to find her extracting a wad of money from her zipper pouch. She peeled off four or five tens and handed them to me.

"Forget it," I said. "It's on the house."

"No such thing," she said. "You're as bad as your dad." She slapped the money into my palm and closed my fingers around it.

She had to bring him up, didn't she? Just when I was feeling so good.

She shut the driver's side door after me and rested her arms across the open window frame. "Arrest Reese. Ha. That's a good one. You've got your Dad's sense of humor too. I could always count on him to leave me with a laugh. I miss that."

I had to go — now. I cranked the ignition over.

"Why don't you stop by more often, Mike? We could reminisce."

Oh yeah. Just what I wanted to do. Remember my old man. How funny he was. How he drank himself to oblivion. How he chose death over life.

Like hell, I thought as I pealed out. Every time I go in there, it makes me wonder why. Why'd he do it? Why was that his choice? "You can choose to die, Dad. It's your life to take. But why did you have to take us down with you?"

Me, Ma, even Darryl.

Thanks, Dad. I hate you.

⁓

Xanadu was sitting in my seat pouting at me when I straggled into Geometry. "I tried to call you," I said, sliding into Bailey's desk in front of her and swiveling around. "The phone number you left was all garbled on our machine." From my shirt pocket, I pinched out the Suprette receipt where I'd written the numbers. I handed it to her. "This was my best guess."

She read it and widened her eyes. She'd taken extra care to put on eyeliner and eyeshadow today. Not heavy. Not necessary. Gray-blue shadow, the color of her eyes. It glittered. Sparkled. She glittered. She didn't know what defective was. "Not even close," she said, uncapping a Flair with her teeth. She was wearing lipstick. Lip gloss, more like. It was all glimmery and slick. She drew a line through the numbers and wrote new ones below.

Mrs. Stargell hadn't arrived yet, which was unusual. The bell had already rung. "I drove out to the Davenports' last night, but you weren't back yet," I told Xanadu. After Nel's, I'd driven straight to their place, circling around for two solid hours, watching for the hearse. I was afraid someone would call Reese Tanner and report suspicious behavior out on the county road.

"Good morning, guys and dolls." Miz S bustled in. "Did everyone have a nice weekend?"

Xanadu rolled her eyes at me and I smiled.

"I see we have people missing still. Has anyone talked to Bailey or Beau since Friday? How is their dad doing?" Mr. McCall had gotten gored by a bull, which was why the B boys were out calving.

From the back, Skip Greer spoke up. "He's still wrapped, but he's able to move around some. Bailey's helping with inoculations today. He says he expects to be back tomorrow."

"Shit," I heard Xanadu mutter. "He's not even coming?"

It made me wonder again about her ride home. What had happened? Obviously nothing. She'd called *me* from Sublette.

"How about Shawnee?" Miz S asked. "I went over to see her Saturday and she seemed fine. Have you talked to her, Deb?"

Deb Pastore said, "Yeah. She had a doctor's appointment this morning. She'll be back tomorrow."

Mrs. Stargell closed her roll book. "I hate to get into the Pythagorean Theorem and trigonometric ratios without Bailey and Shawnee here. It's such a beautiful day, let's go outside and read."

That woke everyone up. There was a flurry of activity as people gathered their books and packs. Xanadu touched my shoulder and said, "Did she say outside to *read?*"

I twisted my head. "She reads. We listen."

Xanadu wrinkled her nose.

"She does this all the time," I said. "She reads to us. She says she wants us to develop an appreciation for the arts."

"Did anyone tell her this was Math class?" Xanadu crossed her eyes. I cracked up. She was so funny.

We herded down the hall in clumps. Xanadu walked beside me. "She's a real head case," Xanadu said, motioning to Mrs. Stargell ahead of us, who'd linked one arm in Deb's and the other in Skip Greer's. "Does she really think we won't take off?"

As in ditch? Nobody ditched. This was Coalton.

"Miz S is cool," I told her. "She grades easy. Plus, you don't want to get on her bad side because she'll call a conference with your parents and make them come to school. She doesn't put up with crap."

Xanadu widened her eyes. "Thanks for the warning." She clenched my wrist and held on. She could hold on forever, it felt so good and warm. Or slip her fingers down into mine, through mine. I relaxed my hand in case she was considering it. But she only squeezed and let me go.

We gathered under the big elm in front, which wasn't giving off shade this time of year. A hawk circled overhead. Miz S said, "Don't spread out too far. My voice isn't what it used to be."

Xanadu kicked off her sandals and wriggled her toes in the greening lawn. Her toenails were painted. Deep, dark red. I sat back, propping on my elbows next to her and extending my legs. There was a slight breeze, but the air smelled of change. A storm brewing in the west. Rain, maybe. Or snow.

Miz S said, "I thought we'd read poetry today."

A couple of people groaned. I didn't. I liked hearing poetry when Miz S read it. She didn't just read; she performed. She opened the tattered cover on a thick black book and skimmed the table of contents. "Here's one I think you'll like." She licked her finger and paged forward. " 'Because I Could Not Stop for Death,' by Emily Dickinson."

Xanadu swung her head toward me. "She's joking, right? Emily Dickinson? Please."

Clearing her throat, Miz S pushed her glasses up the bridge of her nose and held the book out in front of her face.

"Because I could not stop for Death —
He kindly stopped for me —
The Carriage held but just Ourselves —
And Immortality."

Her reading was dramatic, with intonations and voice inflections. Xanadu glanced at me once over her shoulder and stuck out her tongue in a gag. Lifting her long hair up with both arms, she let it fall down her back in raining ribbons. I wanted to reach out and feel every strand, run my fingers through the silk.

"He slowly drove — He knew no haste
And I had put away
My labor and my leisure too,
For His Civility —"

I lay back on the grass, hands under my head. My abs contracted instinctively; hold, hold, let it out slowly. Focus. Control. I tried to focus on Miz S's rising pitch, the tenor of her voice, the meaning of her words. The part about not stopping for Death.

"We passed the School, where Children strove

At Recess — in the Ring —"

Without warning Xanadu lay beside me, her face inches away. "Pinch me if I snore," she murmured. Stretching her arms over her head, she yawned and arched her back. Her breasts rose and fell. She was close. So close. I could slide my leg to the left and touch hers. We were both wearing shorts. Skin on skin contact. Her shorts were blue, stretchy, fitted across her soft, smooth thighs. Mine were boxers, loose, hanging off the edge of my muscular quads. Did she notice? I flexed.

Six inches, that was the distance between us. Why did it feel like miles?

She shut her eyes and licked her lips. I could lean over and kiss her. Touch her nipple.

Xanadu sat up fast as if she'd read my mind. My face flushed and I rolled away from her, scrabbling to sit. I didn't dare meet her eyes.

"Mike," I heard her whisper urgently. She lunged forward and clenched a hand over my shoulder. "There he is."

"He" was Bailey. He'd parked his truck at the curb and emerged, Beau from the passenger side. Bailey checked his watch, said something to Beau, and in step they sauntered up the main walk.

Deb Pastore shrieked, "Bailey, we're over here!"

Miz S choked on "Eternity," the last word. She slit-eyed Deb over the book.

"Sorry." Deb blushed. "I just wanted to get his attention."

A couple of people went, "Oooh." Deb hid her face.

Bailey glanced over at us and hitched his chin. He and Beau parted ways. Bailey strolled across the lawn.

"He is so tall," Xanadu breathed. "And utterly, totally hot."

So are you, I thought. Steaming hot. Bailey appraised the group, his eyes roving the clumps of people. They slowed on Xanadu. On her hand gripping my shoulder.

Yes, I thought. Get a good look.

As I lifted my hand to cover hers, she withdrew it.

"Here, Bailey," Deb piped up. "You can sit next to me." She swept her legs underneath her long skirt to make room for him. I hadn't heard there was anything going on between Bailey and Deb Pastore. But then, I wasn't all that interested. Jamie'd know. I'd ask him. Pray they were a couple now.

Miz S said, "Welcome back, Bailey. How's your dad?"

"Doin' good. Thanks." His head dropped and he removed his Stetson.

"Now," Miz S continued, "I'd like to read 'Oh Mistress Mine' by William Shakespeare." She paused, waiting for Bailey to settle in. Next to Deb. Oh yeah. I saw Bailey sneak a peek at us. Leaning in closer to Xanadu, I deliberately fused my shoulder to hers. Get a good look, Bailey. Back off.

"Oh mistress mine! Where are you roaming?

Oh! stay and hear; your true love's coming . . ."

I knew this poem. We'd studied Shakespeare last year in English. O mistress mine. Your true love's coming. Was Xanadu listening? Your true love's coming.

She flattened out on her stomach, facing Bailey, her chin resting on her hands. I don't know what got into me. My lips began to move. My vocal cords engaged. I mocked Miz S: "What is love? 'Tis not hereafter; Present mirth hath present laughter . . ."

The sudden silence made me stop, and shut up.

"If you'd like to continue Mike, I'm sure we'd all appreciate hearing your interpretation of the Bard."

I died. "No, ma'am. Sorry." Everyone was gawking at me. Xanadu twisted her head around and smiled.

In that moment, I knew I loved her.

The bell rang and we all scrambled to our feet. I waited while Xanadu slipped on her sandals. Then she took off.

I had to jog to catch up. In the main hall, Xanadu bumped right into the back of Bailey, hard. It made him stumble forward. She went, "Oh sorry. I didn't see you there."

When he turned around, she blinked in recognition. "Oh. Hi, Bailey," she said.

"Hi," he said.

"Hey, thanks again for the ride home." She placed an open hand against his arm. "You know, since we live so close, you should stop by after school. Like, every day," she intoned, crossing her eyes.

Under the brim of his hat, Bailey looked at her and smiled. Beside him, Deb Pastore stiffened. Deb glared at The Hand. Xanadu did an unexpected thing then. She moved her hand slowly to my arm, snaking it underneath and crooking her elbow in mine. "Later," she said, to Bailey, tugging me down the hall. The last glimpse I had was Deb Pastore frowning at our backs.

Xanadu said under her breath, "Ooh, that was fun."

For who? I wondered.

"Mike, can you come see me now?"

I jumped out of my skin as Dr. Kinneson ambled up beside me. "I know you have P.E. this hour, but I forgot I scheduled a meeting during your homeroom." She added coolly over my head, "Hello, Xanadu."

Xanadu cut Dr. Kinneson a look. Apparently they'd met.

"You'd better get to class," Dr. Kinneson told her. "You're going to be late."

Xanadu snapped, "I was going. God." She dropped my arm and stormed off ahead of me.

Dr. Kinneson motioned with her wrist for me to follow her. I'd rather have chased down Xanadu, resumed our close encounter of the physical kind, but I didn't think I had an option.

Wrong. I had an option: Follow Dr. Kinneson or die.

Chapter Nine

"I invited the recruiter from Kansas State to come watch you play last week." Dr. Kinneson motioned me to a chair in her office. "He's a friend of my husband's. They went to Penn State together."

She had all these diplomas on her wall that I couldn't read from my seat. A picture of her and her husband sat on the bookshelf behind her. He looked like Denzel Washington.

"Jerry's very interested in your future. Jerry Wesson — he's the recruiter — he's been following you. A lot of coaches from other universities have too, of course. He'd like you to play for K State, though between you and me," her voice lowered. "I think you can do better."

Better than what? Her words were swirling around in my brain. I was having a hard time concentrating with the door closed. I hated closed doors. Hated being closed in, trapped. Did Dad feel trapped? Is that why . . . ?

"What do you mean?" I asked.

Dr. Kinneson folded her hands on top of the desk. "I mean, on a softball scholarship you can take your pick of colleges and universities. You were planning to go to college, weren't you?"

I let out a short laugh.

She looked offended. "What?" she asked.

"College? Me?"

She frowned. "Of course you. Why not?"

I sprawled back in the chair. Feigned attitude. "I'm not exactly college material, Coach. Er, Dr. Kinneson." I crossed an ankle over my knee. The sole of my Nikes was worn through and you could see my bare foot. I dropped my shoe back to the floor.

"That isn't true," she said. "You have a solid B average. You could go just about anywhere you wanted on an athletic scholarship, Mike. To a school with a softball program, which I'm sure is what you're looking for. There are dozens of good colleges and universities with competitive teams. Elite schools."

I couldn't suppress an audible exhale of breath. "Thanks, anyway." I pushed to my feet. "Not interested."

"Sit down," she snapped.

My butt hit the chair. Geez.

"Look at me."

My head lifted.

"What are you going to do with your softball?"

What'd she mean? Like, throw it? Or throw it away?

"What are your goals?" she asked. "Do you want to play professionally?"

"I don't know. I never thought about it." Which was a lie. The biggest lie of my life.

"What do you mean, you never thought about it?"

I used to think about it. But I quit. Dwelling on the impossible was destructive.

"You need to think about it," she went on. "You're good enough, you know."

That wasn't the point.

"Even if you didn't play, you could still get into college. You're smart and talented and you work hard."

I shook my head at the floor. "I don't think college is in my future, Coach — uh, ma'am."

"Why not? Look at me."

Why was she sniping? What had I done to make her mad?

"Why not?" she barked again.

A hundred reasons. The money. Wasn't that enough? The week after Dad's funeral, it all fell apart. I had the application for competitive league all filled out and ready to send. I went to Ma to ask for the money. Except — I couldn't. She was in bed, comatose. Plus, she wasn't acknowledging my existence. So I asked Darryl. I said, "I need you to write me a check for competitive league. Dad said I could go. He said I could try out for a travel team."

Darryl's face went white. Like I'd hit him in the gut.

"Dad's been saving the money," I told Darryl. "It's in his savings account. Just write me a check, okay?"

Darryl took the application I was shoving in his face and skimmed down the page. His eyes stuck on the bottom line. Then, he laughed. He laughed hysterically.

I ripped the app from his hands. "Dad's been planning for me to go, to play competitive," my voice rose to be heard over Darryl's donkey laugh. "I have to if I want to go pro. He's been planning it. He wants me to go!"

Darryl sobered fast. "There's no money," he said. "There's no savings."

"What?"

"There's nothing." Darryl got up from the kitchen table to leave.

"No." I grabbed his arm. "We've been planning this. Me and Dad. He's been saving for me."

"Are you deaf!" Darryl wheeled on me. "There's no fucking money.

He didn't leave us anything, okay? Except the business. The fucking business. He didn't even put money away for his own funeral. Who do you think buried him? Who do you think paid for that fucking headstone?" Darryl's shrill voice cracked. "Who? Who paid for his fucking worthless life?" Darryl stormed out.

I was left to wonder. Who? Who did pay?

Later, I figured it out. Coalton.

I swore I'd never take another penny from anyone in this town. Mike Szabo pays her way. She isn't a charity case.

My dream of going pro died with Dad. I'd play through high school, then hang up my glove. Face reality. Get on with it.

"Listen, Mike," Dr. Kinneson's voice brought me back to the present. She stood suddenly and charged around her desk like she was going to attack me. She stopped just short and held onto the edge of her desk, eyes boring down on my face. I felt like a caged animal, a criminal. "You have a way out of this town, Mike. A guaranteed future. You absolutely cannot waste this opportunity."

"Who said I wanted out?"

She acted like she didn't hear me. "You have so much ahead of you, you can't even imagine. I can help get your name and face out there, get college recruiters interested in you, but you're going to have to want this, commit to it long-term. It's up to you."

Nothing was up to me. He'd made my decision for me.

"Mr. Archuleta says he's talked to you about this before. About trying out for the KC Peppers or the Shockwaves. I understand your financial situation, but there are ways around that."

Don't. Don't blow. Breathe in. Out. Yeah, Coach Archuleta had talked to me. He'd talked a blue streak. He even offered to pay my way. No thanks.

She circled back around her desk and opened her top drawer. Withdrawing a glossy white folder, she said, "There's a softball camp this summer I'd like you to apply for. Jerry says it's brand-new, open only to top flight players. You get personalized instruction, a batting coach, a catching coach. It's three weeks of intensive training. I know you've been working out on your own, strength training, but at your level you need a personal trainer. You can't get that here." She shook her head and added, "They expect so much of you girls these days. Small towns don't have the facilities or resources. But, Mike," she looked at me hard, fixed on my face, my expressionless eyes, "this camp is doable. The recruiters who come to observe are thick as thieves, Jerry says. You're sure to attract attention. He says you have the raw talent — anyone can see that — but what sets you apart are your leadership skills. He says that's what recruiters are looking for. And the commitment, the hunger. Do you have the hunger?"

I used to. I ate up the game. I loved the game. More than she could know. More than anyone could know.

It was quiet, still. A magpie squawked outside her window. She was waiting for an answer. "Where is it?" I asked.

"The camp? Michigan," she said.

"Michigan!"

"It's expensive."

She had to be kidding. Michigan?

Dr. Kinneson handed me the folder across the desk. I made a show of opening the folder and glancing briefly at the papers and brochures inside. Lots of words, promises, hype. No dollar amounts. "How much?" I asked.

She made this clicking sound in her mouth with her tongue, like a human calculator. "With airfare and incidentals, it runs around three thousand dollars."

I choked on a laugh. Pushing to my feet, I said, "Thanks, anyway, Coach." And headed for the door.

"This is your future, Mike." Her voice stabbing at my back. "There are scholarships for players with financial need."

My eyes narrowed. Charity. Handouts. Help for the needy.

"Check with your mother," Dr. Kinneson added. "See what she thinks."

My gut twisted. My mother? Who would that be?

※

Jabba the Hutt was splayed along the entire breadth of the sofa with a TV tray perched between her tree trunk legs. She was eating a Mrs. Smith's cherry pie directly from the tin. Dr. Phil was on. All she ever watched were talk shows — Regis, Dr. Phil, Oprah, Jerry Springer. Since she never left the house, it was her only link to reality. If you call that real.

Two years. Ma hadn't talked to me in two years.

She didn't acknowledge me as I crossed in front of her to head for my room. Or on the return trip to the kitchen to make myself dinner. It'd gotten windy during practice after school. Cold. A storm blowing in. I'd snuck into Ma's room for a pair of Dad's long johns, just in case I might be working in the yard out back of the Merc.

What I'd said to her that day was bad, I admit. The day of Dad's funeral. The words were spoken aloud and I could never take them back. Every day, every time we breathed the same air, I wished I could take them back. She acted like I blamed her for his death. I didn't blame her. That's not what I said.

Darryl oozed into the kitchen. He grabbed a jar of Jif off the counter and looped a leg over his chair at the dinette. Leafing through a new car zine, he dipped his grimy index finger into the peanut butter jar and said, "Where've *you* been?"

"School," I answered. "You've heard of it. You learn stuff, then take that knowledge and apply it to some useful activity in the world. It's called work."

He flipped a page. The peanut butter smelled good. I shoved the box of mac and cheese I was going to cook up back into the cupboard and opened the fridge to fish around for jelly. Miracle of miracles.

Faye's homemade jam was only half gone. I retrieved the loaf of bread and slid across from Darryl at the dinette table.

"You got a call from Charlene," he said. He sucked peanut butter off his index finger.

"Charlene? Why would she be calling me?" Charlene was Darryl's girlfriend. Ex-girlfriend, I should say, from high school. She'd dumped Darryl for Reese Tanner right after graduation. Which was the smartest decision any girl ever made.

"She said you fixed Nel's john so would you come look at her leaky tub. I left the message on the machine."

Huh. I knifed out a mound of peanut butter, not being all that careful about whether I sliced off Darryl's finger or not.

He added, "You getting back in the biz?"

That hacked me. "What biz? Oh, you mean the one you never gave a rat's ass about so it all just dried up and dwindled away? That biz? That the one you talking about?" My voice sounded hard, bitter. Gee, I wonder why. I slathered the PB on a slice of bread and globbed on jelly.

Darryl said, "Look, I told him it wasn't my gig."

"What is your gig?" I folded the sandwich, trying to calm myself. "You don't work." I chomped into it. "You don't take care of the house. You don't fix anything around here." I chewed and swallowed. "What the hell do you do all day? Besides waste gas."

He turned a page in the magazine. With a thumbnail, he loosened the staples and carefully removed the centerfold. Which he handed across to me.

I snatched it out of his grubby paws.

Sliding the peanut butter jar my way, he stood and dumped the zine onto the head-high stack of newspapers and magazines accumulating near the back door. He could at least take them out to the incinerator, I thought. Or do the dishes, fix the roof, clean up the yard. Something, anything. "You know, Dad's survivor benefits are meant for me too. They're not yours to blow on your wastoid life."

He balled a fist in my face. "What do you know about my life, Mike? You just shut the fuck up about my life." We had a brief stare-down, then he slammed out the back door.

I heard him trip over the oil pan he'd left on the porch and curse. The pan clanked into the aluminum siding on the house.

What was his problem?

I could understand Ma's reaction — maybe — but what happened to my brother? When did he check out? What happened to the guy who used to let me tag along with him to the town pool every summer? The one who'd play three-around with me and Dad for hours and hours out back so I could practice my catching and hitting. Where was the Darryl who'd fixed up that old Mustang and won the stock car races in Goodland three years running? Or the guy who'd gotten voted homecoming king his senior year, with Charlene his queen. He'd lettered in track. He'd set a school record for the long jump. Which I'm reminded of every day when I pass by the office and see his trophy all lit up in the display case. Where did that Darryl go? How did he deteriorate so fast? After Charlene ditched him . . . after he crashed his Mustang . . . after Dad died . . .

It was as if Darryl died too. Or went away, same as Ma. Someplace far, distant, removed. They left and they didn't take me with them.

A crash in the living room propelled me off my chair. Ma grunted and groaned. She sounded hurt.

I raced in there. "Ma, you okay?"

She was trying to push to her feet. Grappling with the sofa slip-cover and heaving, falling back. The TV tray had tipped over and spilled what crumbs of crust remained in the pie tin all over the floor. I reached out to give Ma a hand. She slapped me away.

Fine, I thought. I hope you have a heart attack and die.

I hated myself for wishing that, but it seemed to be what she wanted. She finally levered herself up by swaying side to side. She kicked the tray across the room, then thundered down the hall. Her bedroom door whooshed shut.

If Darryl was numbing his pain with anger, Ma was medicating with food.

Anger surged up from my core. How could they? How could they let him do this? They were giving Dad exactly what he wanted — the satisfaction of knowing we couldn't live without him.

Not me. I could. I could live without him just fine.

Chapter Ten

/ called Charlene to see how bad her leak was. Bad, she said. I told her I could stop by either early tomorrow morning before school, or after work tonight, around nine.

"Tonight, please," she said, adding, "Mike, you're an angel."

I made a mental note: The shortest route to heaven is a plumber's license. I wish I had one.

Junior had finished all the stocking out in the yard, so Everett put me to work at the cash register. As I was ringing up Mrs. Ledbetter's ten bags of Meow Mix for all her feral cat colonies, I spied Jamie rushing through the door. Was that snow on his hair?

"Looks like we're in for a doozie," Miz Ledbetter said, tying a scarf on her head. "They're forecasting at least a foot around Sharon Springs."

Great, I thought. That'll screw up the softball schedule. "You want help with that?" I asked her.

"No, I've got it." She rolled her cart to the front and the door opened automatically. My eyes strayed back to Jamie, who'd made a beeline for the candy aisle. He motioned me over. I held up an index finger. Miz Ledbetter didn't need to strain herself loading all that cat food into her car. That was my job.

When I got back, Jamie was ripping into a supersize Tootsie Roll. "You're paying for that, you know."

"ShaneandIaregoingtomeet," he said so fast it took me a minute.

"When?"

Jamie broke off a nub of Tootsie Roll and offered it to me. I declined. He popped it into his mouth. "We haven't set a date, but he's checking out fares to Wichita and Topeka. I told him try Denver, it might be cheaper. I told him I'd drive to wherever he could fly into."

I just looked at Jamie. "You told him you'd drive."

Jamie ripped off another nub, ignoring me.

Jamie didn't drive. He'd tried it once. I took him out on the farm roads so he wouldn't kill anyone, but he said the speed scared him. Speed? He'd only gotten it up to forty. Jamie was strictly a moocher for rides. Wait a minute . . .

He grinned. "Yeah, that's where you come in."

"No." I snatched the Tootsie Roll from him. "I'm not chauffeuring you all over the country just so you can be some pervert's piece of ass."

Jamie blinked. "Excuse me?"

Did I say that? Darryl had gotten to me. Ma too. Everyone lately. "Why don't you ask your mom or dad to take you?"

"Well, now, there's a good idea. I'm sure Geneviève and Hakeem would be thrilled to meet my cyber-boyfriend. Say, we could double. The four of us could have a gay old time clubbing around Wichita." He grabbed back the Tootsie Roll. "Honey, I don't want my mother or father around when I finally hook up with a guy. Know what I'm saying?"

I did. Of course I did. "What makes you think *I* want to be there?"

He gnawed off a nub. "I know you like to watch."

I turned away.

"Come on," he said in that whiny voice that irritates me so much. "You can be my fag hag."

"I have a customer," I seethed. Mr. Blaylock, from the dairy. He'd come in out of the lumberyard with a stock tag. I trailed him to the cash register and Jamie called out, "There's a lifetime supply of curly fries in it for you."

After I rang up Mr. Blaylock, I sensed a presence behind me. "Why are you being such a bitch?" Jamie said. "I thought you'd be happy for me. One of us, at least, deserves to be happy."

I wheeled around and met his eyes. My mouth opened, then shut. I said it anyway. "We both deserve to be happy."

A moment passed between us — an understanding, an acknowledgment. I held out my hand. "That'll be a buck twenty-nine for the Tootsie Roll."

He slapped an invisible dollar bill on me and said, "Keep the change."

When their family got too big for a trailer, the Tanners moved into one of the show homes on First Street. Show homes. Right. None of the homes in Coalton was ever going to appear in *Architectural Digest*. Back in the sixties we had a big population boom — three whole families had migrated to town. They'd restored the most dilapidated houses on First Street. It was front-page news. The *Tri-County Gazette* called it "the redevelopment."

Charlene worked part-time at Tiny's Salon. At least, she used to. Before the baby.

"Mike." She answered the door, looking shocked. "I forgot you were coming."

I thought this was a big emergency.

Charlene reached up to feel the pink rollers in her hair. She had on an oversized, overwashed Garfield nightshirt and leather mocs. "It's freezing," she said. "Get in here." She grabbed my wrist and pulled me across the threshold. "Is that snow?"

A swirl of flurries followed me inside.

"How long's it been snowing?"

"About an hour," I told her. The ground was covered and the streets were slushy.

"I must look a fright." Charlene crossed her arms over her chest.

I blew a tunnel through my hands to warm them. "You don't scare me."

Charlene laughed and slapped my shoulder. If I didn't know better, I'd think she was flirting. I knew better. Darryl looked old for twenty-four, but Charlene looked a decade older. World-weary maybe, with four kids already.

"Mommy," one of them hollered from somewhere in back. "Todd's hitting me with his baseball bat."

Charlene screeched, "Todd, you stop that right now!" About shattered my eardrums. Two kids came tearing into the room, wailing on each other. Charlene collared one. "Wait'll your father gets home. He'll beat the crap out of you."

"Shut up," the kid muttered, noticing me.

"Don't you tell me to shut up," Charlene snapped. "I'll wash your mouth out with soap so fast you won't know what hit you."

"Shut up."

She charged after him through the living room. The other kid, who was smaller, dirtier, stood there and gawked at me. I stuck out my tongue. He didn't react. What was he, brain-dead?

"The shower's in the downstairs bathroom." Charlene returned, her face flushed, a roller hanging loose. "This way." We had to forge a path through the toys and crusty dishes and piles of laundry on the floor.

The basement was dark, dank, semi-finished. Everyone in town had a basement. Coalton was in the heart of tornado alley, so basements or storm cellars were essential. We'd never actually had a tornado set down in town, but five or six threatened every year. Charlene flicked on the light in the bathroom. My eyes adjusted and honed in on the tub. It had a fuzzy scum ring. Gross. Not as gross as the mildew from the faucet clear up to the shower head. Every tile was black and warped.

Bad news.

"It's been dripping awhile," Charlene said.

No shit. The leaky spigot was the least of her worries. There had to be a major rupture in the pipes behind the wallboard for this much buckling of the tile.

"Cut it out!" a voice harped upstairs. "Give it back. Mommy, Todd's got my skateboard and he won't give it back."

The skateboard flew down the stairs and almost decapitated Charlene. "Goddammit, Todd!" she screamed. "You're in time-out." She stormed up the steps, her voice shrilling, "Trent and Troy, both of you, just keep away from your brother. If you wake up that baby, I'll beat your butts bloody. . . ."

I ran my hand along the shower wall and one of the tiles fell off. Uh-oh. I didn't bring any mortar or grout. The sound of sniffling behind me made me spin around. A kid lurked in the shadows. Same one who'd stared me down in the living room. He had to be either Troy or Trent, since Todd was getting his rear end blistered upstairs.

Troy/Trent stuck his tongue out at me. I grinned. At least he was normal. "Hey," I said.

He slit snake eyes and hissed.

Scary. Scary kids.

Charlene bustled back down the stairs. "Sorry. You must be thanking your lucky stars you'll never have kids," she said.

What'd she mean by that? I was going to have kids.

Another bellow from upstairs: "Mommy! Todd shut the door on my finger." Bawling like a banshee.

"Jesus H. Christ —"

"You go ahead," I told her. "I'll take care of this. I might have to remove a portion of the wall to get to the pipes."

"Whatever," Charlene said. "Me and Reese are moving our bedroom down here to get some peace and quiet. We need this shower to work."

"Are you a girl or a boy?" the kid asked. "You look like a boy."

"Trent!" Charlene cuffed him upside the head. Ow. That had to hurt. He wailed. Well, I would too.

"That is so rude. Apologize to Mike. To, uh, Mary-Elizabeth."

I grimaced. "That's okay. I do sort of look like a boy. Check this out." I flexed my arm for Trent. His eyes bulged. Pretty impressive, if I did say so myself. You could see the action through my sweatshirt.

He flexed his skinny arm back. I said, "Dude. You're The Rock." He giggled.

"Thank you, Mike." Charlene let out a long breath and hugged Trent to her leg. "Let's all take a time-out, huh?" She kissed his head, then scooted Trent up the stairs.

I got to work. Halfway through the job of prying off tiles, Charlene reappeared. "So," she said. "How's that sweet brother of yours?" She crouched to retrieve something from under the sink. A pack of Salems and a lighter.

Darryl, sweet? "He's okay," I lied. More bitter than sweet.

She shook a cigarette out of the pack and mushed it between her lips. "Is he in love with anyone these days?" She lit the cigarette and inhaled deeply, like it was the breath of life.

"You mean besides himself?"

Charlene coughed out smoke. "You're so funny. I forgot what a kill you are. No. Ego was never Darryl's problem. Just the opposite." She flicked her ashes into the sink. "He never could —" She stopped.

A stereo blasted overhead, the bass cranked up so high it made the walls shake. "Goddammit, they're going to wake up the baby." Charlene wrenched on the cold water faucet and extinguished her cigarette, then pulled out the sink trap and washed the butt down the drain. As she charged up the stairs again, I thought, That is not a healthy habit for a home drainage system.

Darryl never could what? I wondered. Get it up?

It took a while to cut through the wallboard, since I only had the keyhole saw, and when I lifted out the square of wall, the problem presented itself. Whoever had installed this plumbing had done a half-assed job. It wasn't Dad. He'd never have used galvanized steel pipe in a bathroom. It didn't last long enough, as evidenced by this leak. Leaks, I should say. Three or four continuous leaks. There was more than one botched repair too. Dad would never have fluxed steel pipe to PVC, or even tried to.

I decided to do it right. Rip out the pipe and replumb the whole setup with copper. I'd have to run back to the shop for supplies. Didn't matter. I was psyched about the job.

At the top of the stairs, I found Charlene on the sofa breast-feeding her baby. "I have to run to the shop," I told her, trying not to look.

"He was there when I had Todd. Did he tell you that?" Charlene said.

"What?" I wasn't sure what she was talking about. Or who. She had this dreamy look in her eyes. I inched toward the front door. "I'll let myself back in."

"Darryl, I mean," Charlene went on. She adjusted the baby, squeezing her boob with her free hand. "He took me to the hospital in Garden City and stayed during my whole labor and delivery."

"Darryl?" I stopped in my tracks. "You're kidding. When was this?"

Charlene glanced up, blinked. "Four, five years ago? Todd just had a birthday, so six years ago. Wow, has it been that long? Reese was at some officer training course in Topeka and it was snowing, like tonight. He couldn't make it back. My mom was off visiting her sister. So I called Darryl. He handled everything, like I knew he would. He always was responsible. Good old dependable Darryl."

"Darryl?" My Darryl? We were talking two different people.

"So sweet," Charlene cooed.

Was she still talking Darryl, or the baby?

"I was scared," she said. "It hurt bad, my first labor. Thirty-three hours. He stayed with me, held my hand the whole time. He held me during the worst of it."

"I better . . ." I motioned toward the door.

"I should've married him. Stupid. I was so young and stupid. I should've said yes when he asked."

Darryl proposed?

Charlene kept her eyes on her baby. "All I could think was the insecurity, you know? The instability. A life on the road? No sir, not for me. Darryl and his cars." She sighed. "He loved racing those cars." Her nipple slipped out of the baby's mouth and my eyes strayed to it. Slick nipple, swollen. I couldn't help looking.

I tripped over a Tonka truck. Then stumbled out of the house.

<hr/>

It took three hours to remove the old pipe, install the new, reconnect all the fixtures. While I was at it, I cleaned the faucets and put in new washers. Tomorrow I'd come back with a sheet of wallboard and replacement tiles. Until then, Charlene and Reese could use the tub. I found a can of Comet under the sink and scoured the tub until the porcelain sparkled.

I should've been exhausted, but I wasn't. Exhilarated was more like it. Satisfied and happy with the job. It was late. After midnight. I packed my stuff and crept up the stairs. Reese lay on the couch, blowing a stream of smoke through pouched out lips. He was still wearing his sheriff's uniform. Shirttail out, bare feet. I assumed he was off duty. When he saw me, he quickly stubbed his cigarette in the ashtray on his chest and jumped to attention.

That wasn't a regular cigarette.

"Mike, what are you doing here?" Reese said, fanning the air.

"I came to fix your shower downstairs. Charlene called me. Didn't she tell you?"

He blinked and pawed the air some more. "She must've forgot. She went to bed with cramps." His eyes fixed on mine. We had that moment of understanding. Different kind from Jamie's. "You didn't see this," Reese said, glancing at the ashtray in his hand. Sliding it behind his back.

"See what?" I said.

He smiled sheepishly. I headed for the door. The things I'd been privy to in people's homes while fixing their plumbing and heating . . . If I was into extortion, I could set myself up for life.

Reese kicked through junk on the floor, following me, tucking in his shirt.

"I need to come back tomorrow and fix the wall," I told him.

"Don't worry about it," he said. "I'll finish up."

That's what worried me. "I'll come in the morning. I'll drop by early —"

"I said I'd do it," Reese snapped.

Okay. Fine. He sounded guilty. He should be. For not repairing that tub right in the first place.

Reese jammed on a pair of work boots and followed me out to the truck. The snow had stopped. White cake frosting coated on all the lawns up and down the block. The street was wet, slushy in spots.

"Thanks for coming, Mike, helping us out," Reese said, hanging on the truck door as I slid Dad's toolbox onto the front seat. Reese added, "What do I owe you?"

"Nothing." I hopped inside.

Reese screwed up his face. Removing his wallet from his back pocket, he flipped it open and slid out five bills, which he handed to me. "Buy yourself a burger," he said.

They were five one-dollar bills. I seethed inside. If Darryl had come over and spent three hours on a weeknight to fix their freaking downstairs shower, Reese would've paid him a bundle. He would've had to pay Dad time and a half.

So what? There was satisfaction in a job well done. That's what Dad used to say. "Baby, be proud of your work. It'll be your life's legacy. There's satisfaction in a job —"

"Caught your game with Deighton," Reese cut into my thoughts. He eased the door closed. "You picked off that runner at second like a pro. Man, what an arm."

Deighton. From last week. "Yeah, too bad we lost by a run." To Deighton, no less. The toilet team of the league. Gina had walked three in the seventh and we didn't have time to recover.

"You'll kill 'em next time." Reese winked at me.

My throat constricted. Dad used to say that: "You'll kill 'em next time, baby." Used to wink at me too, the same way. He'd stand behind the bench and cheer me on, give me a thumbs-up, let me know he was there for me.

Reese opened his mouth to say something else, but I gunned the motor. When I peeled out, Reese had to spring back off the curb to avoid my splashback.

She'd left a message on the machine. "Call me." That was it.

Under the thick glow of moonlight through the grimy kitchen window, I squinted at my Timex. 12:19. Too late to call anyone, even her. I still wasn't tired. A charge of electricity streaked through my entire vascular system. I felt edgy, restless, a live wire. I needed to go somewhere, do something.

The water tower. Yeah. Why not?

I decided to walk. Run. Get the exercise, the release.

Even though the snowstorm was over, it was cold, my breath visible in the night air. The extension ladder was slippery. I had to take it slow. Nearing the top, I thought I saw a bat dart under the globe of the tank, but it could've been my imagination. All my senses were heightened tonight.

At my usual spot, I stood at the railing, checking out the state of Coalton. Asleep. Peaceful. Nel's Tavern sign lit up. And the pink pig, of course. Over at Jamie's, there was a light on. His bedroom light. He was such a night owl. What was he doing up? Chatting with Shane? Probably. Planning their tryst. For a moment, I envied Jamie. Envied them both. Then wondered what Jamie was getting himself into.

I could never talk to a stranger like that. Open myself up to someone I'd never met. It was hard enough being honest with Jamie. Give me flesh and blood. Give me human contact. Give me Xanadu.

Jamie's back door swung out and a figure emerged. Him. He was wearing his CHS sweater and, as he crossed the yard, the Mylar in the cougar emblem caught the light. Was he practicing cheerleading? At this hour? I shouldn't talk. How many nights had I gotten up at midnight, one AM, to do curls and crunches? Anything to get through the night, to ward off the nightmare. The recurring nightmare. Two years.

He launched himself onto his backyard trampoline and bounced to the middle. Instead of jumping, he sat down, lay flat on his back, his arms stretched out to the side.

I wondered if Jamie wanted a family, kids. If he'd even thought one day beyond getting laid. It'd be harder for him. Not impossible, though. Nothing was impossible.

Did I say that? No. Those weren't my words. Not my philosophy of life. That was Dad.

He was wrong. A shadow of doubt clouded everything he'd ever said to me now. He was wrong about life. About living. What did he know about living?

My life's legacy? Right, Dad. You didn't leave me a legacy. *I* was your legacy. You left me.

"You should have stuck around, Pops. Should have seen the job I did tonight. Man, you'd have been proud."

You taught me, Dad. You taught me everything I know.

How could you take it from me? The plumbing. The softball. The things I valued most, loved most. The one thing. You. Us. You and me together.

Our time. You ended it too soon, Dad. Too soon.

Chapter Eleven

I lost track of time during my third circuit. I was testing myself. See-ing how much I could take. Armie was always after me to slow down. Lighter weights, he said, slower reps would give me a better workout. He said I shouldn't be working out so much. He said I shouldn't work out at all during softball season.

Armie talked too much.

I was only five minutes late to class, but I got the evil eye from Mrs. Stargell. She had to stop her lesson to erase the absent mark from my name in the roll book. Sorry, I sent her a silent apology. Couldn't be helped.

I headed for my seat and skidded to a stop. Bailey was in it. Xanadu had laid claim to his desk, in front, and she gave me a look like, Wow, where are you going to sit?

Good question. Shawnee was back, so the only vacant desk was clear over by the broom closet. There was a reason that desk was empty. It was smaller than the others, shrimp-size, a castoff from the elementary school. I felt like a castoff myself, wedging through the rows, squeezing into the narrow seat.

Miz S drew a parallelogram on the board and I flipped open my notebook. Xanadu turned and smiled at me. I melted. She had on jeans today, plain old blue jeans. They looked sexy as hell on her, though. What didn't? A light blue, V-neck, long-sleeved shirt exposed her cleavage — oh yes — and highlighted her hair — uh-huh — which was pulled up in a ponytail. She looked different. Like one of us.

I was too far away today, physically and mentally, to care about Geometry. Ratios or hypotenuses or Pythagorean theorems, what did they have to do with my life? Unless there was a connection I was missing to flare nuts or tag outs or tri-sets. A whole hour passed without me. When the bell rang, I glanced down at my notebook. I'd been doodling. One letter, X, filled the entire page. X X X X X.

She was waiting for me outside the door. "How come you didn't call me last night?" She linked her arm in mine. My day suddenly took on meaning. "Did you lose my number?"

"No. I got home late." I loved how she was always touching me, making physical contact.

"Heavy date?" She wiggled her eyebrows.

Right. She was so fresh in the morning. The afternoon. Evening. I realized I was staring and refocused ahead. Bailey stood at the end of the hall, talking with Skip and a couple of other guys. Bailey's eyes traveled the length of Xanadu, taking her in. Deliberately, I pulled her closer, meshing our arms together.

"Hey, Mike," he said when we neared.

"Hey." I hitched my chin. "How's it going?"

"Can't complain."

This was more conversation than Bailey and I had had since elementary. He'd been sitting in front of me all term and hadn't said boo. I take that back. He asked once if he could borrow a sheet of paper for a quiz. Be still my heart.

There was a slight tug on my arm. Xanadu detached herself from me and hugged her books to her chest. "Hi, Bailey," she said, her voice low and sultry.

"Hi," he mumbled. He lowered his head. Then bolted.

Why? What'd he do, piss himself?

Xanadu said, "Oh my God. He's shy. That is such a turn-on in a guy."

I could be shy. I was shy.

She added, "Should I call him? Do girls do that here? Call guys?"

How would I know? "Ask Deb Pastore," I said.

"Deb? Oh, you mean that skank in our class."

Deb wasn't a skank.

"I asked Jamie if they were going together and he said no. Deb's been after Bailey for years and he's definitely not interested."

Jamie and his big mouth.

"So should I?" Xanadu repeated. "Call him?"

We'd reached my locker and I drew a deep breath. Spinning my combination lock, I said, "Do whatever you want."

Xanadu wedged her shoulder against the locker next to mine, facing me. Her books pressed against her breasts, heightening the cleavage. "What I want is for him to call me. Do you think you could give him my number without making it seem too obvious?"

I closed my eyes. Why was she torturing me? *I'd* call her. I'd call her every night. Unless it was too late. From now on, it was never going to be too late. I felt her eyes on me. Waiting, hoping.

"Sure, I guess." I shoved my books onto the shelf. The promise welled up from some distant, detached place inside me. Whatever you want, Xanadu. Whatever you need me to do.

I did the evil deed at lunch. Moseyed by Bailey's table and dropped a folded note onto his mound of mashed potatoes. Just like junior high. How weak. Bailey arched bushy eyebrows up at me.

"I'm only the messenger," I said. The delivery drone who feels like hurling all over you. Blowing some chunks on those potatoes.

I didn't stay to watch him open and read the note. I didn't stay to eat. It was all I could do to keep my head up all the way out the exit.

⁂

Wakeeney was a respectable team. The score was tied 4-4, bottom of the seventh. I was up.

"Sza-bo. Mighty Mike. Sza-bo."

The bleachers were packed, of course, this being a home game. Jamie led the chant.

T.C. was on first, two outs. I bounced the bat off the bottom of my cleat and took a practice swing. "Come on, Mike. You can do it," I heard Gina holler behind me from the dugout. Rather, the lean-to. The rest of the Cougars stood at the edge, cheering me on. My stomach cartwheeled around the bases. Forget what I said about one player not determining the outcome. It was up to me to win this game.

I took my stance. Visualized a hit.

"Sza-bo. Mighty Mike. Sza-bo."

The rhythm of the chant pulsed through my head. Wakeeney's pitcher nodded, narrowed her eyes, and let one rip. Too high. Ball one.

I straightened and took a deep breath. Under the bill of her cap, the pitcher eyed me; tried to psych me out. Me, Mike Szabo. In your dreams. Casually, I removed my batting helmet and smoothed back my bangs. I smooshed the helmet back on. The pitcher began her windup and reared to throw. Just as she was about to release the ball, I held up a hand and called, "Time."

The ump stepped out, throwing up his hands.

The pitcher faltered, stumbling off the mound. The smirk may have registered on my face as I squatted to retie my shoe.

When all the posturing was over, the pitch was dead center and

I smoked it. The crack of my bat echoed as the ball sailed over the heads of the infielders. Like they say in the movies, the crowd went wild.

I don't usually grandstand or even look at the spectators when I cross the plate, but my eye happened to catch the motion of shimmering gold pompoms behind the backstop. Jamie. He was whooping and split jumping in the air. That wasn't what interested me though. In front of him, at the fence, stood Xanadu.

She gazed into my eyes and smiled. My knees went weak. She stuck two fingers in her mouth and whistled, shrilly.

I cracked up. This girl was full of surprises.

She motioned me over to the fence. Hands were reaching through the chain-link and I touched fingers and palms on my way. Xanadu grabbed my wrist and held on. "I have to talk to you," she said, urgency in her voice.

"Okay." I waved to the crowd that was hailing me. God, I loved this game. "What is it?"

"Not now." Xanadu lowered her voice. "In private."

Private? My stomach fluttered. Just the two of us?

She said, "You're a hero."

A hero. Dad called me that. He was the only one who ever called me that. "Baby," he'd say, "you were the hero today. Believe it. You're going pro."

Sure, Dad. Thanks to you I'm not. After our post-game hand slap with Wakeeney, Coach Kinneson cornered me in the dugout. "Have you talked to your mom about softball camp?" she asked.

I pretended to rearrange the stuff in my duffel. I'd pored over the brochures, front to back. The camp sounded cool. The stuff dreams are made of. Someone else's dreams. The glossy folder ended up on Darryl's stack of auto zines bound for the incinerator one of these years.

Coach said, "Mike —"

"We can't swing it." I stood and slung my duffel over my shoulder.

"Are you sure? It's such a great oppor —"

"I'm sure."

"But Mike, there are scholarships."

Was she deaf? I crossed in front of her and jogged out onto the field.

I didn't see Xanadu at the backstop anymore. A flash of red hair disappeared inside the Davenports' hearse. She'd come with Faye and Leland. Jamie said in my ear, "She told me to tell you to call her. Bossy bitch, isn't she?"

I sneered at Jamie. Everyone was congregating on the lawn to walk to the Dairy Delite for a victory celebration. It was tradition. T.C. called, "Mike, your banana split's on us."

"Next time." I waved them off. "I have to get home."

Jamie did a double take. "You're refusing free food? Since when?" Jamie looked at me, through me.

Cram it. I wanted her cell to ring the minute she stepped in the door, the minute I got her alone.

"He hasn't called me," were the first words out of her mouth. "Are you sure you gave him the right number?"

"I gave him your note, like you asked." I assumed her number was on it. Was I supposed to stand by and make sure Bailey could read? I was pretty sure he could.

She exhaled audibly. "Why wouldn't he call?"

He wasn't interested? Yeah, right. "Maybe he's just busy," I said. "With calving and branding and butchering baby animals."

"Shit," Xanadu hissed. "I hate this podunk town. Totoland. No offense, but your lives move in super slo-mo. You could die of stagnation here. How can you stand it? Okay. I'm going to call him. I'll ask about our math assignment. We had one, right? Get him to talk. I know once we start talking, he'll loosen up. If there's one thing I'm good at, it's talking. And coming on to guys." She laughed.

My stomach felt queasy.

"Do you know his number?" she asked.

Silence.

"Okay, that was stupid. I just thought maybe you all knew each other's numbers by heart. I hate to ask you this —"

"No," I said. I wasn't calling him. Not now, not ever. "Why don't you look him up in the phone book?"

"The phone book? Oh yeah, huh?"

I could picture her crossing her eyes, tossing her hair over her shoulder, switching the phone to her other ear, maybe. Licking her glossy lips.

"Jamie was right," she said. "You're a kick-ass player."

My head swelled. "Thanks." She was sure chummy with Jamie lately. Probably because she saw more of him than me. They were in Journalism together, and History and Home Ec. Was it too late in the year for me to rearrange my schedule?

"Hey, why don't the three of us go out and celebrate?" Xanadu said. "Like, on Friday night."

The three of us, meaning her, me, and Jamie? "That'd be cool." I'd rather it was just the two of us, but I'd take what I could get — for now. Let's see, today was Wednesday. Count down the hours.

Xanadu exhaled relief. "Finally. I have something to look forward to. Promise me, no cow pies."

"Ah, shucks."

She laughed. I loved her laugh. She added, "I'll get with Jamie and we'll figure out how to celebrate you in style."

Celebrate me? Nobody had ever "celebrated" me. Well, Dad. When I was heroic. He'd brag on me at home. And, come to think of it, Jamie's mom. She'd baked a sheet cake for my sixteenth birthday in September and surprised me with it in homeroom. It was a little embarrassing, everyone in class singing to me. I'd made a wish and blew out the one big candle in the middle. It was a stupid wish. I knew it would never come true. You can't bring someone back from the dead.

$\mathcal{J}$amie and Xanadu were secretive, whispering behind my back all week, scheming. It made me nervous, anxious. They revealed part of the plan, that the party wouldn't start until later, ten o'clock. Which was fine with me. I was scheduled to work the Merc Friday night.

I kept looking at my watch every few minutes during my shift. Flicking the crystal on the Timex to make sure the hands weren't stuck. I was antsy to bail. Everett didn't even have to remind me to sweep up before closing.

When I got home the house was dark. Darryl must've gone out, or gone to bed. His overactive lifestyle had to be exhausting. The truck was available, that's all I cared about. I took a shower, then called Xanadu to let her know I'd be picking her up in a few minutes. Right after I stopped for Jamie.

"Change of plans," Xanadu said, her voice lowered, conspiratorial. "Don't come until eleven. I'll have to sneak out, and Aunt Faye and Uncle Lee are still up watching TV. Don't come to the house either. Meet me at the road."

"Okay." What was the problem? Wasn't she allowed to go out? Now I'd worry all night she was going to get busted.

I called Jamie back to fill him in on the revised plan. He already knew; he and Xanadu had been in touch. At the designated time, I pulled up in front of his trailer to find him sitting on the front stoop, his cordless phone plugged into his ear. He leaped to his feet, disconnected, and tossed the phone through the front door. Shouldering his backpack, he skipped to the curb. Sly grin on his face.

"What are we doing tonight?" I asked as he climbed into the truck. The grin exaggerated.

"I said —"

"I heard you."

"Jamie, if you guys embarrass me —"

"Just drive," he ordered. "That was Xana on the phone. She says Auntie Petunia and Uncle Fester finally went to bed, so she's heading out. She'll meet us by the power line."

"Why didn't she just tell them we were going out together?" Faye wouldn't have minded. Would she? I got a weird feeling from Faye.

Jamie said, "That'd be too easy. I'm guessing it's a game with her. She wants to see how far she can push it. I'm guessing she's a girl who likes to flirt with danger. 'Flirt' being the operative word."

"She shouldn't be walking alone on the road at night," I said. "Anyone could be out there." Drunks, serial killers. It wasn't always safe in the country. "Why didn't you tell her to wait?"

"Far be it from me. Maybe if you rescue her from the Bogeyman, she'll let you spank her."

I flung a fist and slugged his chest.

He went all limp, feigning death.

She appeared like an apparition, her short white T-shirt reflecting the harsh glare of my headlights. Over the shirt she wore a long, lacy sweater, and tight red leather pants. God. I could take her now. Dump Jamie at the side of the road and celebrate in style.

I pulled up alongside her. The backpack crooked in her elbow looked heavy. What was with the backpacks? They didn't tell me to bring my backpack.

Xanadu opened the door on Jamie's side and he hopped out to let her in. "Hey, guys." She grinned at Jamie — same evil grin as his. What were they up to? She had to scoot way over next to me because Jamie wedged his backpack and hers between them. Did he do that on purpose? Thank you.

"Where to?" I asked.

"The caboose," Jamie answered.

"No way."

"Just drive."

"Jamie —"

"What's the caboose?" Xanadu cut in.

Neither of us replied.

"Come on. What is it?"

Jamie leaned around her and smirked at me. "You'll see."

Kill you, my expression relayed. I didn't want to go to the caboose. We hadn't reached that stage in our relationship yet. If I did take her though, she might start thinking about it. Consider the possibility. I'd been thinking about it.

I eased off the clutch.

Xanadu dug in her backpack and pulled out her portable CD player. "So we don't have to listen to that country crap," she informed us.

Fine by me. I sent Jamie another silent threat: If you tell her I'm into country, you're roadkill.

Ten miles north of Coalton, over the elevated road and past the old homestead, the caboose loomed up out of the scraggly sumacs. I maneuvered the truck down the trampled tire tracks and crunched to a stop. No other cars were around. If one had been, we would've had to leave. Caboose etiquette. Naturally, we'd take note of who was here. Inquiring minds want to know.

"Is this for real?" Xanadu said. "How cool."

The caboose was an abandoned car from the Union Pacific Railroad. Before the tracks were rerouted to the Co-op elevators in town, they ran out this way. A grain car was coupled to the caboose at one time, but it'd been hauled back to the rail yard in Denver, or Wichita.

"I've never been inside a caboose." Xanadu pushed Jamie out the door so she could exit. "What's it doing here?"

Jamie answered, "Providing continuous hours of adult entertainment."

Xanadu plowed through the trees and grasped the stair railing. She stepped up, ascending onto the deck. Jamie followed. I trailed him. He glanced over his shoulder at me and leered. Kill you, I threatened him with a fist. Peering into the little window, Xanadu gasped, "Oh my God. Don't tell me."

The king-size mattress spoke volumes.

Last time Jamie and I had driven out here, in November during our Thanksgiving break, we'd found a bunch of shriveled condoms on the ground around the caboose. Five, to be exact. Jamie added them to his vile collection. He named each one individually: Beau I, Beau II, Beau III . . .

"Do people really come here and do it?" Xanadu asked. She opened the creaky door and entered the cabin, not waiting for an answer.

I collared Jamie, "What are we doing here?"

"A three-way," he said.

I ground a knuckle into his spine and he yelped.

She wandered around the interior, taking it all in. I could read her face — awe and delight. "This is so sleazy," she said, eyes gleaming. "How fun."

"Wait, don't sit on that nasty thing." Jamie hurried over to Xanadu, who was falling to her knees on the mattress. He wrenched her up by the elbow. "You don't know where it's been. Or whose DNA's been deposited. Here. I brought a cover." He opened his pack and pulled out a checkered tablecloth. The three of us spread it over the mattress.

"The Suprette was running a little low on party supplies." Jamie retrieved a cellophane bag full of party hats from his pack. He ripped open the package with his teeth. They were flimsy cardboard cones, Star Wars theme.

Xanadu slid her cone hat on and snapped the elastic band under her chin. I copied her. Jamie put his hat on. We looked at each other and cracked up.

Jamie reached in his pack and pulled out a can of Reddi-wip. "Okay, girls," he said. "Get naked."

Xanadu and I rolled our eyes in unison. Good. We were communicating here.

Jamie popped the top on the whipped cream and aimed the nozzle at his open mouth.

"Wait." Xanadu yanked down his arm. "What's a party without serious liquid refreshment?" She lifted the flap on her pack and extracted a liter of vodka.

Absolut. The brand Dad always kept in his desk.

Jamie gasped, "Girl, you are bad. Give me that." He lunged for the bottle.

Xanadu's eyes sparkled. "You don't know how bad." She relinquished the vodka to him, then produced a bottle of wine from her pack. I assumed it was wine — blood-colored, corked. There was no label on the bottle, so it must've been homemade. A lot of people brewed their own spirits. Xanadu set the bottle next to her and dug out another item. A box. A gift box.

"Oh yeah," Jamie said. "Pick your poison." The third selection was a quart of Jack Daniel's. Jamie raised the vodka to his lips, but Xanadu stopped him again. "This is a celebration of Mike," she said. "We have to make a toast." She opened the gift box and handed me the quart of whiskey.

"Where did you get all this?" I asked as she twisted the cork on her wine.

"I found my aunt and uncle's stash in the root cellar. Is that what you call it, where you store all the jars? I think Aunt Faye must've forgotten it was down there because she sent me to get peaches for dinner. She had to know I'd find the booze."

I almost said what I was thinking: Maybe she trusted you to leave it alone.

Xanadu added, "It ought to be potent. The bottles were pretty dusty."

I unscrewed the lid on the Jack Daniel's and passed it under my nose. Whew. The fumes alone were staggering.

"To Mike." Xanadu raised her wine bottle. "Who always saves the day."

My face flared. "I don't know about that."

Xanadu and Jamie swigged from their bottles. I studied mine, noting how a view of her through the amber liquid turned her hair the color of sunset.

The whiskey burned all the way down. It'd been a long time since I'd drunk hard liquor straight. Since I'd discovered Dad's hip flask in the glove compartment when I was, what, six?

"To Mike," Jamie said. "Coalton's player of the year." He raised the Absolut to his lips again. "Make that the millennium."

Xanadu muttered, "That's a Toto eternity."

The second swig of J.D. went down easier. Most everyone drank; there wasn't a whole lot else to do on weekends. Mainly we stuck to beer though. It was cheaper, more accessible.

Xanadu slid in a disc and cranked up the volume on her CD. The music was hip-hop or rap, no group I'd know. Jamie and Xanadu rocked shoulders in time to the beat. "Let's play musical bottles," Jamie yelled. He handed me the vodka and reached for Xanadu's wine. As I tipped the vodka to my lips, Jamie hollered, "No, keep passing. Until the music stops."

Dumb game. Xanadu seemed to like it though. We circulated the liquor five or six times, then Jamie switched off the music.

The three of us drank from the bottles we were holding. Something was missing here. Oh yeah. Player elimination.

"To Mike," Xanadu said. She clinked my bottle, then Jamie's. "My hero."

"To Mike," Jamie replied. "My queero."

"Shut up." To me, I silently saluted.

The music started up again. "We're going to get so sick," I shouted. Jamie grinned. My stomach rumbled as the Absolut traveled from me to Xanadu. "Did anybody bring food?"

"Fo-od," Jamie sang. He set down the Jack Daniel's and upended his backpack onto the mattress. Fun Size Snickers and Mars Bars and Baby Ruths tumbled out. They had to be left over from Halloween. In the middle of the pile was a baggie.

"Ooh, Jamie. I love you." Xanadu puckered a kiss at him. It made me wish I'd brought candy or something. Right. Ma rooted out sweets like a truffle pig.

I selected a Baby Ruth and unwrapped it. I snuck a peek at Xanadu, watching her, getting lost in her presence with me here tonight. She met my eyes and smiled — a smile so sensuous I thought I'd pee my pants.

"What are you guys doing after you graduate?" Xanadu asked. She and Jamie rolled a joint.

"I'll probably go to the University of Alabama." Jamie struck a match and lit up.

This was the first I'd heard of that plan.

"Why Alabama?" Xanadu took a hit.

Jamie sighed dreamily. "Tell her, Mike."

"Tell her what?"

He widened his eyes at me. "Shane. That's where he wants to go."

Right. Shane, the wannabe filmmaker. He must've been pumping gas in preparation for his SATs.

Xanadu looked from Jamie to me. "Who's Shane?" She offered me the joint and I shook my head no. I was going to be sick enough.

Guess in all their conversations Jamie forgot to mention his one true love. "Shane is Jamie's cybersex fiend," I informed her. "Some guy he met on the Internet. He's too old for Jamie and he's probably a pedophile."

Jamie took the joint and stuck out his tongue at me. It was purple from the wine.

Xanadu twisted to face him. "Interesting. I was having this long distance relationship with a guy I met in a chatroom once. But it didn't work out. You can't connect that way. At least, I can't. I need a body. Give me flesh and blood."

Yes! I thought. A living, breathing, warm-blooded, heart-pounding person.

"What about you, Mike?" She took back the joint, pulled a deep drag, and chased it with a swig of Absolut. She handed the bottle to me.

"I don't know. I never really thought about college until this week." I glugged the vodka and coughed. Xanadu and Jamie wide-eyed me. What? Were we talking about relationships or college? I shouldn't have opened my mouth.

"What happened this week?" Xanadu asked.

I unwrapped a Snickers and popped the whole thing in my mouth. Rude to talk with your mouth full. Xanadu tilted her head like, I'm waiting. So did Jamie. Though he was alternating bites of Snickers from one hand with hits on the joint from the other.

"Coach Kinneson thinks I could get a shoftball . . . a sholar . . . shit." My tongue wouldn't work.

Jamie and Xanadu giggled. I did too.

Xanadu said, "You mean a softball scholarship? You could."

I shook my head. "No."

"Course you could." She touched my thigh. "You're an awesome player. Why not?"

I shrugged. Concentrated on speaking. It was hard with my tongue so thick and her hand so close to my, um . . . "You have to be scouted. You have to play competitive. You have to attend soft . . . ball," I pronounced the words slowly and distinctly, "camp."

"Camp?" Jamie clapped excitedly. "Oh boy. Can I go to camp? I used to be a Boy Scout."

"And the pope is a drag queen."

Xanadu laughed.

Was I funny? I'd made her laugh.

"You can go in my place," I told Jamie.

His face turned a sickly shade of green, like he was going to hurl. I scooted away from him, pulling Xanadu with me. She said quietly, "Why aren't you going?"

I heaved a sigh. "It costs three thousand dollars."

"Holy shit," Jamie hissed. He covered his mouth. "Sorry, Pope." His eyes bulged and he wobbled on his butt, teetering over sideways. He never could hold his liquor.

"Three thousand isn't that much." Xanadu slowly peeled a wrapper on a Baby Ruth bar.

Where did she live? Not in my shack of the woods.

"Don't they have financial aid?"

"It doesn't matter," I said. "I don't really want to go." I exchanged the vodka for Jack Daniel's. It was tasting good now, delicious. Soothing and warm.

"You lie." Jamie shot forward and thrust an index finger in my face. "You're stoned." I scrambled to my feet. I had to pee, bad. I steadied myself on Xanadu's shoulder and felt her hand cover mine. If only we could stay like that, my leg pressed to her side, her hand caressing mine. "I gotta find a tree," I said. My eyes didn't respond as fast as my brain. The door was around here somewhere. Behind me? I whirled and stumbled.

My head felt like a grappling hook. Swing, swing, *clang*. I rammed the side of the caboose. Took a header down the steps, landing in a clump of thistles. A thought registered dimly: Tomorrow that is going to hurt. I groped around for a bush.

When I got back, Xanadu and Jamie were squirting whipped cream into each other's mouths. Attempting to. Jamie had most of it on his face and hair. Xanadu squirted a stream into her own mouth as I flopped down beside her. "Tell me everything you know about the McCalls," she said. Her voice sounded far away, hollow.

"Handth off. Beau'th mine." Jamie's head bobbled.

I smacked his leg. "I knew you still had the hots for him."

Jamie's eyes rolled back into his head.

"You can keep Beau," Xanadu said. "I want Bailey. Bad."

Jamie's eyes focused on mine, momentarily. I retrieved the half-empty bottle of J.D. and swilled.

"I can't believe he hasn't called me yet." Xanadu fiddled with the nozzle on the whipped cream. "I'm not *that* disgusting, am I?"

All I could do was shake my head no. No, no, no. The Reddi-wip can appeared over my face and Xanadu parted her lips, instructing me to do the same. I didn't need instruction. While she squirted a stream of whipped cream into my mouth, she licked her lips as if tasting. Hungry. I was tasting her. I wanted to put my lips on hers and eat her up.

"I'm calling him." She bubbled whipped cream into her mouth, swished it around and swallowed. "I'm sorry, but I can't wait. I don't operate on Toto time." She grabbed the neck of my dad's flannel shirt and jerked me up until my face was flush with hers. "Open," she commanded.

I obeyed.

She filled my mouth with Reddi-wip until I choked. Then she let me go and I fell on my head. I might've passed out. I might've passed on. The whipped cream, the alcohol, the shedding of inhibitions. Me and Xanadu, physically connecting. We did. I felt it. It was real, wasn't it?

If not, this was one heavenly dream.

Chapter Thirteen

*O*kay, I might've been driving a little erratically. I might've been speeding. The road kept disappearing into the sea, then rippling up like the Loch Ness monster in front of me. At least I'd managed to drop Xanadu off safely at the end of the Davenports' drive and leave Jamie at his trailer.

I didn't hear the siren. Did he sound the siren? Reese pulled up alongside me on Main Street. Shit. I was two blocks from home. He waved me over. His cruiser door slammed as I fumbled around to turn off the ignition. Were you supposed to cut the engine? I'd never been stopped by the cops before. The cop.

"Pretty late for you to be out, Mike," Reese said, resting his arms across my open window.

"I got lost," I mumbled.

Reese smiled. His nose twitched and he dropped his arms, stepping back. "Hooey."

Oh that. Jamie had barfed on the floor. I didn't quite make it to the ditch in time. First thing this morning, I was going to hose out the truck.

"Been doing some partying, have we?" Reese stated the obvious.

"Gold star," I said. I licked my index finger and marked him air bingo. Oops, I should stifle the sarcasm with the local law enforcement. "Or is it a silver star?" I pointed to Reese's badge.

Reese was not amused. "I should write you up," he said. "Or make you spend the night in the drunk tank. Unfortunately, Armie's in there."

"Uh-oh, Armie. No one to bail your butt out now."

Reese studied me. He shook his head. My head was spinning like a circulating pump. "I'll let it pass this time," Reese said.

I believe we both knew why.

"You think you can make it home?"

"Oh yeah." I cranked the key. Reese reached in and removed the key from the ignition. Guess that meant I'd be walking.

I staggered out of the truck. Halfway down the block, Reese sidled up beside me. I whirled on him. "I said I can make it."

"I know you did. Consider this a police escort." He grinned and winked.

That wink. I suddenly felt so sick I thought I might blow on Reese's shiny patent leathers. If my head didn't drill a fence post on the Ledbetters' front lawn first.

I woke up on my bedroom floor. The ceiling was a yellow vortex and my stomach heaved. I scrunched to my knees and stumbled to the john, just in time.

No telling how long I was in there, puking my guts out. Every time I stood, the room spun out and my legs crumpled. Finally, I managed to crawl back out the bathroom door — into a roadblock.

Darryl. He did an unexpected thing. He lifted me up by the armpits and shoved me against the wall. "You stupid shit," he said in my face. "You've been drinking."

"Gold stars all 'round."

He shoved me again, hard.

"Ow. Cut it out."

Darryl screamed in my face, "You stupid shit! Don't you start. Don't you ever start. Do you hear me?"

No, I couldn't hear him. My eardrums were ruptured. "Let me go."

"If I ever catch you drinking again, I'll kill you!" He released me and I slid down the wall into a heap at his feet. I tried to pull myself up by Darryl's jeans, but he didn't have any on. Just black bikini briefs. Ew. I wasn't touching those. He kicked me off his leg.

I clawed the wall to stand. Made it.

Darryl clamped down on my shoulder and swiveled me around. It took a few years for my head to catch up. "You're better than him," he said. "Do you hear me?"

"No. Why don't you come closer? *Scream it in my ear?*" I pushed him out of my face. Did my foot connect with his shin? I was being sucked into the vortex again. Falling, falling, *thud*.

The nightmare. Same one I'd had for the last two years. No. It couldn't be. I wasn't asleep.

Or was I?

Sometime later I opened my eyes to find Darryl gone and me flat on my back in bed. Alive, at least, but barely.

<hr />

"You won't believe what he thought." Xanadu's voice reverberated in my empty skull. A brain used to reside there. What time was it? I squinted at the clock on the stove. Four-thirty. PM? Had I slept all day? I was disoriented. Sick. Was it Saturday? I should be at work.

"Mike, are you there?"

"Where?'"

"Get this. He thought you and I were together. Like a couple. Isn't that hilarious?" She laughed.

What? Who thought that? Someone other than me?

"He's coming by later tonight to work on our math. Don't tell him I took Geometry sophomore year. I am *so* glad I finally got up the courage to call him."

Oh, me too, I thought. How could she sound so cheery? Sober? She'd called him. My stomach felt like it'd been reamed out by a backhoe.

"Last night was a blast, wasn't it?" Xanadu said. "I haven't been that wasted since . . ." Her voice trailed off. "You know. Did you get busted?"

A vague memory of Reese helping me home resurfaced. Darryl laying into me. No consequences. "No. Did you?"

"No. Aunt Faye and Uncle Lee's bedroom is upstairs, so I'm sure they didn't hear me come in at *three AM,*" she emphasized the time.

I'd never feel good again. My head was throbbing. My gut ached.

"Mike?"

"Yeah?"

She hesitated. "Nothing. We can talk later. I'll call you after Bailey leaves tonight. If I can. Aunt Faye has this stupid rule about not calling people after nine. I mean, God. How Toto is that?"

"Toto," I said.

She paused a moment. "Thanks," she said. "For everything." Then hung up.

What'd she mean, everything? Her voice suggested . . . Did something happen between us that I didn't remember? No, I'd remember.

She called him.

Darryl slammed in the back door. He tossed the truck keys on the counter and looped a leg over his dinette chair. A cigarette dangled out the side of his mouth. Rubbing his hands together, he said, "What's for dinner?"

I just looked at him. Then snatched up the keys.

"Where do you think you're going?"

"Stop screaming, will you?" Was he? I pressed a forearm to my forehead.

"You're grounded." Darryl stubbed out his cigarette in an old cereal bowl.

Right. "I've got to go to work." I added to myself, If I still have a job.

"Nice present you left me in the truck."

Ugh. The vomit. "Sorry. I'll clean it out."

"Already did." Darryl got up to head for the fridge. "What time are you getting home?"

What was he now, my mother? Ours was such an exemplary role model. "Tiny called from the salon," Darryl said. "One of her sinks is clogged and she wants you to come by and fix it. Somebody named the Redmans — who I never heard of, have you? — are redoing their plumbing and want you to come and give them an estimate on the job. You might've told me you were in the biz again." He glugged from the milk jug.

"You might've asked." Next to the phone he'd scribbled down "Tiny" and the number for the Redmans — who, no, I'd never heard of — on the back of a grocery bill. I'd call after work. I wasn't very lucid at the moment. More to myself than him, I mumbled, "I didn't know I *was* back in the biz."

⟞⟞⟞⟞⟞

I lay on my bed, watching the digital numbers on my clock radio turn over. 9:01, 9:02. Xanadu wasn't going to call. I willed time to stop. 9:05, 9:06. I could've called her, except Faye or Leland might ask who was calling at this hour. They'd think I didn't have manners. Xanadu was right. Nine o'clock was early. The nine o'clock rule was Toto.

9:12. In one minute, I'd call her.

What if Bailey was still there?

I closed my eyes and blocked out all feeling.

I wouldn't call. It was Toto, the nine o'clock rule. But it was part of me. I was the spawn of Toto.

⸻

He was turned around in his seat, his own seat, talking to Xanadu and laughing. I'd never heard Bailey laugh. He sounded like a hyena. Mrs. Stargell smiled at me. "Morning, Mike," she chirruped.

I forced a cheery, "Morning." Not very cheery. I headed for the dunce seat.

Everyone was talking and laughing. What was this, Happy Laughing Day?

I scraped the desk across the linoleum trying to sit. Sit. Stay. Roll over and play dead. Maybe I could inch over into the broom closet while Miz S reviewed the homework. Shut the door and disembowel.

Xanadu waved her arms in the air. What was she doing? She'd swiveled around toward me when Mrs. Stargell began to write an equation on the board. Xanadu drew back her arm and pitched a wad of paper my way. It arced high in the air and I snagged it.

A note. Folded into a wedge. It took a minute to figure out how to unfold the paper without ripping it. I smoothed the page open in my lap. "Sorry about not calling," she'd written. Her handwriting was exquisite, like her. "B stayed until after ten. Then AF kicked him out." She'd drawn a frowny face with a lolling tongue. "Ditch your next class. Let's go somewhere and talk."

I glanced up. She was waiting for my answer.

Oh yeah. Happy Laughing Day.

⸻

We climbed the fire escape to the roof — Jamie's and my refuge when he needed to grab a smoke between classes, and I needed sky. I used to smoke. Let's say I tried it a couple of times and found it held no appeal. Dad smoked. He didn't want me to start. Occasionally, if I was bored,

I'd bum a smoke off Jamie. Mostly I blew rings. I'd flick ash off the end of the butt, or practice holding a cigarette the way guys do to look cool.

There was a shady spot behind the aluminum ductwork over the gym. I directed Xanadu there. Dozens of fresh cigarette butts were stubbed out on the flashing. These couldn't all be Jamie's. Someone had discovered our sanctum. Big surprise.

Xanadu offered me a granola bar. "No thanks," I said. I was too pumped, being alone with her in a private place. My power shake was churning up foam in my stomach.

"Bailey told me what happened to your dad," she said.

"What?" I whirled on her. "What are you and Bailey doing talking about my dad?"

Xanadu cowered a little at my tone of voice. "Sorry. It just came up. I mean, you did. The subject of your dad. I'm sorry." She looked at me; looked deep into my eyes.

Too deep. I had to turn away. Picking up a two-inch cigarette butt and studying it, wishing I had Dad's lighter on me, I said, "Everybody dies. So what?" I flicked the butt down the shingles and watched it roll off the roof.

Xanadu placed a loose hand over my bent knee. "We don't have to talk about it," she said. "I just thought you'd want to."

"I don't." I twisted my head to meet her eyes. Sad eyes. I'd had enough sad eyes to last me a lifetime. "It's old news. It happened two years ago, okay?"

"Okay," she said softly. She added, "Want to talk about your mom then?"

I scrabbled to my feet. "I thought we came here to talk about you. You and Bailey. He thought we were together, huh?" I leaned against the duct. "So you called him, huh?"

"Yeah." She wrinkled her nose. "Can you believe that? The to-gether part?"

I shook my head, wishing I could. Knowing I did.

"He's so sweet. Polite too. Like he calls Uncle Lee *sir*. 'Yes, sir. No, sir.' My dad would shit his shorts if anyone I brought home ever called him sir."

How many had she brought home? I'd call him sir. She could take me home.

Xanadu hugged her knees and smiled. "He asked me out. We're going to the movies in Garden City on Friday. I don't know why we have to wait a whole week."

I checked out. She went on talking: Bailey this, Bailey that. I stood, mind wandering, watching her lips move, her eyes dance. I didn't care what she talked about, what she said or didn't say, I loved being here with her, sharing sky with her. I could stay up here forever.

When the bell rang, I was shocked to realize an hour had passed.

"Maybe I could bum a ride home with him every day," she said, as my consciousness kicked in. "Is that against Toto rules?" She blinked up at me.

Could she hear my silent scream? "I better get back," I said. "I need to work on this history project with Deb." Deb wasn't even in my class.

Xanadu extended a hand for me to pull her up. The heat of her hand, her touch, shot through me. Why him? Why not me? I'd take her home. I'd gladly submit to the extra laps around the bases for being late to practice.

She dusted off her rear. As we treaded back over the shingles to the fire ladder, she clenched my upper arm and tugged me to a stop. "I'm not the kind of person who suddenly drops her friends when she has a boyfriend. I hate girls who do that. And I promise not to blabber on and on ad nauseam about Bailey —" She squeezed her eyes shut. "God. I just did that for an hour, didn't I?" Her head lolled back. "You have permission to slap me."

Never. I'd never lay a hand on her. We poised at the edge of the roof, Xanadu staring off into the ball field, me staring at her. "I don't have a lot going for me," she said, "but I am a really good friend."

"What do you mean, not a lot going?" She focused on me; our eyes held. She had the world. She had me. "You have everything," I told her. "You're . . . you're great."

She nudged my shoulder. "You're biased."

Yeah. She got that right.

She smiled into my eyes. That smile.

I swear, that smile was meant only for me. It wasn't my imagination, and I was stone sober. I watched her descend, her shiny red hair reflecting in the sun. A sentence, a phrase, a word lodged in my brain. Boyfriend. She said boyfriend. She already thought of Bailey as her boyfriend.

Chapter Fourteen

The Redman ranch was south of town, halfway to Garden City. I booked it down there after practice, before work. It was a big job — replumbing a renovation — and I was psyched about the opportunity. I worked up an estimate on the spot, being generous with my labor costs, and submitted my bid. I ran by Tiny's salon before heading for the Merc, but I couldn't augur out her clog. The shampoo sink would need to be disassembled to get at it. I could do that tomorrow. In the meantime I'd gotten another call on a swamp cooler fan. Between plumbing and school and practice and work and working out, it was a crazy week.

I needed crazy. Needed to get my mind off them — the two of them — Xanadu and Bailey, together.

We had a doubleheader Thursday night in Sharon Springs. Jamie caught up with me after the lunchtime pep rally, in his uniform, rustling a pom-pom in my face. "Guess who's taking me to the game tonight?" he said.

"Guess again," I replied automatically.

"Not you. Xanadu."

My stomach leaped. She was coming?

"Somehow she talked Aunt Petunia and Uncle Fester into borrowing the hearse. You want to ride down with us?"

"Coach wants us there half an hour early for a team meeting." Which was a lie. I don't know why I didn't want to ride with them. Yes, I did. What if Bailey came? They might sit together in the car. And in the stands. I'd never be able to concentrate on my game if they were there. I could barely contain my nausea now whenever I saw him talking to her in class. In the hall. At lunch.

I had homeroom last hour so I asked Mr. Decatur if I couldn't take off early for the game. I needed time to clear my head. Focus. Control. Also, I wanted to scope out the Sharon Springs team. This was their first year in the league and I heard they had this hotshot pitcher who was generating buzz with her early stats. Stats could be deceiving, but still. It never hurt to know the competition.

I hustled home. In the driveway Darryl's legs stuck out from under a rusty GTO. He had his radio going full blast. Ma's radio inside was blaring too. How could they stand the noise? The interference? I snitched the truck keys off the counter and took off.

The Wildcats were on the field warming up when I slipped into the visiting team's dugout.

Pop.

My head snapped back.

The catcher stood and lobbed the ball back to the mound. The pitcher was solid, like me. Only large, imposing. Brahma bull came to mind. I thought I was buff, but whew. This girl. She poised in her stance, waiting for a signal from the catcher.

Pop.

That sound. The ball hitting the catcher's mitt. It was music to my ears. Forget spying. I squatted outside the dugout, balancing on one knee. Everyone was watching her.

Pop.

Man, I'd give anything to catch for someone who could throw that fast and hard.

Pop.

Pop.

She was flat-out bringing it, no loss of speed. I could tell by the fire in her eyes she was a serious player. Something else in her eyes too. The way she held herself — her defiance, confidence. I was dying to get in there; connect with her.

"You're early, Mike."

I flinched and almost fell on my butt.

"What'd you do, ditch school?" Coach Kinneson knuckled my head.

"No, ma'am." I stood upright. "I got permission to leave early. You can check with Mr. Decatur."

"I trust you. Our only Ms. Perfect Attendance at CHS." She smiled and dumped her golf bag on the dirt by the dugout steps.

Yeah, I didn't even miss because of Dad. I was proud of that.

She added, "Have you thought any more about camp?"

Why was she on my back about this? I already told her it was impossible. Sighing audibly, so she'd get the message, I said, "I'd really like to go, but no one's throwing money my way, okay?" Did that come out surly? Sorry. But drop it already.

"Maybe you could pass your hat around after the game." Coach elbowed me.

If that was a joke, it died in the dust.

"Mike." She expelled a short breath. "I didn't mean that."

I never minded living at the lower end of the social scale. It's not like Coalton was Beverly Hills. I never felt deprived. Every once in a while, the rich farm kids would square off against us townies, but we put them in their place with attitude. What money Dad didn't guzzle away, he put back into the business. At least, I thought he did. I thought he was putting money away for me. He never let us starve.

Never let us want for much. Darryl and me never wanted all that much. Only for him to be around.

If Darryl had kept up the business, we'd have money. Enough for me to play competitive.

Stop thinking about it. You're not going.

Damn her. Damn Coach Kinneson. She was dredging all this up.

"I've been hearing about this pitcher." She motioned for me to come sit beside her on the bench. "Womack. Is that her name?"

I lowered myself and perched at the edge. You can read her jersey good as me, I thought. Wow, I'd better keep my mouth shut today.

Coach rested her elbows on her knees to watch. "Jerry said the scouts are all hyperventilating to get her signed too."

Womack pivoted and rifled a missile to center field.

"You could have a future in this game, Mike —"

I stood and grabbed my glove. "In case you haven't heard, Szabo Plumbing is back in business."

Coach glanced up at me. "I meant a real future. Away from here."

Who said I wanted away? I loped out into the field before regrettable words spewed out of my mouth. Words that might threaten that perfect attendance record by getting me suspended. Or worse, kicked off the team.

We got shut out. The Sharon Springs' pitcher was too much for us. We lost our composure, lost our cool. Womack scared us. She scared me. And that's an accomplishment.

After the game, as we were slapping hands with the Sharon Springers — proffering insincere congratulations — Womack grabbed my wrist and held on. "Girl," she said, peering into my eyes. She knew. Knew who, or what, I was. She was one too.

"Devon," someone called.

She broke our connection and turned. "Yo."

I watched her lope back to her team and join in their victory whoop. Devon Womack. We'd be hearing her name again.

"Mike, over here." Xanadu waved from the backstop. She'd come alone; sat in a crowd on the top riser of the bleachers. I could finally let my happiness show; let it fly. She'd cheered for me every time I'd snagged a wild pitch or come up to bat. Too bad I didn't show her my best stuff today.

"You were totally awesome," she said as I sauntered over.

"Oh yeah. We kicked butt." I rolled my eyes.

She cocked her head. "Well, *you* were good. Your coach is right. You should go to that camp."

"Would everyone just lay off about the camp!"

Xanadu reeled back. "God."

Geez. What was wrong with me? "I'm sorry." I reached for her, withdrew my hand. It wasn't her fault.

"Sza-bo. Mighty Mike." Jamie jumped on my back for a pony ride. I dropped my shoulder and slammed him into the dirt.

Xanadu said, "We should go celebrate."

Jamie writhed around on the ground, faking a collapsed lung.

"Celebrate what?" I asked, helping him up. "We sucked."

"So? Celebrations don't have to be about winning. They can be about life. Living. Just being alive."

Jamie brushed off his shorts. "I like that. Cuz you never know when you might bite the big one."

My eyes sliced through him like a chain saw.

He gulped. "Sorry. Sorry, Mike. God, what's wrong with me?"

Did he want a list?

"The Mouth here is contagious." He thumbed at Xanadu.

She bent back his thumb until he squealed. I was beginning to like this girl. Love her.

"We could finish what we started," Jamie said. He meant the vodka and whiskey, since we'd only managed to drink half of each. The bottles were stashed inside a toilet tank in the back of the truck. He added, "Tomorrow night. I don't have to work Fridays."

"I can't tomorrow," Xanadu said. "I'm going out with Bailey."

Jamie's eyes met mine. I averted my gaze, glancing over at the scoreboard. HOME: 8. VISITORS: 0. They could clear the board anytime.

"What about Saturday night?" Xanadu suggested.

"I have to work till ten." Jamie pouted. "But we could go afterward."

They waited for my answer. The Merc would be closed by then. I didn't really want to go out drinking again, but what could I say? I wanted to see her, be with her. Always, forever. "Okay. Sure."

Xanadu smiled, that secret smile.

Jamie made a weird face. What? Did he notice? If so, he didn't embarrass me by being an asshole. "Same time, same station." He punched my arm. I slugged him in the gut. He faked a vomit.

"I better get the hearse back before dark." Xanadu sighed. "Uncle Lee got into it with Aunt Faye about me even borrowing it." Grabbing Jamie by his cougar emblem, she added, "Let's go, girlfriend." She yanked him toward the parking lot. I heard Jamie say, "Could I ride in the trunk and pretend I'm a corpse?"

I was moving the rabbit hutches closer to the front by the rolls of chicken wire when Everett hollered, "Mike. Telephone."

Telephone? I'd never gotten a call here. No one would phone for me at the Merc. Unless it was an emergency. What could be an emergency? Another leaky tub?

I hurried inside. Behind the counter, Everett handed me the phone and said, "Not too long. I'm waiting for a call from Goodland on those bedding plants. They were supposed to be here yesterday."

I nodded acknowledgment and put the phone to my ear. "Hello?"

"Mike, I've been looking everywhere for you. Your brother said you were working. How old is he? He sounds totally hot."

Darryl? She must've dialed the wrong number. "He's twenty-four going on fifty." If she was calling to tell me about her date last night, she'd generate more interest from Jamie. I didn't care. I lay awake most of the night not caring, wondering where they'd gone, what they were doing.

"Are we still going out tonight?" Xanadu asked.

"Of course." Had she forgotten? She wouldn't forget. Would she? I was thinking about buying a new pair of Levi's. Dressing up for her. Standing out. Everett had marked all the jeans down this morning. He might let me pay in a couple of installments.

Xanadu let out an audible breath. "Okay, here's the thing. Bailey asked if I'd like to come to dinner at his house tonight. He wants me to meet his parents. Apparently they all eat together on Saturday, then sit around and play cards. How Toto is that?"

She wasn't coming.

"I know we were going drinking . . ."

She wasn't coming.

"I guess what I'm calling about is to ask if you'd be mad if I went to Bailey's. I didn't tell him yes. I told him I'd think about it. I probably should've told him I had other plans, but I couldn't bring myself to say I'd rather go out and get wasted with you guys than play Crazy Eights with the 'rents."

"Why not?" I asked.

She paused. "Come on. You know Bailey."

I did. He and Beau were choirboys. I'd never seen either of them take a drink, not even on the hayride at Coalton Days. Everett cleared his throat in my ear. In the mirror behind the counter, I caught his dour look. Didn't he have pig feed to inventory, dewormer to stock, pasture grass to grow?

"What do you think?" Xanadu asked.

What do I think? I think I want you to choose me.

"Mike?"

I had this vision. I'd make her feel guilty and she'd go with us. All night long she'd be wishing she was with Bailey, resenting me for keeping her from him. Yeah, I wanted her, but not like that. She had to want me too.

"Go to Bailey's," I told her. "The booze'll keep. It's kept this long."

"God, you're so awesome." She sounded happy, relieved. "Thanks, Mike. I'll make it up to you."

Make it good, I thought. This is killing me.

Her door was open a crack. I could hear the rattled intake of breath. She was dead to the world, snoring.

From the top drawer I scooped up Dad's last two undershirts. Something in the back of the drawer drew my attention. Colors. Fabric. His suspenders. His red, white, and blue suspenders. The ones he wore for Coalton Days. I wanted them. I lifted them out and looped them over my wrist.

Ma hadn't stirred, so I took the time to check around again for Dad's work shirts. The navy ones with SZABO PLUMBING AND HEATING embroidered over the breast pocket. He had a stack of them somewhere. In all my snooping I hadn't run across even one. Where were they? Ma's side of the dresser, maybe?

Her first drawer was stuffed with underwear — enormous swaths of cotton and polyester. Gray, holey, ick. It reminded me of the first time — the only time — I saw her naked. I was jolted awake by her screaming.

"Mike! Mike!"

I threw off my quilt and tore down the hall. Their door was ajar and Ma was screeching, "Mike, wake up. The baby isn't breathing." She had the baby in her arms and was wheezing, "Wake up, wake up," Shaking Camilia's limp body. Ma's loose skin jiggled and her rear end hung in layers, folds, and she turned to the side, in profile, and I saw her huge droopy breasts with the gigantic brown nipples and I couldn't help staring at them. Dad lay in bed, his mouth open, snoring. Passed out.

Ma wailed, "Mike, get up! There's something wrong with the baby."

I blinked. "Mommy?"

She whirled and saw me in the doorway. Her eyes were wild with terror. Indescribable hell. She shrilled, "Get out! Get out of here!" She charged me, a raging elephant. "Go away."

I realized suddenly she wasn't calling for me, Mike. She meant Dad. Ma hit the door running and slammed it in my face. I stumbled and fell. Then skittered back to my room and shut my door, burrowing under my quilt, hugging my knees to my chest, shaking.

The sounds of doors opening and closing and Ma screaming. Darryl's voice. "Ma?" Dad's voice, finally. Later, a siren. Heavy footsteps. Shouting. I plugged my ears with my fingers and squeezed my eyes shut.

That's all I remember.

After that, the empty crib. The one still sitting in the corner of Ma's room under heaps of clothes and trash and passing years.

Would Dad's shirts be in the crib? No, he kept them washed and folded. He kept all his things neat and tidy.

She didn't. After Camilia died, Dad did everything around the house.

I eased open the second dresser drawer. A kraft envelope lay under the cup of a huge cotton bra. I slid out the envelope and tipped it. An object fell out. It chinked on the floor at my feet. A ring. Dad's wedding band. She didn't need that. I slid it on my finger. Too big, of course. The drawer below was empty. All her lower drawers, empty. I knew why. She couldn't bend to reach them.

A sound, a feeling, made me spin around. Ma was looking at me.

I gave a little yelp and shut the bottom drawer with my foot.

Her beady eyes studied me. They stripped me bare.

"I . . . needed some stuff." My voice broke. I cleared my throat.

Ma's jaw went slack. Her eyes glassy.

God, was she dead? "Ma?" I started toward her and she blinked back to life. She blinked again, like, Back off. Honing in on the stuff in my hands, she stared as if transfixed.

She was creeping me out. I took a wide berth around her to the door. Pausing in the threshold, I said, "You need anything?"

She didn't move. Didn't answer. Didn't know I was alive.

⁂

"Xanadu has cramps and doesn't feel like celebrating," I told Jamie on the phone.

If he knew the truth about her going to Bailey's house, he didn't let on. He bitched and moaned, "I don't want to spend another Saturday night at home with Geneviève and Hakeem."

It was preferable to my alternative. His parents were human, at least. "So message Shane and wack off together," I said.

Jamie clucked his tongue. "I can't. His computer crashed. He e-mailed me from a friend's house that it won't be fixed until Monday. How will I live without Shane until Monday?"

"Wack yourself." I flipped through the three or four messages Darryl had taken off the machine. Coalton was having a rash of backed up toilets and sinks. The Redmans hadn't called about my bid. I wanted that job; it'd pay for the Levi's, and even the Carhartt coat. More than that. A lot more. It was the biggest job I'd ever done. Alone anyway. I could fit it in somehow. Cut back on my hours at the Merc until school was out. I'd have plenty of time this summer. Just thinking about the challenge made me drool. I wondered if I should call them.

"Shane and I need to talk about how and when we're going to meet."

I tuned into Jamie. "Are you still on that kick? Get off it."

Jamie said, "It's going to happen, Mike. It's only a matter of time."

A matter of time, I repeated to myself. For me and Xanadu, it was only a matter of time. I felt it in my bones. Could I wait? I'd have to.

"Why don't you come over and we'll rent a movie?" Jamie cut into my thoughts. "It'll be just like old times."

Meaning last month. Pre-Shane. "Okay. But no horror. I get enough of that at home."

"How is Our Little Miss Sveltlana and the lovely Kung Pao?"

"I'll be there in ten," I said.

<hr/>

Jamie's mom met me at the door of their double-wide. Dolores, not Geneviève. Dottie to me and everyone else in town. "Mike," she said, "you sweetie. Where've you been? I've missed you." She almost didn't let me through the door before crushing me in a hug. I'd missed her too. She smelled like bacon. Dottie always smelled like bacon.

Grandma Dottie's Gourmet Goodies was the name of Dottie's home business. Her baked goods were in high demand in all the Suprettes around western Kansas. She packaged her goodies in red-and-white polka-dot boxes with dotted-swiss ribbon. Dottie wasn't a grandma — she might never be, seeing as how Jamie was an only child — and the gourmet ingredient in her cooking was supposed to be a secret. Right.

The secret was bacon fat. You could smell it clear to River View. It might seem gross, but the truth was bacon fat added a kind of earthy flavor and moistness to Dottie's cakes and cookies.

The oven timer buzzed and Dottie threw up her hands. "Oops, my lemon bars are done. I think Jamie's in his room. Jamie, hon," she called into the back. "Mike's here."

I liked Dottie. Loved her, actually. She was a regular mom, more mom to me than mine had ever been. Jamie's dad was great too. Bill, not Hakeem. He sold hay balers to farmers and ranchers, so he was on the road a lot.

Jamie padded out dressed in his cheerleader sweater and a pleated skirt. He stopped in the alcove separating the kitchen from the living room and twirled in a circle. "How do I look?"

"Stupid," I said. "Why are you wearing that?"

"We're selecting our uniforms for next year." Jamie admired himself in the hallway mirror. "The pants haven't come in yet, but I wanted to see how the reverse colors looked. Kimberleigh loaned me her skirt." He did a modified split jump in the cramped space. "What do you think?"

"If you show up at one of my games in a skirt, you'll find out how accurate my arm is."

Dottie laughed from the kitchen.

Jamie ignored me. Checking himself out one last time, he said, "Okay, I like it. Give me a sec to change. I picked up a couple of movies at the Suprette." He thumbed into the living room.

The DVDs were on top of the TV — the big-screen TV that took up half the trailer. I wandered over to see what he'd gotten. The aroma of sugar and lemon and bacon redirected my feet to the kitchen. I didn't realize how hungry I was. I'd only had a can of SpaghettiOs for dinner.

Dottie was sliding a cake pan into the oven. "Oh, Mike. Good. I'm trying out a new recipe for lemon bars. Don't tell, but it's really Emeril's recipe that I'm enhancing with my own secret ingredient." She winked at me. "I need a taste tester. Do the honors?"

She had to ask?

She sliced a hunk from a second pan that was cooling on a rack on the counter. As I bit into the lemon bar, she watched intently, index finger pressed to her chin.

"Hmm." My eyes bulged. The crust was warm and chewy; the tangy lemon filling melted in my mouth. I scored her a ten with spread out fingers on both hands.

Dottie beamed and patted my cheek.

I was savoring another mouthful of lemon lusciousness when Jamie flounced into the kitchen. He hefted himself onto the counter next to me and filched the lemon bar right out of my hand. "What are we going to watch?" he said, chomping into it.

The movies. I hadn't gotten that far. Dottie scooped up two lemon bars onto the spatula and held them out to us. I took both and headed to the living room.

"Stop! Thief!" Jamie jumped off the counter.

When I saw which movies he'd picked, I groaned. "We've seen these a hundred times." They were *Dumb and Dumber* and *Titanic*.

"Only ninety-nine." Jamie flopped on the floor and extended his legs out in front of him. "The newest thing I could find was *Mean Girls*, and I hate when art imitates life too closely."

Blockbuster hadn't put Coalton on its regular delivery route. We could get newer than *Dumb and Dumber* though. Oh well. I could use a laugh tonight.

About ten minutes into the movie, the phone rang. Jamie bounded to his feet. "BeShanebeShanebeShanebeShane," he said. He wrenched the cordless off the wall. "Hello? What?" He covered his free ear with a hand. "Oh hi, Dad." His voice went all monotone.

I remoted down the surround sound on the TV.

"Not much," Jamie said. "It's not like I'd ever have a date on a Saturday night. Unless you count Mike." Jamie stuck out his tongue at me and I sneered.

Dottie and Bill knew Jamie was gay. How could they not? They were cool. No drama when he came out. He didn't drive, so if they disowned him Jamie wouldn't get far. He'd probably wind up in the backyard sleeping on his tramp. No, that'd never happen. Anyone in Coalton would take Jamie in. We didn't have homeless people here.

Plus, if we had discrimination, I wasn't aware of it. Jamie and I had grown up here. People knew us; they were used to us. I'm sure they gossiped, but it never got back to me. I never, for one day, felt judged or excluded or persecuted in Coalton.

Jamie joked around with his dad on the phone for a while, then handed it off to Dottie. He resumed his spot beside me on the floor. "What'd I miss?"

I just looked at him. A few minutes later, the phone rang again and Dottie answered it. "Jamie, it's Shane."

Jamie scrabbled to his feet and lunged for the phone. "Shane, I knew you'd call." He listened for a long moment, then held his heart. "I know," he said. "Me too." Jamie caressed the headset to his ear and headed to his bedroom in back.

They must've talked for an hour. The movie was boring. Old jokes. Dottie came in once to ask if I'd like a sandwich, but I declined. It was after nine and she looked ready for bed.

I yawned. So did she.

"Where's Jamie?" she said.

"Still talking to Shane," I answered in another yawn.

She twisted her head and smiled down the hall. Her smile was so full, it was like she was pouring out a waterfall of love for Jamie. I wondered if my mom had ever smiled at me that way. If once, in her whole entire life, she had felt a drop of love for me.

Chapter Fifteen

She didn't call me. I figured she was recovering from her Toto time playing cards with the McCalls. I didn't call her. I didn't want to know what she was doing at the McCalls with *him*. When I got off work at five, there was one message on the machine. Esther Duffy. I groaned. She said her water heater had rusted out and would I come over.

I sighed long and hard. I guess I had nothing better to do, like return Xanadu's promised call. Ask her how she planned to make it up to me.

Only one word described Esther Duffy. Old biddy. I guess that's two words, but they go together. I swear, that lady was born with a burr up her butt. She hated kids. Me and Darryl in particular. She'd storm down to our house and accuse us of stealing her pumpkins or letting her rabbits out of the hutch. I never stole anything from Esther Duffy, or anyone else. Her rabbits were neglected and filthy, so whoever let them out was doing them a favor. I suspected it was Darryl.

I'd forgotten about those rabbits. And Esther Duffy. We hadn't had any contact with her since she moved to the show homes eight or ten years ago. I wondered how she was enjoying the Tanner boys as neighbors.

Esther met me at the door. "Who are you?" she snarled.

Old biddy. "Mike Szabo. You called me about your water heater?"

Her eyes raked me up and down. "Why are you wearing men's underwear?"

I fixed on her mean, wrinkly face. "Because I like them."

We had a staredown. I won. "You look like your dad," she said.

I didn't have anything to say to that.

"Come in, then." She stepped back from the door. "It's a mess down there."

Mess? It was a disaster area. Her basement had an inch of water covering the cement slab, pooling around her washer and dryer, the legs of the water heater entirely submerged. "I'm going to have to pump this first," I thought aloud.

"Do what you need to do." Esther breathed down my neck on the stair behind me. She smelled like rotten meat. "Your dad installed that water heater. Obviously he did a lousy job."

I seethed. That had to be ten years ago. Water heaters corrode. They rust. They fall apart, like people. I almost told her, Lady, find someone else for this job. Almost. There *was* no one else, not in Coalton. Besides, I needed to occupy my time. My mind.

"Excuse me, ma'am." I turned and smiled. "I'll need to get my equipment out of the truck."

She let me pass. I got to work.

Dad's installation was flawless by any professional standards. Standards from ten years ago, though. It wasn't up to current code, or what I knew of it. I figured since I was here, I'd replace all the electrical, update the flex connector to the gas.

"I'll need to run back to the shop for the water heater," I told

Esther. She was lucky we had one in stock. Esther was glued to the TV, some home shopping show.

She remoted down the sound. "He did it to her, you know. They did it to each other."

Was this a soap? It looked like QVC. "I'll let myself out."

"She didn't used to be that big, your mama. She used to be fine. Not petite, mind you. Never small. But she was a nice person. She never was all that social. Didn't come out much. After her baby died . . ."

We've all been through a lot, okay?

Esther sighed. "She was never the same after she lost that baby. And him with his drinking."

Shut up. I pivoted and charged out the back. Drive, I thought. Just drive. Finish the job and get out of there.

The water heater we had was a brand-new forty-gallon Rheem. I hated to give it to Esther, but what choice did I have? If I ordered one, it'd take time. She was an old lady; she needed hot water. I struggled to maneuver the box onto the hand dolly and up into the truck by myself. But I managed. See, Dad? Who needs you?

Hours later, as I was cleaning up, repacking tools, running a final leak test, Esther wandered downstairs with her checkbook. "What do I owe you?" she asked.

I hadn't considered a charge. Five dollars didn't cover the O-ring on a toilet these days.

She said, "Will five hundred do it?"

Five hundred dollars? The water heater was just sitting there, collecting dust. My labor was the only cost. I checked my watch. Nine-thirty. Had I been here that long? Four hours, on a Sunday. "Make it four hundred," I told Esther. It still felt like too much.

She ripped out her check and handed it to me. "Sometimes," she said, "there are two people in the world who should never come together. That's your ma and your pop. Alone, they might've made it.

Together? With their addictions?" She shook her head. "They were a toxic combination."

I just looked at her. "Yes, ma'am," I said.

I was feeling good when I got to school on Monday. Nothing like a job well done. Four hundred bucks in my bank account. A double circuit at the VFW this morning. I was pumped. First thing I saw when I turned the corner heading for Geometry class was Xanadu.

Oh yeah.

And Bailey. Crap.

He leaned down to kiss her.

My muscles cramped. Luckily, the girls' room was three steps away. I barreled inside and leaned against the door. Exhale, flex, hold, hold. Control, action, focus.

She wasn't mine. Not now. Not yet. But someday. Some way. I'd make her love me, the way I loved her.

I'd practically beat the bell tearing out of Miz S's class. I just couldn't take it — his turning around and smiling at her every ten seconds; her poking him, passing him notes. I needed sky. Needed out. We were running track this week in gym, thank God. I could sprint laps. Run it off. For an hour, just run.

Perfume swirled up my nose.

I raised my head off my knees.

"What happened to you? You took off before I could even say hello." She curled cross-legged on the mat in front of me. Her smile faded. "Mike. What is it? Are you okay?" She reached out and touched my knee.

"Just . . . zoning." It was too windy and cold today for track. Gym was held indoors. Rope climbing, a totally wasted exercise — exorcise. My muscles didn't even ache afterward.

She smiled slightly, a sort of half smile, soft smile, which made my bones go rubbery. "I really need to talk to you," she said in a lowered voice. "Alone. In private."

"Okay." I perked up. "We can't go to the roof though. It's too windy."

"Not now. I have Journalism this hour. Did Jamie tell you we have to write a newspaper article for our test? Like, a feature with interviews and sidebars and everything." She crossed her eyes and stuck out her tongue. "I was thinking maybe later. After school?"

I opened my mouth, then shut it.

"You have to work."

"I could get off." Which would be hard. Everett needed me to help stock for Coalton Days.

"That's okay," Xanadu said. "It isn't important. I just wanted to spend time with you."

My heart soared. "I don't have to go in."

"Yes, you do." She tilted her head. "I know you."

She did. She knew me. I wanted to cover her hand on my knee, take it, press it against my pounding heart, pass the tremors onto her. For some reason though, I was paralyzed. I couldn't take action. Don't let go, I prayed. Please, don't let go.

"Maybe we could ditch one day this week and hang out at your house?" Xanadu arched her eyebrows.

I choked. "I don't think so."

Her eyes darkened.

"Not at my house."

She stood. "Okay. Whatever."

I scrambled to my feet. "We can ditch though. Anytime."

Gazing off toward the dangling ropes, she folded her arms around herself and said, "I need to talk about this and I can't with Bailey, you know? He wouldn't understand. I mean, he might, but I'm afraid to tell him."

She was afraid of him. I knew it. She'd be so much safer with me. "We could take off tomorrow," I said. "Go someplace besides my house though."

She peered into my eyes, into my soul. She was wondering, I know, why I didn't want to take her there. She ran her index finger down the length of my arm and raised goose bumps on my skin. "One of these days you're going to tell me your secrets," she murmured.

I almost came.

"Xanadu!"

Both our heads whipped around.

"Where have you been?" Bailey swaggered up to us. "I need my notebook for third period. Hey, Mike." His eyes swept my body, taking in my muscle tee and boxers.

"Bailey," I said flatly.

Xanadu said, "It's in my locker."

"I know," Bailey replied. "I, uh, forgot your combination again." He forced a weak smile.

Xanadu widened her eyes at me.

Really, I thought. All brawn. Not much of that either. Not compared to me.

She held my eyes for an extended moment, sending me a meaningful message. I felt confused, conflicted. One minute I was her world, the next Bailey moved in. I know she was giving me signals, but I didn't know how to interpret them. She wasn't like any other girl I'd known — or wanted this way. She was a mystery, a contradiction. She took off for the main hall with Bailey in tow. Last thing I saw was him looping an arm around her shoulders and her snaking one around his waist. I closed my eyes and hit my head against the brick wall.

The Merc was a madhouse. What was going on? Darryl had gone off in the truck, so I was forced after practice to walk the half mile to work in a blinding dust storm. I was gritting dirt between my teeth as I hung up my sweatshirt on the hook in back. June saw me and rushed over. "Dad needs you up front to help cashier," he wheezed. He added under his breath, "Hate Coalton Days."

They were still a month away, but Everett always got the first jump on the businesses in town with the Merc's spring sale. I lifted my apron strap over my head and tied it twice around the middle.

June slithered away, muttering unintelligible sounds. On the way to the register I passed Tiny juggling an armload of merchandise. She dumped it on the counter. A box of Snausages tipped over and I snagged it before it hit the floor. "Are we out of baskets?" I asked, searching the cart caddy at the entrance. There were still three available.

"No," Tiny said, sounding disgusted. "I was just coming in for dog-gie treats, and then I seen these wind chimes and thought they'd sound pretty outside the salon. Queenie needs a new collar and leash, so I had to get that too. And a windbreaker, which I could've used on the way over. I had to get me a six-pack of pansies, course." She rubbernecked around me. "You're sending me to the poorhouse, Everett."

He smiled sheepishly from behind the cash register. I think he had a thing for Tiny. He was such a crusty old coot. I couldn't see how any woman would be interested in Everett. But then, I wasn't any woman.

A line was already forming behind Tiny. Someone called to Everett how much were the bedding plants and I relieved him at the register. I rang Tiny up. She handed me two twenties, which reeked of per-manent solution, and from the change I gave her, she separated out a five-dollar bill. "For you," she said. "I hope you get to go." She folded the money and dropped it into a can on the counter.

For me? I craned my neck around the cash register. It was a coffee can with a plastic lid, a slot cut out on top. I picked it up and turned it around. A picture of me was glued to the front. It was my school picture from ninth grade. What the hell . . . ?

The can was covered in construction paper and decorated with glitter. Above my picture was printed, in red magic marker, "Mike's Catch-Her-Star Can-paign."

"What the hell . . . ?" I repeated aloud, grabbing the can.

"There it is." Mayor Ledbetter rolled his cart up to the counter. "This is a stellar idea, Mike. Ha, ha. Get it?" He dropped a couple of quarters into the slot. They didn't hit bottom and clink. How many dollars were in there? "Nice to get the whole town involved."

"Whose idea was it?" I snapped.

Mayor Ledbetter arched his eyebrows. "I thought it was yours."

"Mine?" My voice rose. "I wouldn't do this."

Junior appeared behind me with a bag of wild bird seed flopped across his shoulder. "Save this for Renata," he growled. "She's stopping by later. I didn't know your batting average was .647 last year."

"Good write-up in the paper," Mayor Ledbetter said.

"Huh? What paper?" What was this about?

Behind the mayor, Armie dropped a pile of jeans on the counter. He flipped open his wallet and withdrew a ten. "Stick that in there, will ya?" He indicated the can.

Mayor Ledbetter folded the bill and wiggled it in. Armie balled a fist and bounced it off his opposite shoulder. "You go, girl."

"What write-up?" I was stuck on the mayor. "What paper?"

"The *Gazette.*" He waved toward the newspaper rack near the cart caddy.

"I'll be right back." I shoved the can at him and charged across the Merc.

Only one copy of the *Tri-County Gazette* remained in the coin box.

Through the glass window I could see my picture on page one. I dug out a dime and inserted it into the slot.

> "First time I saw her play, I thought to myself, Man, oh man, Emmanuel, this girl has got the goods. She was six and I was . . . well, let's just say awe-inspired."

Was this about me? No one interviewed me or anything.

> Manny Archuleta, in a phone interview from Wichita — where he's helping his mother recover from hip replacement surgery — is speaking about our own superstar. "She was a natural, even as a kid," Manny tells this reporter. "You knew she had the game in her blood. She had a feel for it, an instinct. She's the best player I've ever coached, or had the pleasure to watch develop. She's taught me more about the game than I've ever taught her."
> The game, of course, is girls' fastpitch softball. And the player Coach Archuleta is bragging about is Mike Szabo.

I didn't know Coach Archuleta felt that way about me. Who was "this reporter"?

There was no byline.

> The Coalton Cougars have been on a roll since Szabo's rookie year. For the past three seasons they've placed first or second in the region and continued on to the quarterfinals. Their success is due in no small measure to the infield play and leadership of Mike (Mary-Elizabeth) Szabo.

I cringed.

"Mike!" Everett's voice registered dimly.

> If you've never attended a Cougars game (and you'd be in the minority in this town), you haven't had the pleasure of seeing Mike play. She's the spots and stripes of the Coalton Cougars.

Spots and stripes? Cougars didn't have stripes. Who wrote this? I read faster to get to the end.

Crouched behind home plate, she calls out signals and cheers on base runners. At bat, Szabo is a cat poised to spring on her prey. And she springs to the tune of an astounding .647 batting average.

My breath caught. Who was keeping stats? Besides me. And I only kept them in my head. The article was good. Not because it was all about me. Well, maybe, partly. I'd been written up in the paper before, but not like this.

What you may not know are all the records Mike currently holds. Keep in mind, she's still a junior.

"Mike!" Everett called. "What are you doing?"
I wandered back to the register, still reading.

Most career runs scored: 82
Most runs scored by an individual in a single season: 35
Most hits by an individual in a single season: 49
Most career doubles: 26
Most career runs batted in: 72

Someone was tracking me. The way Dad used to. He knew all my stats. He kept a book, meticulous records. I flipped to page three, where the article continued. My stats ran on for another half column. A name in the last paragraph caught my eye.

"Mike has an extraordinary opportunity to apply her talents and gifts by attending the Carrie Reigners Softball Camp in Michigan this summer. Only the best are asked to apply. Mike is one of approximately two hundred girls on the A-list. We can't let her waste this opportunity because of financial need." Dr. Kinneson went on to say . . .

Damn her!

What was she telling people? That I'm poor? Thanks a lot.

There was a sidebar near the end:

Mike's Catch-Her-Star Can-paign begins this weekend at the Mercantile's spring sale. Drop your spare change into the cans . . .

That's all I saw. Slapping the paper together, I shrilled, "Who did this!" Everyone in the Merc stopped talking and swiveled their heads. I gulped and tried to calm myself.

Coach Kinneson. Had to be. I didn't think she knew how to keep stats. How'd she get those pictures? The other ones, on page three and four. Me in Pee Wees. In Junior League. The team photos. My individual photo, crouched with my glove chest high, spread for a catch.

Coach Archuleta. He had photo albums. He knew our stats. I'd kill them both. They were conspiring against me. I'd make them pay.

I suddenly felt exposed, bared, every eye in the Merc stripping me naked. Every eye in town would be on me. They'd feel sorry for me — again. All over again.

Chapter Sixteen

*I*nterviews. Sidebars. Catch-Her-Star Can-paign. The can, glitter, dotted-swiss ribbon around my school picture. It didn't take a genius.

I slammed Jamie up against the wall of his bedroom so hard the trailer shook. "You're dead, dickhead. Say a prayer."

Jamie looked freaked, which was wise considering the proximity of my fist to his face. "Whatever I did, I didn't do it," he said in a rush.

I twisted his polo shirt at the neck. He faked strangulation. "What didn't I do?" he choked. I released my hold roughly. He stretched out the shirt and gulped for air.

"The can-*paign*." I drilled the word into his skull. "Catch-Her-*Star*?"

"Oh. That."

I knew it. Jerk. I grabbed him again.

"I didn't do it. I swear." He pushed me off. "But I think it's a fabulous idea."

"No one else knew about the camp. Only you and Xanadu. And Xanadu wouldn't do this to me."

She wouldn't, would she? I'd kill her too. No, I wouldn't. I loved her.

Jamie smirked.

He *did* do it.

"What's the problem?" he asked.

"What's the problem? What's the *problem*? It's humiliating." I sank onto Jamie's beanbag chair in the corner of his room. "I feel like a charity case. I feel like the poster child for Jerry's Kids. Thanks a lot." I folded my arms across my chest.

Jamie clucked his tongue. "Nobody thinks that." He resumed what he was doing before I barged in to beat the crap out of him. Glossing his hair in the mirror with pomade or something. He raised his eyes and met mine. "Get over it," he said. "Nobody thinks of this as charity. They just want to help."

"I don't need their help. I don't need their handouts, okay? I've got this big job at the Redmans' . . ." Okay, I didn't have the job — yet. But I would. "I don't even know if I want to go to the stupid camp." I sprawled back in the chair, arms behind my head. "I'm going to be really busy this summer with a replumb job, and the only reason to go to softball camp is if I'm going competitive or want to win a scholarship to college, and why would I want a scholarship when college is so *not* in my future?"

Jamie didn't answer. He was too absorbed in slicking and arranging every hair on his head.

I sighed and shifted to get comfortable. The chair crunched. I crossed an ankle over my knee and picked at the sole of my shoe. "What if I end up having to give all the money back? How am I going to do that? I don't even know who gave what."

Jamie widened his eyes at me in the mirror. "You wouldn't dare. That would offend everyone, even me. If you don't go to the camp, you and I can take off for Puerto Vallarta. We'll hit all the gay beaches. Better yet, let's fly to San Francisco. Shag a couple of hotties off Castro Street."

Jamie's computer beeped. A sexy voice breathed, "Jamie, honey. You've got mail."

"Speaking of hotties." Jamie slid into his desk chair.

I watched as he clicked keys at cyber-speed. My head lolled back against the wall and my eyes strayed to Jamie's ceiling. His glow-in-the-dark stars and moons pasted all over. When we were kids, I used to stay the night and we'd pretend his bed was a spaceship. We'd fly across the heavens, visit other planets. We always come home to Coalton.

"Oh my God," Jamie gasped. "Shane wants to buy his plane ticket right now. No second thoughts. He wants me to pick a weekend." Jamie swiveled around to face me. "What should I say?"

"Say you need a fax of his psychiatric report."

Jamie stuck out his tongue and spun back around. He reached up and ripped his calendar off the wall. "Not this weekend," he mumbled to himself. "I need to color my hair. My tan is uneven. I have to lose ten pounds and bleach my teeth." He flipped to May. "I wonder if you can order Botox online." Jamie sighed. He skimmed down the month. "Okay. Next weekend." He keyed a message on the computer. "No second thoughts."

"I can't believe this," I said.

"Neither can I. It's actually going to happen. Shane and I are going to meet."

"You're going to die. You're going to end up a statistic." I didn't say what I was thinking: You're going to end up hurt.

"Ohmigod, ohmigod, ohmigod." Jamie stared at the screen. He covered his mouth with both hands.

I pushed to my feet and moved to the bed, perching on the edge to hang over Jamie's shoulder. Shane messaged back. Jamie cried, "He can do it!" Jamie wrote back, "I'm so excited." Shane: "Me too." Jamie: "I can't wait." Shane: "Me neither." Shane: "I'm checking Orbitz."

"He's checking Orbitz," Jamie said, hyperventilating.

"I can read."

"Oh my God. I'm having a heart attack." Jamie pressed a palm to his chest.

"What do you think of Xanadu?" I asked to change the subject.

Jamie blew out a shallow breath. "I'm not sure." He chewed his pinkie nail. "She's cool, but there's something about her that bothers me. Oh yeah." He snapped his fingers. "She's straight."

I stood up. "People aren't always what they seem."

"Mike —"

I paved a path through his faux fur rug.

"Mike!"

"What?" I spun around at the door.

Jamie's eyes flickered from me to his monitor. "Oh my God. He did it! Shane got a reservation."

<hr />

What could be more romantic than spending the day with the girl you loved locked up in a plumbing supply shop? I was hoping she'd see the beauty of it. Of course, she'd have to understand what it meant to me and I wasn't sure I was ready to talk about that yet.

We had an oral report to give in History and a fitness challenge in Gym. Today was the worst day of the week for me to ditch. Oh well. Love was about making sacrifices, right? What was perfect attendance, anyway? A worthless certificate.

"I think Bailey's parents have a problem with me," Xanadu said as she hopped into the truck and shut the door. She'd been waiting at our predetermined rendezvous behind the Dairy D. "They look at me like I'm going to corrupt him or something. I'm sure they think I'm this big city slut. Where are we going?" She tucked a foot underneath her and turned to face me as I shifted gears.

"To Dad's," I replied. "I need to see how much ABS he has in stock."

Xanadu said tentatively, "Your . . . dad's?"

What? Oh. "I mean, his shop. His . . . our . . . plumbing shop."

"Okay." Her nose wrinkled slightly.

"We can hang out there," I told her. "If anyone in town sees us ditching, they're likely to call the school."

"You're kidding."

I met her eyes. Minimal makeup. Hair in a ponytail. Cutoffs with an eyelet blouse. Rebecca of Sunnybrook.

"You're not joking," she said.

"The mayor asked if I'd fix the town fountain, since Coalton Days is coming up. That thing springs a leak every year. I thought I'd just replace the whole length of pipe to the water main with new ABS . . ."

She looked at me.

I added, "Not today. I just want to check supplies; see if I have to order anything."

She glanced away, obviously upset. How insensitive could I be?

"I don't know what I did for her to hate me." Xanadu's jaw clenched. "I ate her fucking chicken fried steak without hurling."

"People here are used to each other, that's all," I said. "Bailey's parents just need to get to know you."

"Who cares? That's not really what I wanted to talk to you about." She continued to gaze out the window as I hung a left and tooled down Main.

I didn't want to pry. I was glad we were off the subject of Bailey.

She exhaled a long breath and cranked up the radio, even though it was country. Travis Tritt. She didn't seem to care, or hear.

As the shop came into view, my stomach twisted. Would I always feel sick at the sight of it? It didn't help that I was ditching today for the first time ever.

I drove up the alley and parked in back. "Here we are," I stated the obvious. My voice sounded as far away as I suddenly wished I was. Coming here was a bad idea.

Before I could change my mind, Xanadu got out of the truck. She perched on tiptoes to peer through the cracked window while I unlocked the back door. Inside, the shop was the same as I'd left it. Dark, deserted. I opened the slats on the dusty miniblinds so there'd be enough light to see in the stockroom. To see her.

"I'll be right back. Make yourself at home." Could she, the way I did? The way I used to? This place had been like home to me. Out of the corner of my eye I watched Xanadu wander around the office area, touching things, examining objects. There was plenty of PVC and ABS stacked along the wall in back. Dad must've ordered pipe right before . . . Maybe he'd planned to fix the leak in the fountain before . . .

Stop thinking about it.

I returned to the office where Xanadu had lifted Dad's stuffed pheasant off the filing cabinet.

"He shot that when he was eight," I told her. "His dad, my grandpa Darryl, stuffed it for him."

Xanadu shuddered and dropped the pheasant back on top of the cabinet. Dad was so proud of that kill. Even back then, he'd cherished death more than life.

"Hey, your dad played softball?" Xanadu pulled his trophy down.

"Yeah. He was in a men's fastpitch league. My number, 19, that was his number —"

Her shoulders slumped suddenly and she burst out crying. I plunked the pipe on the floor and rushed over. Removing Dad's trophy from her limp hand and setting it gently atop the cabinet in the same exact spot, I asked, "What is it, Xanadu?"

She almost threw her arms around me. Almost. I know she wanted to. She could have. I wanted to hold her, comfort her, but something kept me from making the first move. Instead, she wrapped her arms around herself. "I can't stop thinking about it," she said. "Tiffany. Her death." A sound like a wounded animal issued from Xanadu's throat and she doubled over, clutching her stomach. I took both her arms and backed her onto Dad's office chair.

She leaned forward, rocking herself. Back and forth. Crying. I balanced on my haunches in front of her. "I don't know how to deal," she said. "How do you deal with it, Mike? Death, I mean." She blinked up, her watery eyes fixing on me.

"I don't think about it." Except at night when the nightmare intrudes. When I see him, his body — falling, falling, *thud*.

I stood up fast, a solid mass of hurt caught in my chest. I couldn't think.

Stop thinking. Stop feeling. Exhale, hold, hold.

"What happened that day?" Xanadu asked quietly.

I was suspended in time, space.

I levered myself against Dad's desk, my knees wobbly. We shouldn't have come here.

"You don't have to talk about it if you don't want to." Her voice soft as a pillow. "All Bailey said was that your dad was drunk and fell off the water tower."

I blew. "Is that what Bailey said?" I stood up straight. I didn't want to talk about this. Not with anyone. Not with her.

Yes, I did. I wanted her to know me, know everything about me. I wanted us to be close.

"Bailey said —"

"Bailey lied." Bailey should shut up. "Yeah, my dad was drunk. He was always drunk. He was loaded that day, sure. But no more than usual." Bailey should tell her the truth, at least. "He was an alcoholic, okay? And he didn't fall off the water tower."

"But Bailey said —"

"He didn't fall." My voice hard, rough.

Xanadu's jaw slowly came unhinged. Her hands rose to cover her mouth. "Oh my God, Mike." She blinked. "He . . . committed suicide?"

I stared ahead.

"Are you sure?"

I glanced up at the pheasant, the trophy, Dad's plumbing license, framed and hung on the wall. Expired. The cracked, filthy back window.

"Mike?"

"I'm sure." Hate you, Dad. I hate you so much. "He wrote out his will the night before he did it. Pretty obvious what he was planning." My eyes met hers.

"Oh God."

Then her arms were around me, pulling me into her, crushing me against her body. No. I won't cry. You can't make me, Dad. But I felt myself falling, falling, losing control. I wouldn't. He couldn't make me.

As much as I wanted to, I couldn't force myself to respond to Xanadu, to hold her in return. Not for this. Not because of him. I'd been dying for this moment, to be together, our bodies melding, but the reason needed to be right. I wanted her to want me, to desire me, yeah. But our coming together had to be spontaneous. It had to be mutual, reciprocal.

"It must be unbearable." She stepped back and gazed into my eyes. Her emotion, her empathy dug so deep into my soul it ached.

"I don't think about it. That's how you get through. You force it from your mind."

Her arms fell to the side. "I can't . . . *not* think about it," she said. "I have nightmares."

I closed my eyes and turned away.

"I won't tell anyone." Xanadu clenched my wrist. "I won't tell Bailey if that's what you're afraid of."

I'm not afraid. That's not it. "He knows. Everybody knows. They're just too polite to talk about it in public."

We needed to get off the subject of Dad. I unlocked her hold on me and charged to the front door; picked up an envelope that had been shoved in the mail slot. It was dusty and yellowed. An overdue notice from Rural Electric, postmarked two years ago. I sailed it to the floor.

Xanadu said, "Have you talked with anyone about this?"

"Like a psychiatrist?" I turned and faked a smile. "The closest thing we have to a shrink around here is Renata, who reads people's horoscopes for ten bucks a pop."

Xanadu's eyes softened. "I meant, a friend."

I wished to hell we'd move on. Talk about the weather, Bailey, anything. "Jamie," I said. "We've talked." As much as we needed to. What was there to say? Jamie understood. You got through it; you got over it. It was cold in here, or hot. My skin prickled. I trudged over to the thermometer to check it, see if it'd click on.

"Jamie's a good friend, isn't he? I can tell you two are tight."

No power, of course. "Not that tight," I said.

"I didn't mean tight, like tight. That'd be interesting, wouldn't it? You and Jamie?" She crossed her eyes.

It made me laugh. "Yeah, *real* interesting."

"I've been meaning to ask you, do you believe in love at first sight?" She sat back down in Dad's chair, tossing her hair over both shoulders.

"Definitely," I said.

She smiled. "Me too. I didn't used to. I can't believe how we just clicked. I mean, the first time we laid eyes on each other, it was like, Wow. I've gotta have this. You're the one I've been waiting for all my life."

My heart propelled out of my chest. Did she mean it?

"He said he felt it too. He couldn't take his eyes off me." She lowered her head and blushed.

Bailey. I felt like throwing up. Change the subject again. Predicting when the drought will end is always a rich topic of conversation.

"Same as us," Xanadu added. She raised her head and held my eyes. Her warmth enveloped me, caressed me.

What'd she mean? Both of us?

"I knew instantly we'd be friends."

Friends? I wanted us to be more than friends. We were more.

"So, Mike. Have you ever . . . ?" She wiggled her eyebrows.

Ever what? Oh. That. My mouth went dry. "Are you thirsty?" I asked. Head down, I plowed across the room. "Dad usually kept a six-pack in the fridge." His mini-fridge was behind her. I had to swivel Xanadu's legs out of the way to get to it. I actually touched her. Sparks of electricity flew between us. Real, palpable. I know she felt it. Goose bumps raised on her skin, and mine too.

In the fridge were a couple of cans of Classic Coke and a quart of Old Milwaukee.

She extended an open hand and I filled it with the beer bottle. Her question lingered. I wanted her to answer it for me. Had *she* ever? Had sex? I didn't care with who. As long as it wasn't Bailey. As long as they weren't doing it, I figured I still had a chance. She liked me — a lot. She knew instantly she would. There was more going on here than friendship. When would she realize it, acknowledge it? The touching, smiling, the intimacy, attraction. When would she act on it?

When she was ready, I answered my own question. At any moment.

She drew a long pull of the beer and screwed up her face. "Ugh. Pretty desperate, drinking warm beer at nine AM."

Xanadu passed the bottle to me and I tipped it to my lips. Not only warm. Flat too. I wanted to spit it out, but the bathroom was clear in back. I gagged as I swallowed. "So. Have you and Bailey . . . ?" I set the bottle on top of the fridge.

A slow smile spread across her lips. "He makes you think he's this shy, virginal type, right? When we started kissing, it was like he'd been saving it up. Saving himself, he said. For me. God, it was unbelievable, Mike."

Why did I have to ask! Stupid. I clutched the neck of the bottle and pitched it in the metal trash can. The glass shattered and beer splattered everywhere. I said, "Let's drive to Garden City."

Xanadu leaped to her feet. "Okay."

I barreled to the door and flung it wide, crashing outside into the blinding light. Why did I have to ask?

Chapter Seventeen

Dr. Kinneson called me to her office out of Geometry. "Where were you yesterday?" she said. "All your teachers reported you missing. Are you sick? Are you okay?"

"No. I mean, I'm not sick."

"Is everything all right?"

"Yes." What could possibly be wrong? Everything was perfect. My dad committed suicide. Xanadu was having sex with Bailey. "I ditched."

Dr. Kinneson's eyes waffled. She studied my face. My face was a study in granite, well rehearsed. She'd never chisel through. "Why?" she asked.

"Why?" I repeated. What kind of question was that?

"Do you have a reason? Was it an emergency?"

Besides needing to be with Xanadu? It seemed vital at the time. I didn't reply. Maybe I shrugged.

Leaning across her desk, Dr. Kinneson added, "What do you think I should do about it?"

She was asking me? I got to decide my punishment? "I don't know. Slap my wrist? Send me to bed hungry?" I smirked.

She didn't smile.

"I don't know," I said again. I'd never ditched before. A class here and there, yeah, when we had a sub. When I needed to be close to the sky. When no one would miss me. Do you miss me, Dad?

"How about you miss the game with Garden City tonight."

"What!"

Dr. Kinneson rolled back her chair and stood. "I think that's fair. One game."

Fair? I couldn't miss a game. It wasn't just a game. "Coach, I'd rather you suspend me. Put me on probation. Make me clean the johns or something. Anything. I can't miss a game."

She opened her mouth to respond, but the phone rang. She answered it. "Yes? All right. Put him through." She covered the mouthpiece. "That'll be all, Mike."

I felt dizzy. Shaken. Damn her. I charged out the door. How unfair could she be? I'd never missed a game in my life. I wouldn't. I'd be letting my teammates down. I'd be letting the town down. If I'd known the price was so high, that it'd cost me this, my pride, I never would have ditched.

What punishment did Xanadu get? None. Because she was a thousand times smarter than me. She'd called in sick.

<hr />

They couldn't believe it. No one could believe it. Me, sitting on the bench. As Coach Kinneson conferred with the ump over the change in lineup, T.C. apparently got elected to ask. She perched next to me on the bench, leaning over so we were face-to-face, and said, "What's up? Are you injured?"

I shook my head at the ground. In sixth grade during a slide into home I'd caught the bag and wrecked my knee. Coach Archuleta had to rush out and help me off the field. I wanted to scream and cry out in pain, but I wouldn't. It hurt so bad.

"Baby, it's okay if you miss a few games," Dad had told me. "Everyone'll understand."

Meaning who? My team? The town? Him?

"I'm fine," I'd assured him, even though I wasn't fine. I was hurt. I didn't want to disappoint anyone. They were counting on me to play. Depending on me to bring home the win.

"You're one tough cookie," Dad had said. He was proud. Proud of my strength and courage. He added, "You're stronger than I'll ever be."

I jerked back to the present. He'd said that. I wasn't sure what he meant at the time. Now I knew. He was weak. So weak. I turned to T.C. "I'm fine. I'm just sitting this one out."

Armie stuck his head around the shell of the lean-to. "Mike, you hurt? How come you're not out there?"

The game was starting, both bleachers spilling over with people. T.C. clenched my shoulder, then loped onto the field. It felt like everyone was looking at me. Waiting. Expectant. I shook my head at Armie. He wasn't going to hear it from me. No one was.

"Coach," Armie called over to her. "Why isn't Mike out there?"

Coach Kinneson said, "She's benched."

"What?" Armie sounded shocked. I felt his eyes burn through me as I stared into the middle distance.

"How come?" Armie asked.

Coach scribbled a note on her clipboard. "None of your business," she said.

My jaw unhinged. Telling Armie that — telling anyone in Coalton that — was like saying, "Fuck you."

Armie bristled. He stomped back to the bleachers and Coach Kinneson muttered to me, "I get the feeling I'm not going to be the most popular person in Coalton tomorrow."

You aren't today, I thought.

It was agony sitting on the bench, cheering for my team, not being out there. When the Buffs saw I wasn't playing, it seemed to energize them. But Cougars tapped into their own current. Fifth inning, they heightened their play. Everyone's game was on. Coalton beat the crap out of Garden City. Without me. It's not like I wanted us to lose, but . . .

Xanadu had come with Bailey. All game long, they sat cuddled at the top of the bleachers. If there was a hell, this was it.

I congratulated my team, shared the victory whoop. Big whoop. "Hey, what'd you do?" Darryl caught up with me as I was gathering my gear. "Murder someone?"

I whirled on him.

"What else would be bad enough that the coach would bench you? Unless you shot your mouth off to her —"

"Shut up."

"The way you do me."

"Shut up!" I kicked gravel at him. Took off for home.

"Pretty cruel," Darryl said at my back. "Not letting you play."

What would you know! I wanted to scream. You don't know.

But he did know. He got it. Coach Kinneson couldn't have hurt me any worse if she'd plunged a knife through my heart.

"Can I go with you tomorrow?" Xanadu asked.

Her words barely registered through my drunken stupor. She'd rested her head in my lap. She was so close, I could touch her face. Brush her lips with my fingertips, lean down and kiss her. "I could show you guys around Denver," she said, reaching up and fondling the ring on the gold chain around my neck. The chain was a payoff from Jamie for agreeing to take him to Denver. He'd whined and bitched and moaned all week and finally I caved. The ring was Dad's. Mine now.

Xanadu slipped her index finger into the ring and smiled tenderly at me. I slugged another shot of tequila.

I liked tequila, I was finding out. She must've known my preference when she excavated a full bottle of Cuervo Gold from the Davenports' root cellar. Who knew what we were celebrating? Who cared?

Jamie was watching me, watching us.

"I could show you my old stomping grounds," Xanadu said. "Show you where it happened."

"Where what happened?" Jamie glugged from a bottle of apple wine.

Xanadu tensed. "Nothing." She let go of the ring and sat up.

Damn you, Jamie.

"What about Bailey?" Jamie asked. "How could you stand being apart from lover boy that long?"

Xanadu sighed wearily. "It's not me. He's got this 4-H crap all weekend. "What is 4-H, anyway? Like a sewing club?"

I burst into laughter.

Xanadu grinned and tipped back her bottle of wine. She swallowed a mouthful. "Could I go with you guys? Please?" she begged.

Simultaneously, Jamie said, "No," and I said, "Yes." I glared at him. "Why not?"

He widened his eyes at me, like, you know. I didn't know. Was this a gay thing? A guy thing? "What?" I said.

He lit a smoke, a regular one, and took a drag. "It'd be too crowded in the truck with the four of us."

"You and Shane'll be naked in back, won't you?" Xanadu said. She winked at me.

Jamie sighed. "I can only dream."

"Anyway, Bailey and I need a break." Xanadu crooked her finger at Jamie to share the cigarette. "He's starting to get on my nerves."

I struggled to sit up. "Yeah?"

Xanadu pulled a deep drag and blew out the smoke. "He thinks he owns me. Why do guys do that, get all possessive? He told me today he didn't like me coming to the caboose and drinking with you guys. I mean, come on. What else are you going to do in Totoland? I told him he could come with us, share the joy, but he made up some lame excuse about wanting to worm the calves before he left in the morning."

Thank you, God. Thank you for worms. I'd never try to own her. She was her own person, a free spirit.

Jamie and Shane could take up residence in the toilet tank for all I cared. Xanadu was coming with us.

_____

I vaguely remember Jamie ordering me to pick him up at six AM sharp so we could get to Denver International Airport by nine. Shane's plane landed at ten-thirty and Jamie wanted time to cruise the concourse.

Did he say cruise? More like work off nervous energy. My brain was fried. Last night's party went on until four AM and I shouldn't have even bothered coming home. The phone rang as I was knocking back my third cup of instant coffee. I lunged to answer it, not wanting to wake Ma or Darryl. I didn't need Darryl hassling me about the truck. Not today. Not on the day I planned to speed up time, spend all day with Xanadu, move her in my direction. Today she would see the light; see me illuminated in it.

"Mike, hi," she whispered hoarsely. Was her throat as raw as mine? It felt like I'd been drinking straight gasoline. Plus, I'd had to pull over twice on the way home to puke. "I can't go today," she rasped.

A veil of darkness dropped over my head. "Why not?"

She expelled an irritated breath. "Bailey called this morning. Aunt Faye was furious because it was like five o'clock. He apologized for being such a butthead and wants to make up for it, so he canceled his 4-H doohickey in Wichita to spend the weekend with me. He's got it all worked out, he says, this elaborate lie he's going to tell his parents so we can spend tonight together. I mean, God. Bailey lying for me? I think it's against his religion or something. Anyway, I guess since I'm the one corrupting him, I better agree." There was a smile in her voice.

My stomach hurt.

"I'm sorry, Mike. I really wanted to meet the mysterious cyber-Shane. And spend time with you, of course."

Darkness. Aching inside.

"You'll tell me all about it, right? I want a blow by blow. Did I just say that?" She giggled.

I needed to hurl. Or do crunches.

"Mike?"

"Yeah," I said. Blow by blow.

There was a clunk on her end, a door slamming. "Shit, Uncle Lee just came in. I better go. Call me as soon as you get back. Bailey better have enough condoms for overnight."

We disconnected. I'd never felt violent toward anyone in my life until now. Bailey should watch his back.

Jamie was huddling on the stoop of his trailer, like he'd been camped out since I dumped him at the curb two hours ago. He sprinted to the street and hopped into the truck.

"She's not coming," I anticipated his question. "She's spending the weekend with Bailey."

Jamie gave me this poor puppy dog look. I almost split his lip with a knuckle whip. I squealed away from the curb, whiplashing his head on purpose. So what? I didn't care. I had all the time in the world.

As I accelerated onto Highway 27, heading north to Goodland, Jamie shrieked, "Dammit! I forgot my camera." He punched his leg, hard. "Dammit. Goddammit."

"Chill. We can pick up one of those disposables at the airport," I said. "You think?"

"I try not to." It damaged my head.

He resumed bouncing his fist off his leg, the way he'd been doing ever since we left Coalton.

In syncopated rhythm with his fist, Jamie's head began to bounce off the headrest.

"Will you stop that," I ordered him. "You're giving me a head-ache." In addition to the nausea and vertigo. "What's the worst that could happen?"

"Are you kidding? He'll hate me. He'll take one look at me and get on the next plane home. The next plane to anywhere." Jamie exhaled all the air in his lungs. "I know he'll hate me."

"No, he won't," I said. "He'll fall in love with you at first sight."

Jamie met my eyes. He seemed to downshift a gear. "Do I look all right?" he asked. "I picked this green shirt because it brings out my eyes, but maybe I should've been more subtle. Worn all black. Or dressed up. What if he's wearing like, Abercrombie & Fitch? I'll die of embarrassment. What if he thinks I'm fat, or ugly? Or shabby, or im-mature, or inexperienced? What if he doesn't come?"

"He's coming," I said. "He wouldn't have bought a plane ticket if he wasn't coming."

"He might've lied to me. Set me up."

Jamie was just now coming to that realization?

"This whole thing could be a scam, like you said. He could be a pe-dophile."

A little late to face the truth, I thought. The turnoff to I-70 loomed ahead and I switched lanes to exit. "I guess it's a good thing you brought me along for protection. If he's a perv, I'll beat the shit out of him."

Jamie laced his fingers together under his chin and fluttered his eyelashes at me. "My queero."

"Shut up." I passed a little old lady going forty and floored it.

Jamie muttered, "I need a smoke." He punched open the glove compartment and fished around. "Hey, didn't I have a couple of joints in here?"

My one lucid act before leaving this morning was to clean out the glove box. If we got stopped, I didn't want to get busted for more than speeding. "Darryl smoked them," I lied.

"Damn." Jamie threw himself against the seat back. "Damn. I should've taken a Xanax this morning. I'll never live through this."

"Look," I told him, "he's probably the gorgeous hunk in his picture. He obviously likes you if he's spending hard-earned gas-pumping money to fly out here and meet you. I doubt he can afford Abercrombie & Fitch. I bet he's as nervous as you are."

Jamie blinked over. "He said he was. We both said how nervous we are."

"Okay. Then you'll have an emotional meltdown together. Your first exchange of bodily fluids."

Jamie sighed. "The weather sucks."

It was gray and drizzly, the gloom pressing in on my dark, heavy mood. Bailey could spend the weekend with Beau. Like Bailey, like Beau. Lying to your parents. Good, Bailey. An admirable 4-H quality. I cranked up the radio to see if there was some good music to distract me, keep me awake, keep me from thinking about it. In the middle of Reba's "I'm a Survivor," Jamie's head began to bobble. He was gone.

He looked so sweet, asleep. Innocent, vulnerable. I hoped for his sake Shane was everything Jamie dreamed of. Jamie had big dreams. Bigger than mine. But then Jamie had always been out of touch with reality.

Chapter Eighteen

I exited onto Pena Boulevard, heading for Denver International Airport. Jamie's eyelids flew open. "Are we here already?"

Already? Three hours on the road, in the rain, hung over? I was trashed. "Ten more miles," I said.

The clouds parted suddenly and sprays of sunshine reflected off the wet pavement. "Oh my God," Jamie gasped. "That's my sign." He pointed up through the front window. "Renata told me my cusp runneth over. She said I'd receive a sign today on my way to Shane."

His cusp? He'd had his horoscope read? Oh brother. The only sign I saw was the turnoff to the West Terminal.

As I poked along the rows of cars, searching for a parking space, I checked my watch. Ten to nine. I'd booked it on the Interstate. We still had an hour and a half to kill before the flight from Birmingham landed.

Inside the terminal, we found a mini McDonald's and bought a Coke and a large fry. We sat at a table watching all the people come and go. The farthest I'd ever been from Coalton was Hutchinson, Kansas, on a field trip in fourth grade to the salt deposits.

Jamie said, "I wish we could meet his plane. What if I miss him?"

I muttered, "You assume he's coming."

Jamie just looked at me.

"Because he is," I added quickly. "What are you guys going to do when he gets here? Where am I taking you?"

Jamie stabbed at his ice with a straw. "You mean if he doesn't have a pulmonary embolism and faint over dead at the sight of me?"

This was tiresome. He was such a girl. "Assuming the best. Say he's a god."

"Assuming the best," Jamie repeated, "you're dropping us off at the nearest Motel 6."

That's what I figured. "Seriously. Do you have a plan? Because if we're just going to drive around, you need to give me more gas money."

Jamie flipped me his version of the finger — a stiff right pinkie. "Assuming he doesn't require immediate medical attention, I thought we'd go where gays hang out in Denver."

"To a bar?" I cried.

"No." Jamie clucked his tongue. "Capitol Hill. That area. I found out online that's where the queer action is. If it was a nice day, I thought we'd have a picnic in Cheesman Park. I printed out a map from the Internet. We could stop at a grocery store and buy sandwiches or something."

Yeah, that was romantic.

"Then we'll go to the Motel 6."

I threw a fry at him.

Every flight arrived in Denver at exactly ten-thirty. No kidding. As Jamie and I wedged through the swarm of incoming passengers, I thought, We'll never find Shane in this mob — if he's here. I had my doubts. We stood off to the side of the escalator that was bringing people up from the concourse trains, comparing faces to the picture Shane had sent Jamie. There were so many people. Too many. No one remotely familiar.

The crowd began to thin. I sneaked a peek at Jamie and my heart sank. Shane had lied. I hated him.

One last time, I craned my neck down the escalator shaft. "Jamie?" a deep voice sounded behind us.

I wheeled around.

"Shane?" Jamie said. This guy about Jamie's height with a backpack slung over his shoulder raised a videocam to one eye. "Saturday, May fifth," he spoke into the camera. "We finally meet. First impression . . . ?" Shane took a step backward and panned the camera down the length of Jamie. "Wow."

I expected Jamie to strike a pose, crack a joke, giggle like a girl. But he just stood there, rigid.

"And Jamie. What is your first impression of Shane?" Shane asked. He lowered the cam and gazed into Jamie's eyes. His voice softened. "I hope he's everything you were hoping he'd be."

Beside me, Jamie melted. "And more," he breathed.

They embraced, eyes welling with tears. Oh brother. Choke me with a camera strap.

They stayed like that forever. I cleared my throat. Jamie finally detached from Shane and said, "Oh, this is Mike." He flipped a limp wrist in my direction. "She's my fairy butch."

I slugged him on the arm. He howled.

Shane stepped back and raised the camera. If he thought he was going to include me in this little biopic, he was sadly mistaken. I covered the lens with my hand and said, "I'm not all that photogenic."

Shane grinned. Not mean or anything. More amused. Okay, he was cute. Sort of boyish-looking with bleached blond hair like Jamie's. Jeans, a long-sleeved tee. Big brown eyes. Wire-rimmed glasses. His cheeks were all flushed, as if he'd run the whole way to get here.

In unison Jamie and Shane said to each other, "I can't believe you're here." They laughed. They hugged again.

A second wave of passengers surged up the escalator and jostled us. Shane took Jamie's arm and led him off to the side. Never mind that I was almost swept away in the crowd. They took off toward the parking lot, both of them jabbering away a million miles a minute. I straggled behind.

At the truck, Jamie opened the passenger door and let Shane in. He caught my eye and smiled so wide I thought his face would fissure. "Mike's our chauffeur," he said to Shane. "She'll take us anywhere we want to go."

"You think." I inserted the key into the ignition.

Shane said, "I really appreciate it, Mike. Thanks."

He had manners. Score him a point.

As I backed out of the parking space, Jamie added, "I don't drive. I'm scared to death of speed."

Shane said, "That's fine with me." He pronounced it "fawn." "A good friend of mawn from high school just died in a car accident."

"Oh my God," Jamie pressed fingers to his lips. "You didn't tell me that."

"A speeding drunk ran him off the road."

Jamie reached over and took Shane's hand. "I'm so sorry." He held it. Easy, natural. Why couldn't I do that with Xanadu?

As we headed for the city, the two of them talked about other things: music, movies, family. Shane's parents were divorced. He had two brothers and a sister, a cat named Russell. He'd come out at fourteen. His dad was still dealing.

We found Capitol Hill, finally, after wandering around downtown Denver for an hour. It freaked me, all the tall buildings and one-way streets and traffic and pedestrians. This was Saturday too. Imagine a workday.

Jamie and Shane consulted the map and directed me east toward Cheesman Park. I spotted what looked like a grocery store. "You guys want to buy your picnic here?"

"Wild Oats," Shane read the grocery name out loud. "Yes, ma'am. I do believe I'll be sowing myself some of those today."

Jamie laughed hysterically. It wasn't that funny. Shane's accent was sexy though.

As we clambered out of the truck, I asked Shane, "What time does your flight leave?"

"One-thirty," he said.

"In the morning?" We wouldn't get back to Coalton until dawn.

"Um, no." He eyed Jamie.

Jamie said real fast, "Onethirtytomorrowafternoon."

I stopped dead in the doorway. "Jamie!"

He scurried ahead of me and snagged a shopping cart. Over his shoulder, he shot me a grin.

Damn him. He might've mentioned we were staying overnight.

I heard him say to Shane, "What shall we get? A jug of wine? A loaf of bread?" They ended in unison, "Thou?" And giggled.

Couple of girls.

I sidled up beside them at the cheese case. "You owe me," I seethed at Jamie. "You're going to pay."

"Put it on my tab." He opened the glass door and selected a round of cheese. Shane must've felt my fire. "Um, I'll go pick out the bread," he said, scuttling off toward the bakery.

"Who's paying for the motel?" I asked Jamie.

"Don't worry about it," he sniped.

He sounded annoyed with me. *He* was annoyed?

"Have you ever had Camembert? Is it stinky?" He sniffed the cheese. "Look who I'm asking." He dropped the round into the basket.

"You're dead. You know that."

He turned to meet my eyes. "No, Mike. I'm alive. For the first time in my life, I am truly and fully alive." He strutted off, leaving me standing there alone. A guy in a ponytail, who'd obviously overhead, grinned like a serial killer.

I hustled after Jamie and Shane. They bought bread and cheese and deli meat and strawberries and chocolate dip and fake champagne and I don't know what all. I tossed in a bran muffin and a bottle of this weird ginseng tea. Shane paid for everything.

We found Cheesman Park not too far from the grocery. There were clots of people sitting under trees or playing Frisbee or walking their dogs. A couple of women strolled by with a baby buggy. Were they gay? I watched them continue down the sidewalk, talking and laughing together. I couldn't take my eyes off them.

Shane paused under a huge silver maple and said, "How's this?" The grass was still moist from the rain. Not too soggy.

"Perfect," Jamie said. "Don't you have a tarp in the truck?"

"Huh?"

Jamie repeated, "Isn't there a tarp in your truck?"

"Yeah."

We stared at each other.

"Well?" he said.

"Well, what?"

He let out an irritated breath. "Do you mind?"

What was I now, his service dog? I huffed and stomped back to retrieve the tarp.

We spread our picnic out under the tree. Jamie made a big production of opening all the cheese packages and breaking the bread and uncorking the champagne. He squealed when it bubbled. Shane recorded the event live for CNN. As Jamie linked his arm in Shane's to drink a toast, Shane shook his head and said, "You are so gay."

Jamie grinned. "I know. Ain't it grand?"

Shane blinked over to me, actually noticing I was there, and said, "So, Mike. Do you have a girlfriend?"

Jamie choked on champagne. Flapping a hand over his mouth as he swallowed, he answered for me, "Mike has an imaginary girlfriend."

Shane looked interested, or confused.

Jamie explained, "She's straight."

I pushed to my feet. Grabbing my tea bottle, I started away. Jamie called at my back, "Mike's holding out for a miracle."

No, I wasn't. Miracles don't happen. Like birthday wishes, they never come true. I wandered over to a group of girls — women — who were stretching a volleyball net between two poles. I leaned against a tree trunk, drinking my tea.

They split into teams. Ten, eleven of them, I counted. Were they all gay? There were more gay women here than I knew existed in the world. The ball came flying at me and I shagged it with one arm.

"Nice save." One of the girls jogged over. I handed her the ball. She said, "You want to play?"

"Sure." I set my tea on the ground.

"Oh look," someone called. "Marty found herself a baby dyke."

Marty answered, "I'm a chicklet magnet. What can I say?" She handed me the ball. "Your serve."

I stepped behind the imaginary line and gave the ball a fister. It streaked over the net. Two players dove for it and missed. The taller one said, "Could I have her, Marty? You promised to share." They all laughed.

I didn't feel offended or anything. More like proud of my skills.

Our team won the first game fifteen to six, then we mixed up players. They were fun, these girls. Women. A blast. Even though I was probably the shortest one, I had enough spring in my legs to spike the net. I was low to the ground so I could scoop serves. I think I earned their respect. I hoped so.

Marty said, "Okay, whoever wins the next game gets the baby dyke as a trophy."

They laughed. So did I. I wouldn't mind being their trophy.

"Mike, come on. We're leaving."

I glanced over my shoulder. Jamie and Shane stood by the tree, Jamie holding my tea and the tarp, Shane the leftover food. "What if

I'm not ready to go?" I wanted to say. But I didn't. This was Jamie's day. I'd have mine.

"Thanks, guys," I told everyone, tossing the ball to Marty.

"We play most Saturdays if the weather's decent," she said. "You're welcome to join us."

I wanted to. I wanted to stay forever and play with these girls.

Jamie and Shane decided they *had* to see this movie, a French flick with subtitles, so we drove around wasting gas until we found the theater. I think they expected me to wait for them in the parking lot. Get real. I made Jamie pay for my ticket. I made him buy me popcorn.

About five minutes into the film, I wished I'd stayed in the truck. Jamie and Shane began making out. Not subtle either. They were really into it. I moved to a seat up front by myself. Imaginary girlfriend. Right. She was real, Jamie. Warm and alive. Imagine her here with me now, kissing me. It wouldn't take a miracle. She needed a break from Bailey. She said so. Here I was, whenever she was ready.

How about when *I* was ready? I was ready now.

After the movie we drove around until we found a motel. Not a Motel 6, but close. The Swiss Chalet. Cheap, but quaint. Shane said, "I'll get us a room."

I reached across Jamie to catch Shane's sleeve. "Two rooms. I'm not going to spend the night with you guys."

They looked at me like, That wasn't exactly in our plan either. Did they expect me to sleep in the truck? Apparently. "Two rooms," I repeated.

Shane nodded. He, at least, had a credit card.

I'd never spent the night in a motel room. It was weird knowing that a stranger had slept in my bed. More than one stranger, probably. The sink dripped. I couldn't stand listening to that all night. I retrieved Dad's toolbox from the truck and got busy. The faucets were washerless, so I dug out Dad's groove-joint pliers and replaced the cartridges.

There wasn't much to do. What do you do in a motel room, alone?

Watch TV? There was cable, and pay-per-view porn, mostly, which Jamie and Shane were no doubt taking advantage of. I couldn't hear anything through the wall. I should call home, I thought. Darryl might be worried.

Yeah, right. He'd be worried about the truck. I picked up the phone and got a dial tone. Then realized it was long-distance and plunked it back in the receiver.

Forget it, I decided. If Darryl or Ma even noticed I was gone, they could send Reese out looking for me. Give the law enforcement something to do besides harass the local youth.

I stripped and took a shower. Weird shower head. No water pressure. I hadn't even brought a toothbrush.

As I lay in bed, staring at the flocked wallpaper, I wondered what Jamie and Shane were doing. Were they kissing? Undressing each other? Were they lying together naked in bed? Doing it? I closed my eyes and thought about her. Xanadu. Doing it. With me. Us. Together.

The world floated away and I drifted.

* * *

They had a teary farewell. Shane asked me to capture it on film, if I didn't mind. I got creative. Later on he'd enjoy the close-up footage of crotch. He almost missed his plane, lingering so long to say goodbye to Jamie. Holding him, touching his face. He took back his cam and kissed me on the cheek before sprinting off.

Jamie was quiet on the way home. He kicked off his shoes and huddled on the seat, hugging his knees and gazing out the side window. I glanced over once to see a tear streak down his cheek.

"What's the matter?" I turned down the volume on *America's Country Countdown*. "Aren't you glad he came?"

Jamie didn't answer for a long minute. "I love him," he finally said. "I don't know when I'll ever get to see him again. Maybe never."

"Don't say that."

Jamie scraped a tear off his face with a knuckle and added, "It's hard. This is so fucking hard."

The ache spread through me. The distance between them, the uncertainty of ever being together. I understood. Same with me and Xanadu. But we were going to be together. I felt it in my soul. It was only hard now.

I wanted to joke around with Jamie, tease him about last night. But he seemed detached, sad. Not the right time.

I dropped in behind a Sysco Food truck and rode his tail all the way to Kansas. When we crossed the state line, I said aloud what I'd been thinking — dwelling on — for the last hundred miles. "I'm telling her."

Jamie blinked awake. He rubbed his eyes. "What? Who?"

"Xanadu," I said. "I'm telling her."

"Telling her what?" Jamie said in a yawn.

I kept my eyes on the road. "How I feel about her."

He swiveled his head. When he didn't say anything, I turned to meet his eyes. "You're going to tell Xanadu how you feel about her."

I nodded.

"Are you crazy!" he cried.

It made me flinch.

"You can't do that."

I resumed concentrating on the road. "Why not? I think she should know."

"And when she does, what? What do you think's going to happen? She's going to say, 'Oh Mike. I never knew.'" He covered his heart with both hands. "'Why, I love you too. I guess I'll turn gay now and dump Bailey for you.' Is that what you expect?"

I scoffed. "Don't be stupid."

"I'm stupid?" His voice rose. "Mike —" He stopped. We passed a sign for Goodland, thirty miles. Jamie said quietly, "Don't do it."

"I'm going to," I said.

I couldn't look at him. Couldn't think about anything else. I'd made up my mind. Miracles don't happen. You make them happen. They're not wishes or dreams or candles on a cake. They're not impossible. Reality is real. It's totally and completely under my control. It was time for action, control. Time for me to take charge of my life.

That night, after Darryl reamed me out royally for not calling — like he actually cared I was gone — I lay in bed on my familiar lumpy mattress, soaking in my poster of naked Maserati girl and reconfirming my commitment. People should know how you feel about them. Before it's too late, you should tell them. Before they're gone and you can't remember the last time he said, "I love you." Or you said it back. You can't remember if he kissed you good night or told you to sleep well, sleep tight, baby. If you took it for granted that he was always there. Then he wasn't.

We were lucky, me and Xanadu. We had time. The time was now. We didn't have the distance to keep us apart, like Jamie and Shane. There was nothing separating us. Nothing but the truth.

I loved her.

She needed to know.

And what would happen when she did? Maybe, just what Jamie'd said. She'd realize she was making the biggest mistake of her life with Bailey McCall. She'd come to her senses. She'd come to me.

Chapter Nineteen

*M*onday morning Xanadu attacked me in the hall. "Why didn't you call me? I left you about a hundred messages on your machine and you never called back."

I downloaded books from my locker into my arms for morning classes and shut the door. "We didn't get home until late yesterday." By then I was wiped, needed to think, plan. "Shane stayed over Saturday night in Denver with Jamie."

"Really?" Xanadu's eyes gleamed. "Did they . . . do it?"

"I assume so. I didn't ask."

"You didn't ask?"

"It's kind of personal. I didn't exactly want the details."

She slapped my arm. "Why not?" She laughed at my expression of horror, which made me laugh. This was going to be easy. As we ambled down the hall toward class, she added, "I guess I don't really want to know what two guys do together either." She wrinkled her nose. "Does Jamie really like him?"

"Well, yeah. He loves him." I didn't say, Why else would he have sex with him?

Xanadu bit her bottom lip and closed her eyes. "That is so cool. God, I'm happy for him."

"Listen." We'd reached the room and I stalled outside the door. "I wanted to tell you —" My throat closed up.

She gazed into my eyes and tilted her head, the way she does. So sexy. "Tell me what?"

I coughed; cleared my windpipe. "Tell you —"

"Yo, Xana." Bailey appeared out of the manure heap and swept her into his arms. He kissed her long and hard. When they separated, he said, "I thought we were meeting out front this morning."

"Oh shit." She bit her index finger. "I forgot."

"I guess I can forgive you. You probably had other things on your mind." He circled her with his hairy arms and rocked her side to side.

Xanadu reached up and tugged his Stetson down over his eyes. "I know what's on *your* mind."

The bell rang, saving me from having to barf on Bailey's boots. As I veered off toward my dunce seat in back, Xanadu snagged my arm and whispered, "We'll talk later, okay?"

I stared at her all period. I couldn't help myself. Her hair was loose today, flowing down her back. She wore low-cut dirty jeans, same as everyone was wearing these days, except on her they looked pristine. Spectacular. A short shirt. No belly-button ring.

I had to tell her.

I tried to catch her after class, but she left. With him. Then later between periods, she was with him again. At her locker, at lunch, after school driving away in his truck.

I was committed. As soon as she knew, she'd see me differently. As more than a friend. Better than Bailey. I'd love her so much more than he ever could.

I'd call her tonight.

No. This wasn't something you did on the phone, profess your undying love to the girl you planned to spend the rest of your life with. I'd tell her before school tomorrow. When we were alone. Away from him.

She didn't show at my locker the next day. I didn't catch her alone once. He was always around, lurking, like a wolf. The scent of him sickened me, primed me for the kill.

After the game tomorrow night, I decided. It was a home game so she'd be there. Yeah, and so would the rest of the town.

Shit.

Friday. When we went out drinking, I'd tell her then. Jamie'd pass out eventually and we'd be alone. Or I'd drop him off first.

Four days. It'd give me time to think about what I was going to say, besides, "I love you."

"I love you, Xanadu. I love you more than life itself."

<hr>

"So, Mike. How much money have you collected?" Coach Kinneson came up behind me as I strapped on my chest protector.

I feigned deafness. What did she think I did, empty the can at the Merc and count it? Get real. My face got hot every time someone folded money to wedge in that stupid can. It was humiliating.

"I submitted your application for the camp this week," she said.

I whipped my head around. "Why'd you do that?"

She skimmed down the roster on her clipboard. "I wanted to make sure you applied in time; that your name got on the A-list."

"Maybe I don't want my name on the A-list. Maybe I don't want my name on any list. I'm not going."

She looked stunned. "I'm sure you'll have enough money by then."

My jaw clenched. I pulled my mask down and charged out onto the field. Why was I so angry about this? It was the money, yeah. The charity. My pride. But there was more. The whole freaking Catch-Her-Star. It's my star, okay?

The rematch with Deighton was a blowout. We avenged our earlier loss. Everyone was in top form, me included. It felt good to get back out there. Play a role. Be a star.

I was buzzed after the game. When I sprang from the lean-to, I saw Darryl loitering at the end of the bleachers, smoking. What was he doing here? He gave me a thumbs-up and I flipped him the bird.

Jamie and Xanadu were waiting for me. "Awesome," Xanadu said. She threw her arms around me. Jamie fluttered a pom-pom in my face. I smooshed it into his mouth.

A horn honked in the parking lot and Xanadu wheeled around. Who else? Wolfhound. "Gotta fly," she said. "We're on for Friday, right?"

"Definitely." I hoped she heard the "we better be" in my voice. I was taking control.

She converged on Bailey and Beau and a group of guys at his truck. I slung my duffel over my shoulder, heading in the opposite direction. I'd planned to hook up with the team at the Dairy D, but now I wasn't in the mood.

Jamie loped up beside me. "Listen, I can't go celebrating with you and Xanadu this Friday." He spit out a strip of Mylar pom-pom. "Shane wants me to call him Friday night after he gets off. To talk, he said. What do you think that means?"

I shrugged. "Form words? Speak them out loud?"

He cast me a withering look. "What if he wants to break up?"

"I didn't know you were engaged." Jamie wasn't coming Friday. Xanadu and I would be alone the whole night. A spike of fear shot up my spine. Why did that scare me, and excite me at the same time?

"You know I really could use some support here." Jamie stopped and flung his pom-poms on the ground. "I'm a total emotional wreck and all you can do is crack jokes."

I slowed. He sounded more upset than mad. "I don't know what it means, Jamie," I admitted. I hadn't had any experience in this arena.

"What was Shane's tone of voice? Was he serious, like, 'We need to talk'? Or light, like, 'I miss the sound of your voice. Let's talk'?"

Jamie exhaled a long breath and bent to retrieve his pom-poms. "I don't know," he said on the way up. "It's hard to tell when the words come across your fucking monitor." He torched me with a glare.

Oh yeah. The joy of cybersex. "Guess you'll just have to wait and see."

"Wait and see if he breaks my heart. What do I have, a sign on my back that flashes, HI, I'M JAMIE. SQUEEZE MY BALLS. MAKE ME SCREAM?"

Kimberleigh called, "Jamie, come on. We need you for comic relief."

Jamie's face lost all expression. "God, to be straight for one day. To know how it's all supposed to turn out."

We didn't go to the caboose. I took Xanadu to the water tower instead. As the extension ladder clanged against the metal frame, she gazed upward, shielding her eyes. "Are you insane? I'm not going up there."

"Don't worry," I told her. "I'll catch you if you fall."

"Ha, ha," she deadpanned.

"Here, give me your pack. I can carry both of them. Trust me. I do this all the time."

She met my eyes and held. "Why?"

I didn't have an answer for that one.

Xanadu touched my arm. "Okay, I think I know," she said. I almost died. If she did know, I wish she'd tell me so I'd have the words to explain it.

She handed me her pack and stepped up onto the first rung of the ladder. I followed close behind. At the top she waited for me by the gate, looking freaked.

"It's okay," I reassured her. "It's safe." With me, you're always safe, Xanadu, I wanted to add.

She grabbed the bottom of my shirt and shuffled after me to my usual spot on the walkaround. I set down the packs and sat, motioning her beside me. She hesitated, looked around. Slowly, she crept to the railing and peered over the side. "Is this where he . . . ?"

"No. Other side." Where the sun sets. Where I never go.

"It's high up here." Her eyes swept the tower, the fields, the highway out of town. She stepped back. She sat and scooted against the water tank. Next to me, our arms touching. "Kind of creepy, Mike."

"Not to me. I think it's peaceful. The stars, the wheat, the farms. When I come up here I feel . . . I don't know. Free. Like a cloud. Like sky. No edges, no limits. No walls to close me in."

She tilted her head slightly and smiled.

All the blood rushed to my face. It was hard revealing so much of myself to her. But I needed to. I wanted her to know me. To know I trusted her.

I felt her shiver.

"Are you cold?" I reached over and unzipped my pack.

"A little."

Damn. I'd forgotten my sweatshirt. I was so psyched about seeing her, being with her, that my brain had disengaged. It'd been a balmy day, but the night air was crisp. It was always chilly up here at night. I knew that. Damn. Her arms prickled with goose bumps.

My muscle tee would be enough for me. I took off Dad's flannel shirt and held it open to her.

"No, I'm fine —"

"Wear it. It's all warmed up for you."

She blinked at me, then slid her arms into the sleeves. The shirt was way too big. On me it hung to my knees; on her it looked sexy as hell.

The sky was clear and calm, the air smelled earthy and fresh. Out in the fields, blue and red strobes from all the circular sprinklers created a moving quilt of twinkling stars. "It really is beautiful," Xanadu breathed.

"Yeah." I stared at the side of her face. "It is."

She turned to me and held my eyes. My heart hammered a hole in my chest. Do it now, Mike. Do it. "I brought you up here to tell you something." My voice sounded shaky, weak. I hated that. Be strong. Be confident.

She waited.

Blood roared in my ears. My hands felt clammy and I wiped them on my new Levi's. "I, uh . . ." Couldn't speak.

"What, Mike?" Her fingers brushed my quad.

A bolt of lightning shot through me.

"You can tell me." Her voice was soft, sensuous. "You can tell me anything at all."

"I love you." Did I say it? Did I speak the words aloud? Or did they lodge in my throat, get mangled, trickle off into the night? I didn't want her to think I was insincere, or unsure. With more conviction, more finality, I said it again: "I love you. I'm in love with you."

There was a moment when the world stopped spinning underneath me. When my heart was sure to rotor right out of my chest.

One word: "Oh."

Oh? That was it? She removed her hand from my leg. My eyes followed her hand, up her arm, to her face, her eyes. They dropped. A tiny smile curled the tips of her lips. "I think I knew that. I mean, I've known it. Mike —" Her voice changed.

"Don't say anything." I stood up fast. "Think about it." I suddenly felt like running, jumping. Not off the tower. Off the ends of the earth. Into a tornado, a centrifuge, a cyclone swooping me away from here.

"I have thought about it," she said quietly.

My ricocheting brain crash-landed on the tower. "You have?"

She nodded. "Yes. I love you too."

My heart sang.

"As a friend."

No. She wasn't supposed to say that. We were beyond that. Of all the things she could've said: I'm not ready yet. Let's see where this takes us. I'd like a little time to get used to the idea. I never knew. Now that I do know, I love you too. I love you, Mike.

"What did you bring to drink?" My voice disembodied.

"Mike —"

I bent down to open her pack. Inside was a full bottle of Wild Turkey. I yanked it out and unscrewed the lid.

"You understand, don't you?" she said. "I mean, I'd be honored to be your girlfriend, if . . ." She paused. "Any girl would be lucky to have you. I'm just not . . . that girl."

I guzzled. Lucky. Lucky me. The dark amber liquid burned all the way down.

"I hope this doesn't change things between us," Xanadu said, watching me.

I coughed and took another swig. I wiped the dribble off my mouth. "Why should it? Nothing's changed."

She held out her hand for the bottle. Reluctantly, I relinquished it. She patted the spot next to her. I drew a deep breath and sank to sit. Too close. I inched away. I needed the consuming love I felt for her to dull, diminish, die away. "You're the best friend I've ever had, Mike," she said. "I need you in my life." She reached over and took my hand, raised it to her lips, and kissed it.

I wrestled the bottle from her and finished it off. A new world record for speed drinking. Oh yeah.

I don't remember getting off the tower. I don't remember getting home. At some point I must've blacked out because I finally felt at peace.

"I love you too," she'd said. "I need you in my life." The words churned in my brain. My damaged brain. They leaked and pooled. They cesspooled. Swirling, picking up speed, intensity. It wasn't my imagination, and I wasn't drunk when she'd said it: "I love you too." She'd touched me, kissed my hand. She wanted me. I know she did.

An excruciating pain in my shoulder made me cry out and I jerked upright. Darryl was screaming in my ear, yanking my arm and yelling, "Goddammit, get up. Are you deaf?"

I clicked into semi-consciousness. My mind was thick, slow. My gut had ruptured.

"Ma's bleeding to death," Darryl said. "Get the fuck out of bed and help me."

Chapter Twenty

"We have to get her to a doctor." Darryl clenched my pits and hoisted me to my feet. I felt feverish, disoriented. My ears pricked. A sound: Ma in her room, gagging.

Darryl said, "Jesus Christ. You smell like a brewery. Goddammit!" He raised a hand to hit me, but smacked my bedroom door instead and stormed out.

I stumbled after him down the hall.

She was lying on her side, her head hanging off the mattress. She wheezed and choked. There was a pool of blood on the floor, more dribbling down her chin.

"Ma?" I knelt beside her and slid an arm around her back. "What's wrong?"

She gurgled and coughed up another spray of blood, splashing my bare legs. "You're going to be okay," I heard myself say. She was dying. Where was Darryl? "Ma?"

She reached around and flung my arm off her. My brain screamed, Fine! Die! See if I care.

She whimpered like I'd spoken the words aloud. "I didn't mean it," I said, in case I had.

"Fuck." Darryl rushed in. "Doc's gone to Nebraska fishing all weekend. We'll have to get Ma to the hospital in Garden City."

I stood on wobbly knees. No. Please, no. Not the hospital. Darryl added, "I don't know if we can get her in the truck." His wild eyes searched mine. "Maybe we could clear out enough room in back to lay down some blankets."

"I'll get my quilt." I weaved down the hall. Not the hospital. Not again.

Somehow, Darryl got Ma to her feet and out the front door. She barely fit through the frame. She'd never squeeze into the back of the truck. Even if we could push her through the double doors, there was too much equipment back there — the snake and air compressor and water pump. Darryl helped Ma down onto the front stoop and said, "We'll be ready for you in a minute, Ma. Stay here."

Where's she going to go? I almost asked. You think she'll run away? I wished she would. I wished I could. Where would I go?

She was still coughing and spraying blood all over the place. I glanced back briefly to see her fleshy arm shield her eyes from the light. From the world. She shriveled into herself, if that was possible. I couldn't remember the last time she'd been out of the house.

Darryl started throwing stuff out the back of the truck. The air compressor came flying by my head and I yelled, "Don't bust that."

"Just help me!" he screeched. He lifted a toilet tank under his arm and hauled it out. Bottles of wine and whiskey rolled onto the driveway.

Darryl's fiery eyes incinerated me on the spot.

"Look, I'm sorry —"

"Darryl!" Ma cried.

We both jumped.

"Where are you?"

"Get me a couple of cinder blocks from the back," Darryl ordered. He leaped out of the truck and rushed back to Ma. I staggered up the drive, squelching the urge to hurl. The only free blocks I could find were saturated with motor oil and sticky with cobwebs. I hefted a block up in each hand and hobbled back to the truck.

"Make a step for her," Darryl said. He supported Ma by one of her flabby arms.

Between us, we got her smooshed inside, don't ask me how. Darryl spread out my quilt on the floor. She groaned and rolled over onto it. She was bleeding and sweating like a pig and the stench and stain of her would be on my quilt forever. Grandma Szabo's quilt. It was the only thing I had left of her.

"You ride with her," Darryl said.

"Okay."

"No." Ma reached over and grasped Darryl's sleeve. "You."

Her beady eyes met mine and went black. Darryl snapped at me, "Can you do this? Can you do this one fucking thing for me?"

I snatched the keys out of his hand. "Shut up. Don't ever talk to me again."

<hr>

U.S. 83 was deserted. Why? What day was this? I couldn't have slept all day Saturday, could I? I would have felt better than this. It had to still be Saturday. No cops in sight. I floored it. I knew where the hospital in Garden City was by heart. I turned up the radio, but I could hear over it Darryl talking to Ma in back. She was weeping now. Through the rearview mirror, I saw him prop her up against him, on his chest. He smoothed her greasy hair down, held her as she gurgled up blood all over my quilt.

What I'd said to her echoed in my head. It was the day of Dad's funeral. I'd lit into her. She was in bed as usual, weeping. "Get up," I'd snarled from the doorway. "Get up and get dressed. It's time to go."

When she didn't reply, didn't respond, I'd charged in and yelled right in her face, "Get up!" I'd punched the pillow beside her head. She'd flinched then. "Get your fat ass out of bed for Dad's service. He was your husband, dammit. The father of your children. All three of them, living and dead."

Ma'd glared at me. This spittle, like venom, dribbled out the side of her mouth.

Pay your respects. Is it so much to ask?

She'd rolled over and curled into a lump. She hadn't spoken to me since. Not one word. Not to say, "hello," or "goodbye," or "brush your teeth," or "go to school." I was dead to her. More dead than Camilia.

So what? I didn't care. She could die too.

I didn't mean that. She was my mother.

I squealed the truck into the emergency entrance and slammed on the brakes. Darryl said over the seat back, "Go tell them we need help."

I hurried up the wheelchair ramp. Please, God, I prayed. Don't make me remember. There was a black lady at the receptionist's desk keying into her computer. The harsh lights, the smell. "My mom's outside in the truck," I told the lady, my chest seizing. "She's real sick. She's —"

"Rudy," the lady barked at a guy in scrubs who was passing behind me. "Can you help this little gal out?" The phone rang. The receptionist didn't take her eyes off me as she spoke into her wired mouthpiece, "Hello. St. Joseph's Emergency."

Rudy grabbed a wheelchair from an area near the door. "She won't fit in that," I told him.

His eyebrows arched.

"She's . . . big."

He said, "How 'bout a gurney?"

I shook my head. "You'll never get her on it. If we can get her up to her feet, she might be able to walk in."

Outside, Rudy peered into the back of the truck. His eyes bulged. Darryl got out and he and Rudy discussed it. They decided to use the quilt to slide Ma as far as she'd come, then leverage her up with brute force.

On the first pull my quilt ripped. The sound made my eyes well. Sorry, Grandma. They got Ma to the end; squeezed her legs out. I reached up to help her down, but Darryl muscled me out of the way. Fine. You do it. He propped Ma up. She had blood all over her face and down the front of her shift, on her socks, her arms. I just stood there, helpless. Wanting to hold her, help her. Mean something to her.

"Park the truck," Darryl commanded. "Then come back."

I opened my mouth to snap a retort, but swallowed it. Darryl looked strung out. Rudy, meanwhile, had managed to wedge Ma through the Emergency Room's sliding glass doors. She didn't seem to be coughing as much, or spitting up blood. Good. I felt relieved. For Darryl's sake, anyway. He still loved her. She loved him. They could have each other.

The parking lot was practically empty, just like the last time I was here. Forget about that. Block it out. When I got back inside, the receptionist informed me Ma was in Examining Room 2, right down the hall. She added, "You can't miss her."

Her face seemed to flood with embarrassment. "I didn't mean —"

"It's okay," I said, smiling. I didn't want her to feel bad. Enough people felt bad. I didn't need one more person feeling sorry for me.

It was claustrophobic in the examining room, too crowded for all of us to stay. I told Darryl I'd wait in the lounge.

The sounds were what finally got to me. The screeking carts and the phone ringing and the constant din of voices, the whoosh of doors opening and closing, someone sneezing. I took the same seat I'd sat in when Dad was wheeled in off the ambulance. It made me shudder, the clammy feel of vinyl against my bare legs. The vise grip in my stomach clamped down. Waiting, wondering. Where did they take him? Why?

Why, Dad?

I couldn't just sit — again. I wandered over and stood by the window, gazing out onto the parking lot. Last time it was dark. Quiet. 3:00 AM. 3:06 AM. Time of death. Dead on arrival. I don't know why they even bothered with the ambulance. "Can I get you something to drink?"

I jumped out of my skin.

The receptionist lowered herself to the windowsill, smiling wide. She had a nice smile. "Juice? A cup of coffee? I'm on my break. Thought I'd head down to the cafeteria for a snack. You want to come?"

"No. Thanks. I'm all right."

"A sweet roll? Your mom may be a while."

"I'm fine."

She pushed to her feet, rubbed my arm, and left. She was kind. Probably Ma's age. Probably a mother. A better one than I got.

The sounds all quit at once. It was dead as a morgue. My head hurt. I felt claustrophobic. Sick. Wanted to barf. I decided to wait outside in the truck; maybe take a nap. Not on my quilt. I'd have to burn my quilt now.

Next thing I knew Darryl was pounding on the driver's side window, yelling at me to get up. "The doctor wants to talk to us together," he said.

Bleary-eyed, I followed him inside. We passed the examining rooms, a maze of supply closets, unplugged machinery, cramped offices. The doctor was sitting at his desk filling out papers. He stood and introduced himself. Dr. Good-somebody. Good-fellow? Good-hollow? He leaned across his desk and shook my hand.

"Your mother's going to be fine," he said. He motioned us to sit. Me and Darryl both chose to stand. "It looks a whole lot worse than it is. These things always do. She probably ruptured a blood vessel and started hemorrhaging. We packed her nose and gave her something to calm her down. It can be unsettling, seeing all that blood and having it run down the back of your throat."

I was processing his words.

Darryl said it for me, "She had a bloody nose?"

"A ruptured vessel." The doctor nodded. "But yes, basically."

"A bloody nose?" Darryl repeated. "Shit," he hissed.

"You were right to bring her in," the doctor said. "She could easily have gone into shock."

"Can we take her home now?" Darryl's voice hardened.

"I'll get someone on staff to help. She should be fine. You can re-move the packing in a few hours." Dr. Goody-Good made a call, wrote something in Ma's chart, and replaced his fountain pen in his breast pocket. Folding his hands over the desk, he said, "Your mother is morbidly obese."

Darryl and I both made the same choking sound in our throats. Like, tell us something we don't know.

"Her blood pressure's slightly elevated, which could be a result of her panic attack. It isn't dangerously high, but in her current condi-tion, she's at increased risk for any number of medical problems: heart disease, stroke, diabetes, osteo —"

"Can we go now?" Darryl cut in. "Mike has to be at work."

I do? I looked at Darryl. Oh yeah. I do.

"Your mother has a serious condition. Life-threatening. Have you considered gastric-bypass surgery? It's an operation where —"

"I know what it is," Darryl interrupted again. "You staple the stom-ach shut so she can't eat."

"Basically. And reroute the intestine," the doctor added. "It's prov-ing to be an effective procedure for the morbidly obese."

"I know," Darryl said.

How'd he know? I didn't know.

"Most major hospitals have an obesity-surgery center," the doctor went on. "Kansas City —"

"Kansas City." Darryl's head bobbed. "Too far away."

"There's one in Denver too."

"Look, we're in Coalton, okay? We don't have any insurance. It's an expensive operation, but even if we could afford it, Ma doesn't want it. I've already talked to her. I've begged her, pleaded with her to do it. I've been trying to get her to do something, anything, but she won't. She cries if I even bring up the subject."

I just stared at Darryl. When had he done that?

"I can't force her to want to live, okay?" he said. Tears rimmed his eyes. He added, "She won't listen to me. Neither of them will listen to me. Fuck." He sniffed hard. "If we could just get someone to help us out to the truck, I'd appreciate it." Darryl turned and left.

Abandoning me there, alone with Dr. Do-Gooder.

He smiled. "Maybe you could talk to her. You know, woman to woman?"

I burst into laughter. It wasn't even funny.

On the way home I cranked up the radio in the truck to run interference on all our thoughts. After Darryl put Ma to bed, I lingered in the hall outside the door, listening to him try to soothe her. "You get some rest, Ma," he said. "Jerry Springer'll be coming on satellite in about an hour, so I'll make sure you're up. We can take that gauze out of your nose then. I'll wash up in here later; don't worry about that." He stepped into the hall and eased her door shut.

I was about to make a joke like, "Next time she has a bloody nose we'll just shove a Hoagie up it," when Darryl attacked me. He slammed me against the wall and hissed in my face, "You're still drinking, you little shit. I thought I told you to stop."

I pushed him off me. "You told me. So what?"

He lunged at me, knuckling a fist, missing my face, but not the wall. The plaster cracked and the whole house shook. Darryl and I both gaped at the hole he'd made.

"Nice," I said, my head nodding. "Who's going to fix that? Same person who's been promising to get to the roof?"

I expected Darryl to come after me. Beat on me. Bloody me. Maybe I wanted him to. Maybe I wanted him to bash my head against the floor and knock some sense into me. Physical pain. I could take that. I understood it.

This hurt inside I didn't know how to relieve.

Instead, Darryl went limp. His hands spread out and pressed against the wall behind me, over the hole. He hung his head and just started bawling.

Chapter Twenty-One

I headed for the VFW. Sweat it out, I figured. Burn it off. Get all the ugliness out of me.

Jamie showed up sometime around my third circuit to bribe Renata into letting him use the tanning bed for free. I heard him in there, sucking up to her, telling her how accurate her horoscope reading had been. As I headed for the lockers, Jamie called, "Hey, Mike. Wait up." He whispered urgently to Renata, loud enough for me to hear, "Hide that. Don't let her see it." Renata moved an object off the coffee counter to the shelf below.

What? Who cared? I wasn't in the mood.

Jamie caught up with me at the door. "We need to talk."

"I have to take a shower."

"Good idea. You reek." Jamie plugged his nose and followed me into the changing room.

I shoved him out and slammed the door. He was still chatting up Renata when I emerged a few minutes later. Spotting me, like he'd been lying in wait, he said, "Go ahead and warm up the bed, Renata. I've got to consult with my fag hag."

I stormed outside.

He raced to catch up.

I whirled. "I really hate that, you know. You can flaunt it if you want, if you think that queer act is so fucking cute, but leave me out of it."

"Whoa." Jamie reeled back a step. "Who peed in your Wheaties?"

I exhaled a long breath. My muscles hurt. I hurt. I shouldn't have done the last set of lat pulls. I should've stayed in bed and zoned.

My knees gave out and I sank to the park bench in front of the VFW. Jamie eased down beside me. "What happened?" he asked. "You look like shit."

I let out the breath I'd been holding ever since we left the hospital. "I had a crappy morning, okay?" I told Jamie about it. He listened, clucking his tongue in all the appropriate places. The knot in my stomach loosened. Not that I needed sympathy, his or anyone else's.

"So Sveltlana's adding a bloody snot rag to her cosmetics carousel," Jamie said.

I don't know why that made me laugh. I smacked Jamie in the chest. My eyes filled with tears, I laughed so hard. Then I wasn't laughing.

Stop it. I grit my teeth; swiped my eyes. Get past it. Control it.

Jamie said, "I wondered where you were. Xana said she called your house for, like, three hours straight and no one was there."

"You talked to her?" I blinked real fast and fixed on Jamie. "What'd she say?"

He held up his hands. "Don't get all jealous. She wasn't after my bod."

What would I say to her? Forget about last night, what I revealed? Nothing's changed? But it had changed; everything changed. She knew my true feelings now. She'd always know. We'd have it between us.

Across the street, Miss Millie tripped on the curb. Her Pekingese,

Pooky, took a dump. That dog had to be thirty years old. It looked as drunk as her, wobbling around on spindly legs. Jamie called out, "Good morning, Miss Millie." He said under his breath to me, "Break out the beer nuts. It's Millie Time."

"What'd she want?" I asked.

"Who?" Jamie said. "Oh . . . her." He shrugged a shoulder. "I'm not sure. She hemmed and hawed around for a while. Finally she said it was personal and that she could only tell you."

Huh. Maybe she'd been thinking about it, considering the possibility. The probability that I'd be better for her than Bailey.

Jamie stood and stretched his arms over his head, yawning audibly. "She did say Bailey was taking her shopping in Goodland today, so you wouldn't be able to call her back until later."

My stomach hurt again. I doubled over to keep my guts from spilling out all over Main Street. Bailey shopping? I couldn't see it. Shopping for what? A new 4-H pin?

Jamie pulled his shades out of the side pocket of his baggy pants and slipped them on.

"I told her," I said, clenching my middle.

It took him a minute. "You're kidding. What'd she say?"

I hesitated. Why did I start this? "She said she already knew."

Jamie was quiet. Stunned? Shocked?

I twisted my head up to find out.

"You *are* obvious," he said. "She'd have to be blind not to notice."

I annihilated him with eye daggers.

Jamie sat back down, extending his legs out stiff in front of him. "What else?"

I slid to the edge, copying his pose. I beckoned the sun to bake me, soak me, bathe me in warmth. I closed my eyes. "She said she loves me too."

Jamie did a full body twist, almost falling off the bench. "She actually told you that?"

As much as I wanted to leave it, let him believe what he would, I couldn't. "She said she loves me as a friend."

Jamie's whole body sagged. "Ow."

I pushed to my feet.

"Hey, want to get blitzed tonight?" He shot up beside me. "Geneviève has a bottle of schnapps in the cupboard she sips on whenever she talks to Grandma about me."

"No." I started for home.

Jamie grabbed my arm. "Forget it, Mike," he said. "She isn't worth it. She's a slut."

I spun on him. "Don't say that. Don't you *ever* say that about her. Do you hear?" I grasped his wrist and wrenched it down off me.

A long moment passed. "You're hurting me," Jamie said, not taking his eyes from mine.

My fiery gaze traveled down to his wrist, to my hand clenching it in a vise grip. I let go roughly.

"I was kidding." He held his wrist against his chest. "God."

It didn't sound like a joke. Still. What was I doing hurting the only friend I'd ever had? "Look, I'm sorry," I told him. "I'm not myself." I stepped off the curb to cross the street.

I heard him mutter, "Yeah. Whoever that is anymore."

⎯⎯⎯⎯⎯⎯◆⎯⎯⎯⎯⎯⎯

I dreamed about her. I'd been dreaming about her almost every night since she'd arrived. It was a welcome relief from the nightmare — falling, falling, *thud*. In one dream she'd open a door and step into my room. My bedroom, except it wasn't this pit where I lived. It was a harem. She was a harem girl, dressed in silk, satin, velvet, and gauze. Her hair was braided with lace and gemstones and pearls. She sank into my Persian carpet in her bare feet as she floated toward me.

I lay on a round bed draped in pure linen with my samurai sword at my side. She drew back the curtain and knelt on the bed. She crawled toward me. She pulled me to a sitting position, then, one article of clothing at a time, undressed me. My jacket, my shirt, my undershirt. I did the same for her. She was beautiful naked, her skin pale and silky and soft. I was beautiful too, for once. We embraced each other. We fit together perfectly.

It was a stupid dream. Incongruous, anachronous. How did a samurai sword fit with a harem girl? There was no connection. No logic.

But I craved the dream. I longed for it to replay every night. I never wanted to wake up, never wanted that dream to end.

I was stacking fertilizer bags on a palette when Xanadu appeared out of the mist. First thing I saw were her painted toenails, plain leather sandals, one foot holding down the bag I was trying to lift.

My head rose and she smiled into my eyes.

That smile splintered my heart into a million pieces. She was so damn sexy. I swiped a stream of sweat off my forehead and said the only thing I could manage. "Hey."

"Look." She held out her right hand, fingers spread. "Bailey bought me a ring."

My eyes dropped to her outstretched hand. The ring was gold with an opal in the center and two tiny diamonds.

"It doesn't mean we're going together or anything." Xanadu examined the ring in the fading dusk. "He just wanted to buy me something special. Oh God, Mike. I'm so happy." She pressed the ring to her heart.

He bought her a ring.

She said quietly, "I never thought anyone would love me. I never thought anyone could, not after —" She stopped. Her chest heaved.

He bought her a ring.

"Mike, you got that fertilizer loaded?" Everett hollered. "The truck's here with the mare motels and I need that space in back." His silhouette framed the rear doorway.

"Almost done," I called to him.

Xanadu grimaced. "I better let you get to work." She reached down and took my hand. Raising it to her face, she rested her cheek in my palm. Her face was cool, silk, satin. Why? Why did she do this? Didn't she know every time she touched me she set me on fire? Didn't she get it?

"I haven't told him," she said. "I know I should, but I'm afraid. I don't know what he'll do when he learns about my past. Do you think I should tell him?"

I don't care. I backed away from her a step. "Don't ask me." It came out harsh. I didn't want to talk about him. Not ever.

"You think I should, don't you?" She glanced away, across the yard, toward the flatbed. Her eyes narrowed, like she was mad at me.

"You don't have to," I said. "You don't have to do anything you don't want to, Xanadu." Except . . . love me, I thought.

Her eyes fixed on me, hard. "No, I should be honest with him. You'd tell him, wouldn't you? You're always up front with people. I wish I could be like you, Mike. Just put the truth out there for everyone to see. Deal with it."

"Mike!" Everett yelled.

"Okay!" God. Get a life.

I hefted up a bag of fertilizer.

"Aunt Faye's getting suspicious about the booze, I think." Xanadu trailed me to the rows of pallets against the chain-link fence. "Friday should be our last time. I don't want her banning me from the root cellar or locking the door because . . . well . . . Bailey and I have been using the cellar." She bit her lip.

I flung the bag on the pallet and it burst apart. Shit. Just slice through my heart with a samurai sword, why don't you?

"If Aunt Faye and Uncle Lee sent me home, I'd die. My whole life is here now. With you and Bailey. I don't ever want to go back." She paused and squinted into the setting sun. The giant red orb, blood red, oozing. "We'll have a big blowout on Friday, okay? The three of us. Not Bailey." She crossed her eyes. "He's such a prude. You know what? I don't even care. He loves me. He's good for me. He —"

"I have to finish this, okay?" Go. Go now, I prayed. Before I lose it in front of you.

"I'll call you later." She touched my arm, burning a hole to my soul. Then she crunched through the gravel and disappeared inside the building.

The Sharon Springs Wildcats arrived in a caravan of trucks and SUVs. As the players dumped their gear in our visiting team's lean-to, Cougars stood in a line of solidarity out front. We zeroed in on our target: Devon Womack.

I looked over to T.C. and she shrugged.

No Womack. We were so ready to psyche her out too.

My hopes soared. We might actually have a chance to win this game if Womack didn't show. A lone VW zipped into the parking lot and ground to a stop. The door opened. Crap. It was her.

She lingered at the side of her red Bug, tying her shoelace. A white car pulled in beside her and Devon straightened. This huge smile spread across her face. She sauntered up to the driver's side door as a girl got out of the car and said something to Devon, which made her laugh. Then — shock me with a live wire — they kissed.

Right here in broad daylight, in Coalton, Kansas. Two girls kissing. My eyeballs bounced off the scoreboard, I'm sure. Did anyone else see?

They held hands as they approached the lean-tos. Now people were gawking at them. When they got closer, I noticed the other girl, Devon's girl, had on a KC Peppers T-shirt. The Peppers were a competitive team out of Olathe, Kansas.

I knew the Peppers. I'd been following the tourneys. Ever since I was little, I'd followed them. I knew all the competitive teams: The Shockwaves out of Kansas City, the KC Peppers out of Olathe, the Colorado Stars. I'd visualized myself on the field, in the uniforms, number 19. I'd fantasized about it. But it was out of my field of dreams now.

Dad was the one who'd kept that dream alive. The dream died with him.

I couldn't take my eyes off them. Devon and her girlfriend. Their fingers intertwined at their sides. Like they held hands all the time.

Devon glanced up and saw me looking. Her eyes narrowed. The Peppers girl headed for the bleachers, and Devon veered my way.

"Yeah?" she said, coming right up to me. "What?"

"What what?" The softball in my hand I smacked into my glove.

Devon leaned into my face and spoke ominously. "She's mine. Got that? Hands off."

The ball dribbled out of my mitt and thudded in the dirt. "I never . . . I'm not . . ."

Devon grinned. As I bent to retrieve the ball, she added, "We're going to kick your ass today."

"Bite me," I replied automatically.

"I would, but you're not my flavor." Another grin twisted her lips and she jabbed my shoulder. She took off. My eyes strayed to the stands, to the KC Peppers girl, joining the Sharon Springs Pep Club. God, she was hot. How'd they hook up?

"Mike!"

I put my eyeballs back in my head. Xanadu stood behind the backstop, waving. I raised my glove to her. Bailey wasn't with her, which lifted my spirits. Maybe he got castrated by a bull.

"Let's go." Coach Kinneson clapped behind me.

"Hey," I said to my team as they trotted out onto the field. "Game on?"

In one voice they sounded, "Game on."

Kicking the collective ass of a team requires tremendous quad power. The Wildcats were weak today. Especially Womack. I don't know what was with her — she was probably showing off for her girlfriend. She couldn't get a ball over the plate to save her rep. We scored five runs in the first inning and won by eight. We were stoked. It was a needed reminder to take one game at a time, to never be intimidated. A single player does not make a team. A game isn't won until the very last out.

That's what Dad taught me. Never give up. Never give in. Nothing's impossible. "Believe it, baby. Believe it and it's yours."

Dad, I want to believe. I want to believe so bad. Once, just once, I want to believe you were telling me the truth.

Chapter Twenty-Two

*X*anadu loaded an Alan Jackson CD before passing me the bottle of strawberry wine. Her tastes were changing. I took that as a sign. She said to Jamie, "Did Mike tell you about my ring?"

Jamie choked. Lowering his fifth of scotch, he wiped his lips and said, "Ring?"

Xanadu stuck out her hand for Jamie to ogle. Did she have to wear it on her left hand? Wouldn't it look better on her toe? Or in the plastic bubble from the gumball machine?

Jamie turned to me. "You got her a ring?"

I spit-sprayed the inside of the caboose.

Xanadu laughed. "No, you idiot. It's from Bailey."

Jamie tried to meet my eyes, but I was busy guzzling.

Xanadu said, "This is a farewell party. Did Mike tell you?"

"Are you leaving?" Jamie said flatly to Xanadu.

"No. My suppliers are becoming suspicious." She opened a package of Ding Dongs that I'd snitched off Ma's TV tray. Ma'd been asleep on the sofa when I left the house. Or dead. I didn't check her pulse.

Xanadu broke the Ding Dong and handed me half. "We're depleting my aunt and uncle's stock of booze. I keep filling the bottles with water, but . . . I don't know. I feel kind of guilty about stealing it."

"Really," Jamie said. "When did you grow a conscience?"

"What's that supposed to mean?" Xanadu and I snapped together.

Jamie raised his bottle to his mouth and swigged.

Xanadu and I looked at each other and shook our heads. Jamie could be a jerk. He proved it by adding, "Tell us the truth, Xana. We're quitting because Bailey doesn't approve of you having sex with us on Fridays."

She let out a little huff. "Get real."

"Oh, I am real. You're the fake. All you are is Bailey's Barbie."

"Shut up," I snarled.

"Bailey's lay."

Xanadu intercepted my lunge for Jamie's throat. "If Shane asked you to stop doing something he disapproved of, you would," she said. "Wouldn't you?"

Jamie shook his head. "I don't think there's anything he disapproves of. Let me think." He pressed a finger to his chin. "Nope. He loves me just the way I am."

"Proof he's sniffing diesel." I took another glug of wine.

Xanadu laughed. She jabbed me in the arm. "I know I shouldn't cater to Bailey's every whim, but alas, I'm in love." She sighed. "If I wasn't so hot for Bailey, I could sure go for Beau."

Jamie bristled. That shut him up.

I closed my eyes. Concentrated on the slow buzz creeping into my brain. On her nearness, her heat. She could be "that" girl, if she let herself. My girl. Xanadu kicked my foot. "How'd you know Ding Dongs were my favorite?"

My eyelids fluttered. She smiled at me. I know everything about you, I thought. I know you better than you know yourself.

She sprawled across the mattress, her head landing in my lap. "You'll never believe what I dreamed about last night. You and me. Us. Together."

"Yeah?" I said. My breath caught.

"Yeah. It was like a lesbian action dream." She laughed. "I think you're putting ideas in my head."

I gripped the neck of my bottle and raised it to my mouth. She added, "If I was with you, I could be myself, huh? I could do whatever I wanted." She reached up to fondle Dad's ring. "You'd love me no matter what."

No matter what, Xanadu. No matter what. I caught Jamie looking at me, at us, a scowl on his face.

What?

"What?" I voiced it. Xanadu's words tumbled around in my brain: lesbian action dream, lesbian action dream, no matter what.

Jamie's gaze settled on Xanadu, who'd curled up on my quad, hands folded under her cheek. I couldn't help myself; I touched her hair. I brushed a long tendril of the silk away from her face. Her beautiful face. My fingers lightly traced the swell of her cheek.

I was giving her ideas.

Later, as we were dropping Xanadu off, I was drifting in a dream. I was so wasted I could barely see, and Jamie was stumbling around. We hoisted Xanadu between us, dragging her to the gate. "You guys." Her half-closed eyes alternated between Jamie and me. "You're the best friends I've ever had," her words slurred. She flung her arms around Jamie, then me. She squeezed me hard.

For the first time ever, I hugged her back. I held her close. She didn't resist or push away; she stayed in my arms, her breasts pressing against my chest. Her hair smelled of soap and cigarettes and nighttime and possibility. I nuzzled her neck.

Jamie jerked her off me.

"Hey —"

"We have to leave," he growled, deep in his throat. "Geneviève wants me home before the butt-crack of dawn." Spinning Xanadu around ninety degrees, he shoved her in the direction of the farmhouse. Rougher than necessary. She stumbled and almost fell. I lurched to catch her, but Jamie grasped my arm and yanked me back toward the truck. "We're out of here," he seethed under his breath.

"Stop it. What's your problem?" I karate-chopped him in the neck. Xanadu swayed a little, then called, "See you guys." She started jogging up the driveway. I wanted to run after her, but Jamie stepped in front of me. Xanadu wheeled around and air-blew us a kiss. She seemed more sober than she'd let on.

"What's with you?" I asked Jamie as we climbed into the cab from opposite sides. My eyeballs were sloshing around in my head. I squeezed the lids together to stabilize the rocking boat.

Jamie didn't answer. He was giving off vibes — angry, upset.

"What?" My lids snapped open.

He still didn't answer. I cranked the key and shifted into first. Gravel spewed as I shot out of there.

A movement, too fast to react. I felt the thump under my tires. Slamming on the brakes, I downshifted and opened the door, staggering out to see what I'd hit.

It was a rabbit. A little bunny. Under the front tire, it was limp and bloody. I dug it out. Dead. Tears sprang to my eyes.

I'd never hit anything in my life. Never. I'd never killed another living thing. Gently, lovingly, I lay the rabbit under a bush at the side of the road.

As I climbed back into the truck, I was shaking. "I killed it," I said to Jamie. "A rabbit."

He didn't say a word.

I poked along the county road more aware than I'd ever been

sober. Jamie sulked the whole way. "Look, we don't have to stop going to the caboose just because Xanadu doesn't want to anymore, if that's what you're mad about." I killed a living thing. A helpless little bunny. What if she was pregnant or something? What if she had babies somewhere? What if they needed her? "You could get Renata to buy us a six-pack. You could probably get her to —"

"She's playing you," Jamie said.

It took a few seconds for his words to filter in. "What do you mean?"

"I mean, she's playing you. I bet she has from day one. The way she touches you and smiles at you. She's still doing it. Even more. She should've backed off after you told her. She knows what you want. She's using you. She's a player. She's playing me too."

"Shut up. She wouldn't do that."

He twisted to face me. "You don't even see it. You refuse to see it because you want it so bad."

Because it doesn't exist.

"She's a goer."

"Shut up! Shut the fuck up."

Jamie's face pinched.

I drove, concentrated on the road, on not being responsible for any living creature leaving this earth. As the stoplight came into view, Jamie murmured, "I'm glad this is the last time. I don't want to hang around with her anymore. I hate her. She is a slut. I can't stand the sight of her."

I jammed on the brakes. "What do you know? You don't know her, not the way I do."

He looked at me. "Maybe. But I know you."

"No, you don't. You don't know shit. You don't understand anything."

Jamie said solemnly, "Oh yes, Mike. I do. I do understand." His eyes held mine. "I know exactly what you're doing," he said. "You're deluding yourself. You're pretending this is real, or could be. Do you think I haven't been there? I have. We've all been there. You're not the only queer who's fallen in love with a straight person." He broke his penetrating gaze and glanced away. "At least Beau didn't play me."

"Get out."

Jamie blinked back. "What?"

"Get. Out." The hatred in my heart underscored the words. I lunged across the seat, across his lap, and wrenched open the door.

Jamie exhaled a weary breath and slid off the seat. Clutching the handle on the open passenger door, he said, "Are you pissed at me because I'm right? Or because I called you a queer?"

I jammed my foot on the accelerator. The door tore from Jamie's hand and banged against the side panel. Through the rearview mirror, I saw Jamie move to the middle of the road. He stood, arms outstretched.

What? If he thought I was going to answer his ridiculous question, he was the delusional one.

I'm not, I told myself. I'm not like him.

⸻

Squeezing down hard, I lifted my legs. Up. Down. Up. Down. I was going to get so ripped. My fourth circuit. Feel the burn.

"Take it easy, Mike." The pressure on my ankles released and Armie hovered over my head. "You're gonna crash. What are you lifting?" He calculated the amount I was leg pressing. "A hundred and ten? Jesus. That's suicide." He began to ratchet down the weight.

I rose to sit up on the bench and felt woozy. I hung my head between my legs, gulping in deep breaths. My quads were spazzing bad. Sweat drenched my undershirt.

"You're done for the day." Armie draped a towel over my head. "I don't want you coming back here alone. From now on, you have access to the equipment one day a week and only if I'm here as your spotter. Go hit some softballs."

He swaggered off. Jerk. I wanted to chase him down and beat the crap out of him. I could too. I could take him. If I wasn't so dizzy. And my knees didn't buckle when I tried to walk.

I stood in the shower until my muscles relaxed, recovered. I cranked on the water full blast. The sting felt good, soothing, familiar. I turned off the cold completely and let the hot needles prick my skin. My hands crossed over my chest, cupping my breasts.

Proof I wasn't like Jamie. I wasn't a guy. I wasn't queer.

Yeah, okay, I was gay. Did that make me queer? I hated that word. It implied something like, "not normal." I was normal. I was gay. So what? That was fine. I wasn't *that* gay. There were degrees, weren't there? Jamie was off the scale. I was barely pushing the gauge.

Could you be a little bit gay? A hollow laugh might've escaped my throat. How deluded was I? Jamie was right.

The boiling water finally made me gasp with pain and I wrenched off the faucet. I noticed a slight drip and made a mental note to repair the plumbing for Armie. I owed him that. He was right; if I kept up this pace, I'd damage myself.

I toweled off, remembering a conversation I'd had with Jamie a few years back. He was just coming out. We were lying on his living room floor after school, surfing the Dish networks for a decent movie. This had to be sixth, seventh grade. We always hung out at Jamie's house, since Ma lived at mine. Dottie had fixed us a hot sandwich — meatloaf with ketchup. I remember that. I loved Dottie's sandwiches, her home cooking. I loved Dottie.

"Listen to this, Mike," Jamie had said. He was reading from a book he'd checked out of the library. "It says there are three stages to coming out. One: Admitting to yourself you're gay."

I surfed channels, half watching for movies, fully tuned into what he was saying.

"Two: Accepting the truth of it."

I stopped on *Tomb Raider*. I loved Angelina Jolie. She was hot.

"Three: Embracing your difference, your identity, and your sexual orientation." He'd closed the book and turned to me. "I think I'm at two: Accepting it. Where are you?"

A cold claw had gripped me. Without looking at him, I'd said, "What makes you think I'm gay?"

I remember he'd laughed. He'd laughed uproariously. "I guess that answers my question," he'd said.

Yeah, mine too. I hadn't come very far, had I?

Chapter Twenty-Three

Xanadu called me the minute I walked in the door. "Can you talk?" she asked. She always asked that, Can you talk? Like there were people around listening, caring. Like I'd ever say no to her. I still hurt, my muscles from working out, my head from thinking too hard. My heart too. It ached.

"He asked me to go with him to a family reunion in Colby," she said. "Isn't Colby some kind of cheese?" She laughed.

I smiled. Jamie was wrong about her. I knew it in my bones. She had feelings for me if only she'd face the truth. She was dreaming about me. Lesbian action dream. Sex dream.

"Where is Colby?"

"North of here," I said. "About thirty miles." I checked my messages from Darryl. Ledbetter. Fountain. Why hadn't the Redmans called about the replumbing job? They had to have reviewed the bids by now and been ready to get going. It'd been weeks.

"I'm going to tell him today," Xanadu said.

"Tell him what?" I asked.

She made a sound, like an irritated scoff. "You know. About my past. What I've done. Who I am. He's going to hear all about the real me." Her voice changed. "The real me. Won't he be surprised."

I hoped, prayed her confession, her reality, included me.

She went on, "His whole family'll be there though. It might not be the best time. Bailey's mother creeps me out, the way she looks at me when she thinks I don't see. Like she wants to throw a bucket of water on me so I'll melt. Isn't that how Dorothy killed the Wicked Witch? So Toto. Anyway, I really need to tell him and soon. It's driving me crazy."

I knew the feeling.

Xanadu said more intimately, "I'm glad I have you for moral support. What are you doing today?"

"Me? I, uh, promised to fix the town fountain this weekend for Coalton Days."

"What are Coalton Days, anyway?" she asked. "Bailey and Beau keep talking about them like it's some huge deal."

Bailey should shut up. Likewise Beau.

"Is it a big cow pie–eating contest or something?" Amusement in her voice.

"No. Well, yeah. It's a celebration. Town history. Tradition. All the businesses put merchandise on sale. Saturday we have a parade and an arts-and-crafts festival. A tractor pull. Then Sunday people get together at the park to eat and play games — horseshoe pitching and bingo, that kind of stuff." I was talkative, babbling.

"Bingo?" Xanadu said. "Are you serious?"

I shut up.

"Oh God. You are. I should know by now you guys are never joking."

When I didn't respond, she let out a long sigh. "Okay, I'm going to Colby. God. What should I wear? Bib overalls?" She laughed again.

I couldn't bring myself to tell her Everett's most popular clothing item was bib overalls.

⟶•◆

I was hungry. Weak. Needed carbs, protein. My canister of protein powder was down to one last scoop and we were out of eggs. On my way to pick up the PVC pipe for the fountain, I decided to make a pit stop at the Suprette. Replenish my Whey and get a dozen eggs. I might buy a whole precooked chicken and a bunch of bananas if they were ripe and on sale. I'd never been so hungry.

Deb Pastore was cashiering and waved to me. She'd worked part-time at the Suprette since ninth grade. Half the town was here today. Saturday morning — Coalton's unofficial grocery day. Observed by everyone but the Szabos, of course. The Szabos got their groceries delivered. La di da.

The day-old bakery goods were on display up front by the register. Next to them were cards and candles and bug spray. Everything was fifty percent off for Coalton Days. I should buy Xanadu a candle, I thought. A gift. A Valentine's card on sale. Behind me I heard a crash, then a bloodcurdling scream.

"Todd, I'm going to kill you! I can't leave you alone for one minute and you're destroying the Suprette. Wait'll I get you home."

Uh-oh.

Charlene stormed out of the canned foods aisle with her over-loaded shopping cart. The baby, who was strapped in a baby seat, was wailing like a banshee. "Deb," Charlene called, "my little monster just wrecked the soup display. He's putting it all back together though. Aren't you, Todd?" She threatened him with slit eyes. I wondered where the other two monsters were lurking.

Deb and I made the exact same face. Scary mother. Scary kids.

To avoid a run-in, I hustled to the meat case.

The chickens in the rotisserie looked fresh. That charbroiled aroma. I slid a juicy one off the skewer and bagged it. The bananas were too green, so I settled for a tub of banana pudding.

It would've slipped my attention altogether if the flickering fluorescent light over the register hadn't caught the glitter. "You're making a killing here," Deb said, smiling at me. She lifted the coffee can off the top of the register and shook it. Change clanked around.

"The mayor puts in a ten-dollar bill every time he comes in," she said. "In fact, almost everyone contributes. Nel tells me she had to put out three more cans at the tavern to keep up with all the donations."

I paid. I bagged my groceries. I walked out. I slammed the truck door. Squealed onto Main.

How many were there? Three, four? Were there cans all over town? I'd finally hid the one at the Merc behind the cigarette tray. The Suprette and the tavern. Where else?

The VFW, the coffee counter, Renata hiding the evidence. Is that why people had been so nice to me lately?

No, they were always nice. But they'd been smiling more, feeling sorry for me more.

Dammit. This town didn't owe me. Nobody owed me.

I veered off Main Street toward Highway 83. The softball camp was maybe, maybe a possibility. But if I was going, it'd be on my terms. Me paying my own way. My choice. My life.

At Rock Hill I exited and followed the graded road eight miles, the way I had the previous time. Past the five blue silos, the oil rig. Why hadn't the Redmans gotten back to me? It was rude. The one time I called, no one answered and I didn't leave a message. I should have. I should've said, "This is Mike Szabo, from Szabo Plumbing and Heating. I came by and gave you a bid on replumbing your house, remember? I haven't heard back. You might've called and I missed it, since the tape in my machine is scratchy, and my brother is a retard, and my Ma can't get off her fat ass to answer the phone."

There were two orange vans parked in the Redmans' drive. At the barn, a tractor and a Jeep Cherokee. I eased in behind one of the vans. I took the front porch steps two at a time and knocked on the storm door. No answer. "Hello?" I called.

A shadow materialized in the living room. "Oh." Mrs. Redman opened the door. "I didn't hear you through the racket." She squinted her eyes. "I know you."

"Mike Szabo." Last time I was here she was all dressed up like she'd just gotten off work. Today her clothes were paint-smeared and baggy. She had a smudge of green on her nose. I was tempted to reach up and wipe it off.

She was pretty. She'd told me, when I came to give her a bid, that she and her husband and three kids were moving in because her parents couldn't keep up the place anymore; the house was a shambles. It didn't look that bad to me, but what did I know, living in a snake pit? They were planning an entire remodel, rewiring and replumbing, adding a third bathroom. It was the biggest job I'd ever bid on. Okay, the only job.

Dad had done the cost estimating. I'd helped order supplies and made sure everything got delivered to the job site, but he had crunched the numbers. Before he crunched himself.

"I was wondering if you decided on a plumbing contractor," I said.

"Um . . . yes. We did." Mrs. Redman looked sort of sheepish. "Applewood, out of Garden City." She eyed the vans over my head. I turned to look. APPLEWOOD PLUMBING, HEATING, AND AIR CONDITIONING, the panel on the side of the van read. The rushing sound from an acetylene torch drew my attention back to the house. A guy yelling from the basement, "Rafe, grab me another roll of solder from the truck, will you?"

"I'm sorry," Mrs. Redman said. "I guess I should've called. I've never done this before — gotten estimates, hired contractors."

"No, that's okay," I heard myself saying. "I should've called you sooner." Damn. Why hadn't I called? Maybe if I'd called the next day to follow up, she would've hired me.

Backing down the steps, stumbling a little, I said, "Well, good luck with your house."

She smiled. "Thank you." Then headed back inside.

On second thought . . . "Ma'am?"

She reappeared.

"If you don't mind my asking, was my estimate way higher than Applewood's?" Because it couldn't have been. I'd barely priced the job above the materials cost, figuring I had most of what I needed in stock. A company like Applewood charged union rates. Two vans, three or four guys. Their bid had to be twice mine. Three times.

"Actually," Mrs. Redman winced, "your bid was so low we didn't think you were serious."

"What?" My heart sank. "I was. I mean, I am. Serious. I could do this job for a lot less than Applewood. I'd do a good job. Our work is guaranteed."

"That's what Mom said. She's the one who suggested I call you. She has this friend in Coalton . . ." She studied me for a moment, then her eyes glazed over.

What? She knew about me? About Dad? So what? What did my history have to do with my plumbing skills? Wait a minute. If she knew about me, she'd give me the job out of pity. No, that wasn't it. It was something else —

Oh, I got it. "Your husband didn't think I could do the job, is that it? Because I'm a girl?"

Mrs. Redman met my eyes. "No, that *isn't* it. I'm the one who didn't think you could do the job."

I about fell off the steps. "Why?"

She scanned me up and down. "Look at you. You're, what? Sixteen?"

"Eighteen," I lied.

"Eighteen. Even so, I understand you don't have any employees. It's just you. You're not even licensed in the state. I checked. Are you still in high school?"

"Yes, but the year's almost over. I don't need employees. They jack up the cost. If I need help I'll ask my brother —" I choked. That was stupid. He'd never help me. It's not his gig. "I'd have worked full-time for you," I told her. "Day and night if you needed."

She let out a weary-sounding breath and peered off toward the barn. "I hired a more established, reliable firm. You can understand that."

"Ma'am, Szabo Plumbing and Heating has been in business since 1932. We're well established. I'm completely reliable. Ask anyone in Coalton —"

"I don't have to justify my decision to you," she snapped. "We went with Applewood."

I felt myself shrinking. "Yes, ma'am." I backed off her porch. "Sorry."

I wouldn't. Wouldn't cry. It was one job. So what? I didn't need it. Who needed it?

I needed it. Because there was no way, no way in hell I was ever going to accept money from people in Coalton. Money was help. Szabos didn't need help. I didn't. Once I started accepting help, it was all over.

"Are you speaking to me?"

"No."

Jamie plopped down beside me on the lawn in front of the school. "Geneviève's lemon-bacon bars were a bust. She says the world isn't ready for that much moistness. I say the world isn't ready for their desserts to spark a grease fire. She's leaving me the recipe in her will. And honey, I'm leaving it to you." He dropped a block of aluminum foil in my lap. "Peace offering."

I'd skipped lunch to grab some sky. I needed space.

"Hi, guys." Xanadu loped up and knelt down next to Jamie.

He scrambled to his feet. "I just remembered." He pivoted in place. "Whatever it was I forgot."

She frowned at his retreating back. "What's his problem?"

"He has so many."

She slapped my knee and smiled. Then held on and squeezed. My mood shifted, lifted. I'd been in a black hole ever since yesterday, losing the Redman job. This sense of self-confidence Dad had inspired in me, this I-can-do-anything-I-put-my-mind-to attitude, anything I want, was slowly seeping away. What I wanted seemed suddenly out of reach. It was stupid to want that camp. Forget it.

"What's that?" Xanadu eyed the foil.

"Lemon bars," I said. "Grandma Dottie's secret recipe."

"Oh yum." She didn't ask about the secret, just snatched the package out of my hand. "I am ravenous. Bailey was supposed to buy me lunch, but he had to stay after class and make up some lame assignment in English —"

"Xana," his voice carried out from the building.

She raised her eyes over my head and her face lit up like fireworks. If I had a fire extinguisher, I would've doused that flame.

He rushed over. "Hey, babe. Sorry I'm late."

"Prove it," Xanadu said.

Bailey arched his eyebrows. He lowered his voice. "I will. Tonight."

She pushed to her feet. "We'll talk later, Mike." She touched my shoulder, then leaned down to my ear. "I still haven't told him. I'm such a coward. You need to give me courage."

Try liquid courage, I thought. It's stronger and it lasts longer.

She absconded with my lemon bars.

It didn't matter. She could have everything of mine. Everything, if once, just once, she'd look at me with the same burning desire she had for Bailey.

"Hello, Mike. Mind if I join you?"

I shielded my eyes against the noonday sun. What was this, Grand Central? "Pull up a chair," I said to Mrs. Stargell.

"Don't mind if I do." Her joints creaked as she descended to the lawn. She sat, extended her legs out in front, and smoothed her flowered dress over her bony knees. "Would you like half my sandwich?" she asked. "It's liverwurst."

Liverwurst wasn't my favorite. At the moment, though, tree bark would taste good. "Thanks."

She peeled back the Saran Wrap and handed me a wedge. "Dr. Kinneson and I were talking about you during my planning period today." Mrs. Stargell took a bite.

Why didn't everyone just shut up about me? I suspected I wasn't Dr. Kinneson's favorite person these days. But she'd dredged up everything. She was interfering in my life.

"I'd like to tell you a story," Miz S said.

My stomach chose that moment to grumble.

"Eat." She pointed to my sandwich.

I chomped into the middle. Soft white bread. Mustard. For liverwurst, it wasn't bad.

"When I was in college, my senior year, I had an opportunity to go to England for three weeks on a study tour." Miz S took a bite of sandwich and chewed. She wiped the crumbs from her lips. "A group of select students were chosen for their particular interest in British history and art and literature. I was one of the chosen few. Along with the tour, we'd read great works of the masters and visit museums and attend concerts. We'd travel the countryside to see the birthplaces of Lord Tennyson and Byron and even the Bard himself. It was the chance of a lifetime." She paused for another bite. "And I didn't go."

I widened my eyes at her.

She lowered her sandwich to her lap, staring off into the distance, looking lost. Like she forgot she was telling the story to me.

I said, "Didn't you have the money?"

"What?" She blinked fast and returned from wherever she'd gone. "Oh no. It wasn't that." She raised her sandwich to her mouth, then lowered it again. "My folks would've mortgaged the farm to have me go. But I was in love."

My chin hit the ground, I'm sure. Miz S in love? I couldn't picture it.

She sighed dreamily. "I'd met Terrence. My future husband. The first one."

First one? Whoa. This was getting interesting.

"Terrence and I were hot and heavy. Ooh, baby. We were all over each other like gravy on grits."

I choked.

She looked at me and laughed.

"Sorry," I said. I shoved the rest of my sandwich into my mouth to plug it.

"We were a real item in Leoti. That's where I grew up. I was loathe to leave Terrence. He, of course, didn't encourage me to go. Three weeks apart? Lordie, we'd die of separation anxiety. Long story short, I forfeited the opportunity. I'll tell you, Mike, to this day, I regret that decision. What I missed — traveling overseas, expanding my world, living my dream — it went up in smoke. Poof." She popped apart her fingers, and crumbs flew. "What I'm trying to say is, you should take advantage of this opportunity you have to attend softball camp. Right now. Today. You may not get another chance to pursue your dream. I didn't." She forced a smile, kind of wistful.

Her words swirled around in my head. My opportunity. My dream.

Right, Dad. My dream died. Again. Because of you. I should have left it dead and buried.

"Whatever happened to Terrence?" I asked.

"Who?"

"Your first husband."

"Oh. Him." She cocked a limp wrist. "He flew the coop. As did the second, and third."

Third?

Unexpectedly, Miz S looped an arm around my shoulders and pulled me close. She smelled of chalk and liverwurst and rose water, and I had the strongest urge to wrap my arms around her and hold on tight. Like I would a mom. The one I never had. But my arms wouldn't respond to my heart.

"Don't do anything you'll regret, Mike," she said, rocking me gently. "Some decisions you can never take back."

Hear that, Dad? You made your choice. You can never take it back.

I decided to skip Coalton Days. Xanadu was right. It was Toto. A hick-town hoedown. Who needed it? Besides, I'd gotten up at the crack of dawn every day this week to work on the fountain. It was a bigger job than anticipated. Not only did the pump need to be replaced, the pipe to the water main had to be chiseled out from under fifty years of tree roots, then new pipe cut, laid, reconnected. I couldn't do it after school because of my *real* job. My paying job, which paid shit. And the hundred dollars I'd quoted Mayor Ledbetter didn't cover the replacement cost of the PVC. Thanks, Dad. You could've taught me how to bid on jobs before you bought it.

"What do you mean you're not going to Coalton Days?" Jamie had a hissy fit on the phone. "You have to go. It's tradition. I already signed us up for the sack race."

"Ask Beau to hop in the sack with you." From the back of the house, I heard the toilet flush and Ma crack the floorboards in the hallway.

Jamie whined, "Please? It's no fun without you. Anyway, I have to talk to you. I need to show you something I can't show to anyone else."

What could that be? His limp dick?

Jamie added, "What are you doing today that's so important?"

What *was* I doing? It was Sunday. The Merc was closed. I was banned from the VFW. It wasn't like I had a hot date. The TV blared to life in the living room and I pictured myself holing up here all day with Bloody Mary. Or Derelict Darryl. "For a little while," I told Jamie. "But only so we can retain the world title."

"Praise Ra," he said. "I thought I'd have to give up the trophy. It's holding my condom collection, you know."

Chapter Twenty-Four

The year Dad died Coalton Days had been canceled. Not only because of him; it'd rained that entire week. The sidewalk sales were washed out and the park had become a mucky swamp. Nobody felt much like celebrating anyway. Today the weather was warm and balmy, a perfect spring day.

The stores along Main were all closed. Even Hank's Hardware and Tiny's Salon. I hoped I wouldn't run into Xanadu and Bailey. Bailey and Xanadu. Ever since he got her that ring, they'd been like French horndogs. Not Xanadu. Bailey. He couldn't keep his paws off her.

The Old Farts band was tuning up in the gazebo. They weren't too bad, except all they knew were polkas. The gazebo was decked out in bunting, the traditional red, white, and blue.

"There you are." Jamie rushed out from behind the bake sale table. He called over his shoulder, "I'm taking a break now, Geneviève." Dottie fluttered fingers at him. She was busy collecting money for a box of Grandma Dottie's that Dr. Kinneson and her husband were buying.

Dr. Kinneson spotted me and waved. I waved back. She didn't act too mad at me. I hadn't changed my mind. Dreams were for other people. People who could afford them. People who had a farm to mortgage for their kids.

Our last softball game of the season was tomorrow after school. Maybe afterwards she'd get off my case. I'd have to figure out a way to give the money back. All of it.

Jamie was standing in front of me, gawking.

"What?"

"You, making a fashion statement." He snaked a hand down my chest.

I'd decided to wear Dad's suspenders. I don't know why. Patriotism? Tradition? "What did you need to show me?" I asked Jamie.

"Patience, my dear. All will be revealed."

I exhaled indifference.

Jamie headed for the picnic area, but I pulled him up short. Too many people. I steered him in the direction of the fountain instead.

It was working great, better than it ever had. Shooting ten-foot cones of recycled water over the bronze statue of John Coalton, our town founder. Darryl had done a research paper on John Coalton for his senior project or something. He'd dug through *Gazette* archives and talked to old-timers. He unearthed the fact that our founder had been run out of Oklahoma for bilking old people out of their life savings in a land fraud scheme. That history lesson dropped a few chassis in town. We didn't celebrate John Coalton anymore. The statue remained though. He was our legacy, like it or not.

I sat on the brick ledge surrounding the fountain and Jamie hopped up next to me. He pushed up the cuff of his long-sleeve shirt and shook his hand at the ground. A silver bracelet slid down his arm. "Shane sent it to me," he said. "Isn't it awesome?"

The bracelet looked expensive, like real silver. Not that I'd know fake from real. "Nice," I told him.

"He had it engraved." Jamie jimmied the bracelet off his wrist. Underneath, next to the skin, was one word: FOREVER.

"Forever." Jamie repeated aloud. "That's a long time."

"Longer than a one-nighter in Denver," I said.

He pressed the bracelet to his heart. What was it with all the love jewelry? Didn't anyone send flowers anymore? Flowers expressed sentiment. Then, after a week, they died.

"There you are."

Our heads shot up.

"I've been looking all over for you guys." The sight of Xanadu still made me melt. She had on her red leather pants today — so fine — and a loose knit, see-through shirt. What I saw was a skimpy bra. Was she reverting to her old self? Her true self? The bellybutton ring was back. The pants showed every curve and crevice of her. Her hair was loose, free, blowing in the breeze away from her face like a supermodel. Like my Maserati girl.

She smiled into my eyes. I felt a rise between my legs. "What's that, Jamie?" Her eyes drifted down.

"Nothing," Jamie snapped. He fumbled to put the bracelet back on. It slipped out of his hand and plinked to the ground, rolling away. Jamie dropped to his knees and groped for it, scooping up the bracelet like we were going to tackle him and take it away. Xanadu curled a lip at me, like, What is with him?

Who knew? Love did strange things to people.

"Hey, guys." Bailey sauntered up behind Xanadu. He was holding a package of beef jerky. Ripping off a chunk between his teeth, he said, "How goes it?" sliding one arm around Xanadu's bare midriff and offering her a bite.

She pushed his hand away. "Ew, I hate that stuff."

Bailey looked offended. "Why? It probably came from the same cow as your pants." He smirked.

She elbowed him in the ribs and grinned up at him.

It wasn't that funny. "I'll take one," I said, not waiting for him to offer.

Bailey had to detach himself from Xanadu to pull out a strip of jerky from the package. "Jamie?" Bailey extended the jerky to him.

"No," Jamie grumbled. "Thanks."

"What's a hayrack ride?" Xanadu asked out of the blue.

Bailey knuckled her head and said to me, "I keep telling her it's the highlight of Coalton Days. She doesn't get it." He explained to Xanadu, like she was a moron, "Everett and June load the flatbed with hay and drive a bunch of people around."

"That's it?" She made a face. "You're joking."

I think Bailey wished he was.

"He made it sound like it was a religious experience."

Bailey's eyes dropped. "She'll understand once we do it," he mumbled. "Beau said June wants to get started earlier this year, around eight. I said I'd spread the word."

"Count me out," Jamie said. "I have other plans."

Bailey's jaw dropped in unison with mine. What other plans? Jamie miss the hayride? Even if Beau was history, we always went on the hayride. It was tradition. Last year the tradition was margaritas. Jamie and Deb had smuggled in a couple of thermoses and passed them around. Other people filled canteens and water bottles with beer. Bailey was right, the hayride was the highlight of Coalton Days.

"You remember our plans." Jamie widened his eyes at me.

What plans?

He growled low in his throat.

"What?"

"Forget it." He turned and stalked off.

"Why is he mad at me?" Xanadu asked. "What did I do? He's been dissing me all week. If he even sees me coming, he deliberately walks the other way." She slit eyes at his back. "Is he pissed off because we're not getting smashed every weekend? God, you know, I'm sorry if I don't want to steal from Aunt Faye and Uncle Lee anymore. I have a police record already, okay?"

"You do?" Bailey said.

Xanadu blanched. "That was a joke." She fixed on my face. "What did I do to Jamie?"

"You didn't do anything," I said. "He has PMS."

Bailey cracked up. So glad he found us amusing.

The jerky suddenly tasted like cardboard, so I stuck it in my back pocket for later. Xanadu perched next to me on the ledge and Bailey invited himself to scoot in beside her. She had to remove her purse from her shoulder to accommodate him. For some reason, she handed me the purse.

It was beaded. Black and green and clear glass beads. I wanted to open it, inhale the scent of her, search around inside for evidence and understanding of her.

She said, "Did I tell you I decided to finish my senior year here?"

"No." My hopes soared. A lot could happen in a year. "I'm glad." Euphoric.

"Me too." She nudged my shoulder with hers. "I'm going to need a summer job though. Dad says he can't keep sending me money, and Aunt Faye and Uncle Lee shouldn't have to support me totally. I was thinking maybe I could get a job at the Merc. Wouldn't that be fun, the two of us working together?"

It'd be a dream, I thought.

"Could you talk to your boss? Ask him if he has a position for me? Tell him I have experience hauling horse food off a flatbed." She grinned.

I snorted.

"Serious," she said.

"Sure. I can do that." Everett didn't need summer help, not with me and June there. He told me earlier in the week he expected this year to be slow with the economy and the drought. Warning me, maybe, that he might have to cut back my hours. I could work part-time, though. Split my hours with Xanadu. Anything to be with her.

She bumped shoulders with me again. I bumped her back.

Bailey leaned around the front of her and asked, "When are you going to softball camp, Mike?"

Was he still here? "I never said I was."

He arched his eyebrows.

"Everyone just assumed that's what I wanted."

Bailey said, "You don't?"

Xanadu interjected, "I hate when people do that. Assume they know what you want. Assume they know *you*, when it's obvious they don't. How could they?"

Exactly.

She unlatched the purse in my lap and dug inside, pulling out a camera. "I wanted to get some pictures of us to send home to my friends. My friends," she intoned. "Right. To Mom and Dad and Loni, at least." Eyeing the surrounding area, she pointed and said, "Let's do it by that tree over there."

My eyes followed her finger. *"No!"* I said.

Xanadu flinched. Did I react out loud? I just meant not *that* tree.

How could I explain? When I was six, Dad and I had planted that tree on Arbor Day. A red oak. It was a sapling then, a baby. The tree was tall now, a perfect canopy that would shade the entire picnic area come summer. In the fall our red oak was the most glorious tree in town. I hadn't noticed how much it'd grown. Two years. How much I'd missed coming here on weekends, during the summer. Sitting under our tree to think or read or soak up sky.

"Mike?" Xanadu's eyes drilled the side of my granite face. "Are you all right?"

I swallowed hard. "Dad and I planted that tree together," I said, not looking at her.

"Oh. I didn't know. I'm sorry. We can take pictures somewhere else."

I turned and met her eyes. An image of her materialized in my mind, against my tree, red hair on red oak. "No. Let's do it." I pushed off the ledge to my feet.

Xanadu handed the camera to Bailey and stood beside me. She took her purse, then my hand.

She took my hand. And she held it all the way to my tree. She didn't care how many people saw. She didn't care if Bailey saw.

"Take one of me and Mike together," she ordered Bailey.

Through the heat, the blood coursing through my veins, I heard him ask, "How do you work this thing?"

Xanadu ducked under a branch and snaked an arm around my waist. "It's self-focusing. Just point and click."

"Where's the clicker?"

"God," she said under her breath. "He's so clueless sometimes." She told him, "The red button on top."

Can't you see? I almost said. He's clueless all the time.

"Okay." Bailey raised the camera to his eye. "Smile."

Xanadu rested her temple against mine.

Click.

I think my eyes were closed in the picture, but I didn't care. We could stay this way forever. The warmth of her breath on my face, our arms around each other's waists. Her soft skin, hot skin.

Xanadu shifted so we were front to front, cheeks touching. "Take another."

I was holding her with both hands now.

Click.

She threw up a leg and, in reflex, I caught it across my arms. Leaning back, she stuck out her tongue and dropped her head down.

Click.

A couple more silly poses.

"Will you take one of me and Bailey?" she asked.

I'd take him out. What could I say? "Sure."

Bailey and I exchanged places. He pulled Xanadu into his arms and held her head to his chest with his big hairy paw. I raised the camera to my eye, framing only her face. The slight smile. Not unhappy, but not thrilled about being manhandled.

Click.

She spun around and moved back against him, leaning into him, his arms enfolding her. Thick arms, tanned. Pound for pound I was more buff than Bailey. I could work on my tan; it was early in the season. He'd gotten a head start with the calving.

Click. I might've cut off his head.

He wedged his chin on top of Xanadu's scalp. She tilted back her head and smiled up at him. She smiled. And kept on smiling.

A memory resurfaced. Déjà vu. Jamie and Shane. How they smiled at each other, shared smile. Intimate eyes. Me, taking their picture. Me, not in the picture.

A bolt from the blue knocked me back a step. "Mike." Dad's voice. Dad, speaking to me. "Look, baby."

Xanadu and Bailey filling the camera's viewfinder.

"Can't you see?" Dad said.

I could. I could see Xanadu kissing him, Bailey kissing her back. I could see what passed between them. The connection. The bond. The love. In that instant of clarity, I saw the truth. She loved him.

She loved him in a way she would never love me.

I handed the camera back, mumbled an excuse, fled, flew, escaped. The blur of grass under my feet, the ground moving, splitting, opening a chasm between us. Them. Her and me. The distance impassable, impossible. The longing, desperation, the broken coupling, the draining of my hopes.

I was gay. A dyke. A baby dyke. That's how I felt, like a baby. A toddler taking her first steps and stumbling. Falling. Trying again. Succeeding. Grasping the power, the strength, the freedom to run, run, running off half-cocked, not watching where I was going or what I was doing. Not seeing the truth. Not aware of the danger. Like a wild child, forgotten, oblivious to the stairs. Running, falling, falling, *thud*. No one to catch me. No one to care. To pick me up, hold me, comfort me, rally me to try again. Keep going, baby. Anything is possible.

No, it isn't, Dad. You're a liar. "You're a liar. A fucking liar."

I hated him. I hated him for giving me hope.

I slammed through the back door.

"Who's that?" Ma sounded startled.

My lungs hurt. My head hurt. Everything about me hurt.

"Who is it?" she demanded.

"It's me," I snarled. In a weaker voice, calmer voice, "It's me." Whoever I am. Whatever I am. I inhaled what strength and dignity I had left and headed to my room.

She was propped on the sofa, sitting, I guess, her rolls of fat spilling over two full cushions. Her TV tray had toppled front first and her Donettes were broken all over the floor. The picture on the TV screen crackled and buzzed.

I looked from the TV to her. She gazed off into space, her beady eyes black as death. On the floor by her feet lay the remote control.

I sauntered up to it. Bent over, picked it up. I held it out in my open hand between us. "Say please," I said.

Her jaw clenched.

Say it, I screamed inside. Say please. Say Mike. Say help me. Say stay. Say anything to me.

Nothing. No reaction.

Slowly, I set the remote on the sofa cushion, too far for her to reach. "What is it with you?" The pressure busted free, spilling out in a rage. "Two years, Ma. It's been two years! You haven't said a word to me in all that time. Not one word."

She blinked.

"Is it *worth* it?" My voice rose.

She shriveled in place.

"Dammit. Goddammit. All my life. What did I do? What did I do to make you hate me?"

No movement, no comprehension.

Dammit! I wheeled around and stormed for my room.

"Thief."

"What?" I stopped.

"Thief," she repeated.

I turned around. "What do you mean? I didn't —"

"You're stealing from me," she stated flatly. Her eyes focused and fixed on my face. It felt like two ice picks boring through my pupils.

I couldn't hold her gaze. "I'm not stealing. I just . . . I wanted some of his things." My eyes raked the floor.

"You're stealing."

"No!" I glanced up. "I'm just borrowing."

"You're stealing him from me."

Her narrowed eyes sliced me in half. She added, "You always did."

She was crazy. I didn't know what she was talking about.

Yes, I did. Maybe. "You can have it all back," I said. "What do I care?" I yanked up the chain around my neck and threw it on the sofa. I charged to my room to get the stuff — the clothes, the lighter, the pictures, watch, everything I'd taken. I tore the suspenders off my body. She could have him. She could keep him, I thought. There's nothing left now. He left me nothing of value.

I stomped back in and crossed the room. She shielded her face with her forearm, cowering, like I was going to hit her.

I wanted to. I wanted her to hurt the way she hurt me.

But she was Ma. My mother. I wouldn't hurt her.

I piled the stuff beside her on the sofa. I placed the remote in her lap. Easy. Gently. "Here," I said.

She was shaking. Protecting herself with her hunched up body. I realized suddenly she was afraid of me. My own mother was afraid of me.

"I'm sorry," I said, my throat constricting. Sorry for whatever I did to you. Sorry for you. Sorry for me. As I backed out of the room, she snatched the remote and clutched it to her chest. She fumbled around for a channel. "Sorry," I repeated. Sorry for being born.

I curled on my bed like a baby. No covers. My quilt was trashed. I thought about working out the pain with curls or crunches. A hundred crunches. A thousand. There weren't enough crunches in the world.

It didn't matter. There was no pain to work out anymore. No feeling at all. Only numbness.

I craved a beer. A quart of Old Milwaukee. Absolut. The hard stuff, yeah. Burn my brain. Rip me bad. Find a tower.

They'd be going to the hayride tonight. This would be the first year I missed. So what? She'd be there with him.

She'd changed me. Ever since she came into my life, every day of my life was different. Out of kilter, out of joint. My inner connections were compromised. They were leaking. Every junction, every elbow, every vee, wye, ess, they'd all pulled loose, pulled apart. As if they — I — had lost the glue that'd held everything together. My whole system was breaking down, and I didn't know how to repair it. Or replace it. I'd been waiting so long.

Waiting. It was the waiting that was unbearable.

What was I waiting for? A miracle? That he'd come back and show me how to fix it? Fix me. That she'd love me. Heal me.

Xanadu.

I rolled over onto my back and stared at the water spots on my ceiling. A picture of Dad flashed into my mind. Him giving me a ponyback ride to bed. Neighing through the kitchen, the living room, the hallway. He'd buck me off onto my mattress, then lean down and touch his nose to mine. The sweet odor of booze on his breath, the cigarettes. The smell of Dad. The comfort, certainty. I'd wrap my arms around his neck and nuzzle into it; feel his stubble of whiskers against my cheek.

"Good night, baby," he'd say. He'd hold my face between his strong hands and kiss my forehead.

"G'night, Daddy."

We'd both whinny. And laugh. I never stole him, Ma. He was never mine to take. You can't own a person. You can't take her from someone she loves.

"Hey, chest hair." Darryl pounded on my door. "You got company."

I blinked back to the moment. Company? Who, Jamie? He'd come to rub it in about how delusional I was. He was right. I was so out of touch with reality, I lived in a fantasy dream world, worse than his.

The door swung open and Darryl stood aside. Xanadu rushed into my bedroom. "Oh God, Mike." She flew across the room and flung herself on top of me. "He hates me."

Chapter Twenty-Five

Darryl lingered in the doorway, hanging onto the knob, eyes popping out of his head. He opened his mouth to say something, but I guess he changed his mind. He stepped back into the hall and shut the door.

Xanadu was bawling, really bawling. I struggled to sit up. She was weighted onto me, holding me down. Her head burrowed into my neck and her arm pinned my shoulder to the bed.

"What's wrong?" I said quietly.

Her chest heaved.

A strand of hay stuck in her hair and I plucked it out. "Xanadu?"

She cried louder.

I stroked her head. "Tell me what's wrong. What happened?"

She rolled away from me to lie flat on the mattress and swiped her nose with the back of her hand. "He hates me," she said. "I told him about . . . ," she paused, her eyelashes slick with tears, "you know. Everything. He thinks I'm evil and horrid. He thinks I'm possessed, that I'm Satan." A tear slid out the corner of her eye and down her cheek. "He got all mad; asked why I hadn't told him before, why did I wait so long? Why did I do it? 'Why did you *do* it?' he says. Fuck, I don't know why I *did* it." Her voice rose. "I don't know!" She covered her eyes with her forearm and sobbed. "I made a mistake." She hiccuped.

I didn't know what to do. She was so close, her body generating heat, moisture. I propped on an elbow and rubbed her arm.

"He said he couldn't handle it." She sniffled. "He couldn't handle being with me anymore." Her voice broke and a flood of tears gushed from her eyes. She closed her fists, curled her wrists under her chin in the curve of her neck, and her whole body vibrated.

What could I say? I'm glad? I wasn't glad. She loved him. He betrayed her. I despised him.

Tenderly, lovingly, I brushed back her hair.

"I thought I could trust him, you know?" She twisted her head to look at me. "The way I trust you. God, Mike." She arched upward and disintegrated in my arms again.

I held her. Held her close. I felt her hurt, deep down and unrelenting. I wanted to do major damage to Bailey McCall. I could too. I could take him. One face-altering blow with my fist . . .

Xanadu murmured into my hair.

"What?" I drew back from her slightly.

She swallowed hard. "Can I stay here tonight? With you?"

My heart beat a pneumatic drill. "Sure."

She rested her forehead on mine. "I better call Aunt Faye so she doesn't send the fucking FBI out looking for me." Xanadu rolled over to the edge of the bed.

While she punched numbers into her cell, I gathered all the Power-Bar wrappers and weights and dirty clothes off my mattress and kicked a bunch of crap into the closet. I'd missed a pair of Dad's boxers and an undershirt. So what? I heard her say, "No, overnight with

Mike. If you don't believe me, here, you talk to her." Xanadu shoved the phone at me.

I'd never used a cell phone. Where did you talk?

"Hello, Mike? Is that you?" Faye's voice.

"Um, yeah." I didn't even see microphone holes. "I'm here," I spoke into the numbers.

"Is Xanadu staying over there, or are you covering for her?"

I gulped. "No, ma'am. I'm not. I mean, she's here. She's kind of upset because she and Bailey . . ." I glanced at Xanadu, at her vacant expression, her eyes taking in my nudie posters on the wall. "Broke up," I finished.

There was a long pause. "Where are *you* sleeping?" Faye said.

I eyed my bed.

She added quickly, "Never mind. All right. Tell Xanadu to be home by seven tomorrow morning in time to get ready for school."

"Okay." The phone buzzed in my hand.

Xanadu smiled at me. Her eyes softened. "Thank you," she said.

She perched on the edge of the mattress and kicked off her shoes. Standing, she shimmied out of her leather pants. She lifted off her shirt. The skimpy bra was black. She slid in under the top sheet and fluffed my pillow. After a minute, her eyes found mine.

She lifted the sheet.

I hesitated. Dad's face flashed, so clear and vivid. His voice: "Nothing's ever going to hurt my baby. Not if I can help it."

"Mike?"

I shimmied in.

She was so near I could feel her heart pounding, her lungs expanding and contracting. She ran a hand down the side of my face and said, "You're the only one I can trust. The only one."

I don't know who kissed who first. Her soft lips on mine pressed deeper and harder, pressing, moving into me. She used her hands, her mouth. I let her. I helped her. I loved her.

When I woke, Xanadu was gone. The room was bathed in the warm glow of dawn. I could still feel her skin melded to mine, the heat of our bodies bonding us together. I heard her breathing, smelled the sweetness of her. I closed my eyes and drifted away.

She wasn't at school on Monday. Bailey was there, looking like he hadn't slept in a week. Good. Last night was the first time in two years I didn't bolt awake at three AM from the nightmare. Falling, falling, *thud*.

I thought about calling her at lunchtime. I got as far as the reception desk, then bailed. She was tired. Needed sleep. We hadn't slept much either. I'd see her later today at the game. She'd come to my game, I was sure of that. She'd want to watch me play.

She'd want to be with me now.

The game was against Scott City. They were fourth in the standings, out of the running. Quarterfinals started Saturday, but I wasn't thinking that far ahead. Coalton Cougars were 15-4 this season, second only to Sharon Springs.

You could tell by the intensity of their warm-up, Scott City didn't come to take batting practice. Last game of the season, they wanted to win. I respected that. It was going to be hard to keep my head in the game.

As I watched the stands fill, I limbered up with side stretches and knee bends. I didn't want to work up a sweat. She was still on my skin. I didn't want to wash her off.

Where was she?

The pep squad had squeezed into the middle section of bleachers. I still didn't see her. I would though. She'd be here. She was my girlfriend now.

Girlfriend. Wow. I had a girlfriend.

Behind the backstop, Jamie caught my eye and rustled a pom-pom. I wanted to yell at him, "You were wrong. You were wrong about her. Wrong about me too. Wrong about everything. Anything is possible."

One more scan of the bleachers.

"Mike, what are you doing?" Coach Kinneson called from the lean-to. "We're ready to go."

Everyone had finished warm-ups and returned from the field.

I jogged over. Hey! Coach Archuleta was back. We all crunched him in a hug.

He smiled, that crinkly, reassuring smile of his. I'd missed that this season. His trust in us, my faith in him. T.C. said, "You're just in time, Coach A. You only missed the whole season."

He tugged T.C.'s cap down over her eyes. "You don't need me," he said. "Look at your record."

It wasn't about stats; he had to know that. My eyes strayed to Coach Kinneson, who was staring back at me. She seemed . . . hurt? Because we liked him better? No. More sad. Bereft, as if she'd lost the whole season. Or lost me.

"Now that we're together," Coach Kinneson switched to automatic, "I'd like to congratulate you girls on a tremendous year. First of all, you survived me."

There were titters of anxious laughter.

"Second, you managed to pull together as a team and get yourselves into the playoffs. I'm proud of you. Every last one of you. There wasn't a game we played that you didn't put out a hundred percent. Maybe that first game with Sharon Springs."

We groaned.

She added, "If you work hard toward any goal, success is guaranteed. Isn't that right, Mike?"

"What?" My face flared. Why was she asking me? "I, I guess."

"You guess?" she repeated. There was challenge in her eyes.

Gina piped up, "The team party's tomorrow night at my house. Who all's coming? My dad needs to know how many steaks to buy."

We raised hands and Gina tallied the count. Dr. Kinneson shook her head at me. What?

The ump lumbered over to the lean-to. "We're ready to go, Coach."

"One minute." Coach K. held up an index finger. She nodded at Coach Archuleta. "We thought about waiting until tomorrow, but Manny and I both agreed we should celebrate it now, as a team. The vote was unanimous. Mike Szabo is this year's MVP."

"What?" My head jerked up.

T.C. intoned, "Again? How boring."

Everyone laughed.

"Wait a minute." I held up a hand. "I didn't vote. When did we vote?"

Coach Kinneson dropped a jaw. "Didn't anyone tell Mike about the vote? You girls."

They laughed again. They'd tricked me. "You're dead," I said. "You're meat."

Coach Kinneson reached into her golf bag and lifted out a trophy. It was tall. She presented it to me.

A trophy. Bigger than any of the others I'd won. The gold plaque at the bottom read: COALTON COUGARS, MOST VALUABLE PLAYER. Underneath the date and my name: MIKE SZABO.

She'd gotten my name right. All my other trophies were stored on the shelf in my closet because they said Mary-Elizabeth. I smiled at Coach and she smiled back. This wave of sadness washed over me.

Regret.

The umpire grumped, "It's game time, Coach."

Coach Archuleta tossed me my face mask. "Show me what I missed," he said. Meaning all of us, I'm certain.

We hustled onto the field. Everyone on the team clapped me on the shoulder or touched gloves with me. My pride swelled. I loved this game. I loved all of them. As I strapped on my shin guards, I glanced up into the stands one last time. She wasn't there —

Yes! She was. Sitting on the top riser. I tried to catch her eye, but she was wearing shades. So beautiful. So mine.

Nothing could ever compare with the happiness I felt at that moment. The sky's the limit, as Dad would say. Believe it, baby. Punching my glove and swaggering out onto the field, I chanted with Jamie and the crowd, "Sza-bo. Mighty Mike. Sza-bo."

Scott City gave a respectable showing. They only lost by a run. Never count out a team, especially one with something to prove. Same goes for a person.

Did Dad say that?

No, I did. My own personal philosophy.

We flung our gloves into the air and hugged each other. Great season. MVP. The reflection off a windshield as a vehicle pulled into the parking lot blinded me momentarily. The stereo was blaring an Alan Jackson song: "Who's Cheatin' Who." The music cut out. As I snagged my glove in midair, my eyes were drawn to the truck. To Bailey opening the door and stepping out.

I craned my neck around to find Xanadu in the bleachers. She wasn't there. She was at the backstop, breaking away from the milling crowd. Heading for the parking lot.

Bailey started toward her.

She walked faster, then he did. She trotted, he sprinted. She ran.

"Hell of a season, Mike." Reese Tanner clenched my shoulder.

Beside him, Mayor Ledbetter said, "Looks like there's a camp in your future, young lady. When's it start?"

"What?"

They hung over me, suffocating me.

"The camp," Reese repeated. "Where is it?"

"I don't know," I stammered, backing off. Bailey was kissing her. My heart was knocking so hard, it was cracking ribs. I couldn't catch my breath.

Through the sea of well-wishers and back-slappers, I staggered to the lean-to to grab my gear. Everything was spinning.

"Mike."

I dropped my trophy into my duffel and zipped it up.

"Mike."

She loomed at the edge of the aluminum shell, smiling tentatively. "Great game. You were awesome, as usual."

My eyes strayed over her shoulder to Bailey, who was standing off a short distance, talking to Faye and Leland.

"Listen, um. This is so weird."

I met Xanadu's eyes.

"I guess he had to get over the initial shock, you know, of me being a supplier. Not to mention drug-head and murderer." She dropped her eyes to the ground. "God. Can you believe it?" A smile tugged her lips. "He still loves me. After all that, he still loves me."

My brain screamed, What about me?

"Anyway." She folded her arms loosely around herself and kicked at a glove someone had left propped against the bench. "About last night. You knew I was upset about Bailey, right? I wasn't thinking straight. Straight." She let out a little laugh. Then her face grew serious. "It didn't mean anything, okay?"

Bailey called, "Xana." She jumped. Lowering her arms, she smiled again, shyly, and said, "I better get going. His mother and father want to *talk* to me." She rolled her eyes. "Persecute is more like it. Why did he have to tell them? Now everyone'll know." Her eyes darkened. "God, I hate small towns. I don't know how you stand it. So Toto." She reached out to touch me, but I was too far away. "Call me later, okay?"

She didn't wait for an answer. Just turned and jogged away.

Out of the lean-to, in the opposite direction, across third base, in front of the scoreboard, I walked, loped, broke out, ran.

It didn't mean anything, okay?

My legs pumped, arms pistoned. Didn't *mean* anything? The wind whipped at my face. It didn't mean anything, didn't mean anything. Okay? Okay? My chest hurt. Wheezing, coughing, gasping for air. I slammed the ladder against the tower, my hands shaking so hard I could barely grip the rungs.

At the walkaround, I stumbled over the bolts on the metal floor. I lost my balance, fell to my knees. I couldn't stand, couldn't balance, couldn't force myself upright. I crawled to my spot.

Jamming my back into the water tank, I hugged my knees and felt myself sinking, sinking.

Didn't mean anything mean anything mean anything, okay?

"No!" I screamed at the top of my lungs. "No. It's not okay!"

Chapter Twenty-Six

A tidal wave of tears surged up from a deep well inside of me. They gushed from my eyes and sluiced down my face. Mike doesn't cry. Mike Szabo does not cry.

She does not cry because she does not feel.

It didn't mean anything, okay?

To who, Xanadu? To who?

I bawled. I bawled like a baby. Not since I was four and fell off the roof and broke my arm had I bawled like this. "Don't cry, baby," Dad had said. "Big girls don't cry."

Don't they, Dad? Don't they cry? This hurt. It hurt more than a broken bone. Bones fuse, they heal. This hurt would never heal. It ruptured my core, the fiber of my being, it ripped away at my soul.

Didn't mean anything, okay?

"No! It's not okay!"

I don't know how long I sat there, hunched over, heaving out my guts. Hours? Days?

Control. Gone.

Action. Over.

The gate screeked.

I curled up tighter. Go away. Please. Go away.

Footsteps. The whoomp of a body flopping down next to me.

"Go away." My voice sounded small, frail. Not me, not Mike. Just go, I prayed. I don't want you to see me like this.

"Wow, I haven't been up here since I was a kid. Dad forbid it, you know. Too dangerous, he said. What do you call that? Irony?" Darryl snorted.

I lifted my head. It was too heavy for my neck. "What do you want?" I snarled. "I don't have the truck."

"That must be because I do. I got your stuff too. That big ole honkin' trophy." Darryl smirked. "Jamie said I could probably find you up here. What did you guys do, steal a ladder from Hank's?"

I buried my face in my knees again.

"People kept telling me you guys were coming up here. Phew." Darryl let out a short breath. "It's a long way down. I forgot how far."

"If you're scared, get off."

"I'm not scared. I'm just saying . . ."

I whipped up my head and glared at him. Take the hint. Leave.

Tapping a Marlboro out of his crumpled pack, he grasped the cigarette between his teeth and offered me one from the pack. I shook my head. He flicked his lighter and a flame sparked to life. Lighter fluid. I closed my eyes. Leaned back against the water tank.

Darryl took a deep drag. The smoke smelled good. I don't know why; I hated cigarettes. "Maybe if you told me what was wrong, I could help you," he said.

I laughed. Bitter sounding, acrid tasting in my mouth.

"Believe it or not," he went on, oblivious, "I do know a thing or two about life. I've been around the block. Okay, I admit, it's a short block." Darryl chuckled at his own joke. "Could be I have a few insights though. I could maybe give you a different way of looking at things."

My tears welled again. Darryl's voice — the intonation, the inflection, even the words — sounded so much like Dad.

He nudged my foot with his. "C'mon. Try me. What are big brothers for?"

Hating, I thought.

I inhaled his smoke and held it in my lungs. We all have to die of something, right? Why not cancer? He wasn't leaving; he was settling in. "Okay." I whirled on him. He asked for it. "All right. Question number one: Why was I born this way? Question number two: Why can't she love me? Question number three: Why did he —" My throat closed up. I forced out the words. "Have to die?" I collapsed in a heap again.

Darryl didn't try to put his arm around me or anything, for which I was grateful. We weren't that way. We never had been. I didn't need physical comfort, anyway. I needed a spiritual guide, an angel. A savior.

Darryl finished smoking his cigarette, letting me cry it all out. Through bleary eyes, I watched as he stubbed the butt on a bolt and flicked it, skittering it across the walkaround. He turned toward me. "Could you come up with some harder questions?" he said.

I torched him with a death look.

He elbowed my shoulder. "Never mind. I'll take a crack at these." Scratching his bald spot, he shifted to get comfortable. "Why were you born this way? Well," he expelled a long breath, "I don't know, Mike. Why are any of us born the way we are? Take me, for instance. How come I got all the looks and brains and personality in the family?"

He waited. If he was hoping I'd laugh at his stupid joke, sorry. I didn't have it in me.

"Okay, take me again," he continued. "Why was I born such a

loser?" He lit another cigarette and dropped the pack into his pocket. As he blew out smoke, he said, "I thought for a while I'd made myself this way. A self-made wastoid. Isn't that what you call me? Isn't that what everyone says? You're right. But I don't think it's all me. In the end, it is. We're responsible for how we turn out. But I sure inherited Ma's lack of motivation."

That was the truth.

"You were born special though," he said.

I scoffed.

"No, I mean it. Everybody knows it. All the time I hear people say, 'That Mike. She's one special little gal.'"

I just looked at him.

"They do. Everybody loves you."

Not in the way I wanted to be loved. Not by the people I needed to love me. The one person who could've saved me.

"I think we don't get a choice in the born-that-way department," Darryl said. "All we can do is make the most of what we're given. Does that answer your question?"

"No."

"Question number two. Why can't she love you? I assume you mean that girl who slept over last night. Xanadu, that her name? Sounded to me like she loved you pretty good."

Oh my God. All the blood rushed to my face.

"Yeah, the walls in that house aren't solid steel. And, of course, there's that hole now."

I ground my face into my knees.

"Don't worry. I'm not a peeping Tom."

It didn't mean anything, okay? *Okay?*

"I was at your game today," Darryl said. "I try to make it to most of them."

He did? That surprised me. I'd seen him a couple of times.

"I saw what happened when Bailey showed up."

I died. Again, I died.

"Some people aren't made to love each other, Mike. Take Charlene, for instance."

Why didn't he just shut up? Why didn't he leave? Why didn't he take the fucking hint?

Darryl hooked an arm around one bent knee and took a drag on his Marlboro. "Charlene and I clicked; we really did. After a while, though, I knew it'd never work out for us. We both knew it. She wanted things in life — a home, family. She had this vision of who she'd become, who *we'd* become, as a couple. She bought into the extended family plan." Darryl flicked his ash. "Man. Can you imagine if that was me living the life of Reese? All those kids?" He sucked in a long drag, held it, and blew smoke out his nose. "Me, a father. What a joke."

I don't know, I thought. Darryl'd be an okay father. Not great. He'd keep those kids in line, anyway.

"Reese was a helluva catch for Charlene," Darryl went on. "He's steady and responsible. Ambitious guy. I never could've given Charlene everything she wanted. Everything she needed." Darryl faced me. I was peeking out at him from under my arm. "Understand?" he asked.

No. I hid my eyes. Yes. I didn't want to, but I did. I could never give Xanadu what she wanted, what she needed. She wasn't like me, physically, emotionally. I would always leave her unfulfilled and yearning. Eventually, she'd go looking elsewhere. She'd go looking for guys.

I raised my head a little. When did my brother grow a brain?

"Question three."

"Look, just forget it." I scrambled to my feet.

Darryl scrabbled up after me. "No reason," he said at my back. "No fucking reason that I could ever come up with why he did it."

I hung over the railing, staring down into the nothingness. The dirt, weeds. I felt like hurling. Or hurtling.

"Did you hear me?"

"He didn't fall, did he?" I heard myself say.

Darryl appeared at my side. "No. No, he offed himself."

I knew it. I'd always known it. I'd even said it out loud, acknowledged the truth. Still, I didn't want to believe. My dad committed suicide. Why?

Darryl and I locked gazes for a brief instant and quickly averted our eyes.

"I don't know what the hell was going on with him," Darryl said. "He never talked about personal stuff. We don't do that, you know? Expose ourselves that way. We never have. For, like, a year afterwards, I went around and talked to everyone Dad ever knew, everyone he spent time with, and I asked them why. Why'd he do it? Did he talk about problems he was having? At work or at home? Maybe with this worthless-piece-of-shit-of-a-son who'd never amount to anything."

I cut a glance at Darryl. It wasn't his fault. It wasn't either of our faults.

"The only person who could tell me anything was Nel, and all she said was Dad would come into the tavern lots of nights and go into the storeroom. He'd sit back there on the beer boxes and cry. Not even drink. Just cry."

Dad? I'd never seen him cry. Not once in my whole entire life. "Don't cry, baby," he'd said to me. He was always laughing and joking around. Not only with me. With everyone. He fooled us. He had us all fooled.

The silence grew. Darryl and me breathing together.

"It wasn't you," I told him. "If it was anyone's fault, it was Ma's."

Darryl shook his head. "No."

"Yes."

"No!" he barked. "Okay, yeah, she was starting to go off the deep end even before it happened. When I was in high school — junior high — she began to change. Decline, I guess you'd say. She'd tell me at breakfast she was coming to watch my track meet and never show up. Or we'd be out shopping for groceries and she'd have these panic attacks. I practically had to carry her home. She'd hide in her room and eat all day. Finally, she couldn't leave the house. She didn't have the strength, or the will. Whatever it took. She didn't make it to my graduation."

Yeah, I'd lit into her about that too. How much strength did it require to get your fat ass out of bed and attend your only son's high school graduation?

No wonder she hated me. Feared me.

"She's sick, Mike," Darryl said. "Same way Dad was sick. Depressed or whatever. I don't know. I'm no psychiatrist. All I know is, she's killing herself same as he did. Only slower, over time. There are lots of ways to die."

That sounded familiar. Ma already seemed dead to me. Inside. "She accused me of stealing him from her," I said.

"What?" Darryl frowned.

"Dad." I turned to him. "She said I stole him from her."

Darryl scratched his head. "Huh. I could say the same thing about you."

"What?"

"He loved you most. You know that. He didn't know I was alive."

"That's not true —"

"The two of you were inseparable," Darryl said. "You were always his baby. His favorite. After you were born, he forgot all about me. Me and Ma both."

That's a lie. "What about Camilia?"

"Who?"

"Our sister."

Darryl looked vacant.

"Our sister, Camilia? The baby who died?"

"Oh. Her."

"Yeah, her. What was that, immaculate conception?" Dad didn't forget about Ma. I never stole him.

Darryl said, "I forgot about the baby."

"You forgot a lot of things. Dad loved you. Just . . . in a different way. He went to your graduation, didn't he?"

Darryl snorted. "I wish he hadn't. He was drunk off his ass before he even got there. He embarrassed the hell out of me."

He did? I didn't remember that. Dad never seemed drunk to me. He put on a good act.

"Well, Ma loves you," I told Darryl. "She hates me, but she loves you. She's scared of me."

Darryl met my eyes. "Who isn't?" A grin creased his face. He sobered fast and added, "Ma doesn't hate you. She hates herself. It's the Szabo family curse. We're all born hating ourselves."

I didn't have a response for that. The way I was born . . . The way I am now . . .

"How'd Camilia die?" I asked.

Darryl blinked at me. "I don't know. Why? You think Ma killed her?"

"No!" God.

"You blame her for everything else."

"I do not. I blame you."

We both cracked smiles. I looked away.

"So, how did she die?" I pressed. "Do you know?"

He shook his head. "A heart defect or something. Why are you dwelling on this?"

"I'm not. I just wondered, okay? You wanted me to share so I'm sharing." A heart defect. Defective hearts. That's the Szabo family curse. "She should've gotten help," I thought out loud. "Him too. They should've gone for professional help when they needed it. Ma should still go."

"You're right," Darryl said. "But I think you know as well as I do, we don't ask for help. It's not our way."

Not our way. Our way was killing us. We were slowly dying. Of loneliness, isolation, withdrawal.

A redtail hawk swooped off the top of the water tower and dive-bombed the ground. It scooped up a bull snake and flew off.

"Score," Darryl said. He took the last drag of his cigarette and flicked his butt over the side of the tower. We watched it flutter to the ground and disappear in the long prairie grass. Resting his elbows on the railing, Darryl gazed off into the distance, beyond the town, the wheat fields. "Know what he said to me that morning? The day he did it?" Darryl didn't wait for me to answer. "He said, 'Take care of Mike and your mom. I'm counting on you.' "

I fixed on Darryl. He cupped his hands around his mouth and shouted to the sky, "How'm I doin', Pops? I bet you're happy you left me in charge."

Darryl's head lolled back and a strangled laugh issued from his throat.

The eerie sound sent chills up my spine. "Hey, you're doing okay," I told him. "You're doing good. The bills are paid at home. There's food on the table, a roof over our heads. Sort of a roof."

"I'm a fuck-up, Mike." He wheeled on me. "I always have been. I always will be. Dad knew that. He *knew* it." Darryl's Adam's apple bobbed.

He made me so mad. He *was* a fuck-up. A self-made loser. His whole life was one self-fulfilled prophecy. "If Dad knew, how come he left the business to *you*?" I said. "Why didn't he give it to *me*?" My voice broke. "I loved that business. I would've carried it on. Dad knew that. He *knew* it." I swiped an arm across my nose.

"You were fourteen, Mike."

"So!" I practically screamed at my brother. "I could've handled it. I would've quit school to run that business."

Darryl said, "Yeah. I'm sure that's what he was afraid of." He peered deep into my eyes. My burning eyes. Stupid tears. Darryl reached over to touch me, but I lurched away. He said, "The business is yours, Mike. It's not going anywhere."

"It's *not* mine. He left it to *you* in the will."

Darryl's jaw clenched. "I'll give you the fucking business. Here." He made a grand gesture of handing it off to me; brushing his hands of it. "Everybody knows you're Szabo Plumbing and Heating. You always have been. You always will be. It's just . . ." He trailed off.

What? Darryl wanted his cut? Fine, whatever.

"I thought you'd want to do more with your life is all," he said. "Get out of this town, make a name for yourself. Go to that camp and get recruited. Earn a softball scholarship for college. Have a future. Be somebody."

I am somebody. I was. Mike Szabo. Szabo Plumbing and Heating.

"Do you know you have nearly a thousand dollars in your account already? I deposited three hundred more at the bank this morning."

"What?" I sniped at him.

"The town council agreed to match whatever money I collected dollar for dollar. If that isn't proof people around here love you, I don't know what is."

I reeled back a step. "Wait a minute. You started the Can-paign? Catch-Her-Star? That was you?"

Darryl held up his hands. "Hold your applause. It was the least I could do. You don't listen to me about anything else." He grilled a stiff finger into my arm. "Like boozing your life away."

I slapped him off. "I hate you. How'd you even know about the camp?"

"That folder you left in my auto zines. I called over to Dr. Kinneson and she filled me in."

Darryl? This was his doing? "You decorated all those cans?"

"Well," he said. "I had help with that."

Jamie. I'd kill him. I'd kill him and Darryl both.

Darryl said, "It's kind of weird, but I felt like finding that folder was a sign. Sort of a kick in the pants from Pop, like this was the way I was supposed to take care of you. Since you never take stock of my sage advice."

"Shut up." I stared at him, my brother. The old Darryl was back. The one with substance, heart.

"What if I don't want to go?" I said. "What if I don't want people's charity? Did you ever think of that?"

Darryl didn't answer right away. Finally, he drew out a long, "Yeeeah. And I thought about how Pastor Glenn's always preaching the joy of giving. How everyone would love to feel the joy of giving toward you. How sometimes we need to ask for help, and even accept it when it's offered."

"Did you ever think how I might let them down? How I might not be good enough? How I might disappoint them?" There, it was out. The tears welled again. I knew what it was to be let down by someone you admired, someone you loved. Your hero. MVP. Most Valuable Person in your life.

Darryl was gaping at me, slack-jawed.

"What?" I rubbed my eyes.

"I can't believe it. The great Mike Szabo? Not being good enough? Sorry, I don't buy it. I don't even think you believe that."

"Shut up." What did he know? He didn't know anything.

Maybe a couple of things. He didn't know me.

The wind kicked up and prickled my arms with goose bumps. Darryl shivered. We stood together, quiet, the wind whistling through the metal slats of the tower. Finally, I said what I was thinking: "That article for the *Gazette*. You write that?"

He shrugged. "Guilty. So crucify me."

"I could never lift you to the cross, not with that gut. I'm trying to tell you it was good. You did a good job on the Can-paign, okay?"

Darryl looked shocked.

"Have you been keeping my stats?"

"No," he admitted. "Well, not all of them. Manny helped. And Dr. Kinneson."

I'd kill them too. So much help. "Did you ever think about being a writer?" I said. "Seeing as how you've got all these keen insights into life."

Darryl smiled. "Maybe I'll apply for a job at the *Gazette*." He had a nice smile, my brother. I saw it for the first time in a long time. Saw him. He wasn't a total loser. He had potential. He should use it.

Something else I noticed. "Where'd you get that shirt?" Dad's blue work shirt. "I've been searching for those."

Darryl winced. "I took them. Don't tell Ma. I don't know. I wanted something of his. Something personal"

I closed my eyes. Yeah.

The two streetlamps along Main came on as dusk settled over the town. "So," Darryl heaved a long breath and turned to me, "Any more questions?"

I shook my head. I didn't think I could take much more truth today.

Darryl exaggerated a shiver and said, "This place gives me the willies. Why do you come up here?"

"To get closer to . . ." Sky. Dad.

Darryl nodded, like he got it. "I'm going home." He took a step back. "You coming?"

"Not yet." I had some crying left to do. Crying I'd never done for Dad. Two years. It needed to get out.

Darryl clomped across the walkaround and paused at the gate. "You're not going to jump, are you? I can't afford another fucking ER bill."

I sneered at him. "Don't worry about it. I'm sticking around. If only to make your life a living hell."

He laughed. "You're doing a good job at that." The gate screeked and he disappeared.

The sky was turning pink. Pink and pewter and gold and dragonfire red. Colors blazed the sky, swirling and spiraling over my head. Suddenly I was moving, walking, circling the tank to the west side.

Here was a whole different world. Miles and miles of fields — brown now, but late in summer they'd be filled with sunflowers. I'd forgotten about the sunflowers. Their beauty, their expanse. To the south, River View. Was that the last thing he saw, his final resting place?

Oh Dad.

I lowered myself to the walkaround, dangling my legs off the edge. Now, when I wanted to, I couldn't cry. Guess I was all cried out. It'd hit me later, I knew. I wouldn't fight it anymore. I needed to get beyond it.

The sun began a slow descent, infusing the sky with dazzling hues of brilliant color. A spectacular show. They probably didn't have sunsets like this in Michigan.

Michigan. It seemed so far away. I was going to Michigan. I had to go. Not to make a name for myself, like Darryl said. I had a name. Mike Szabo. Mighty Mike Sza-bo. Darryl was wrong about Szabos hating ourselves. I didn't hate myself. Not for being born. Not for the person I was. I was a good person. I tried to be, anyway, kind and generous. Giving. I could be more forgiving, maybe, toward Darryl. Toward Ma. I'd try.

I didn't even hate myself for being gay. I just wanted to get to the place where Jamie was. Stage three. Past wishing I'd been born different, to accepting that I was. Finding the joy in that. It didn't seem so far to go.

It was away from Coalton though. To a bigger place, more populated, where I'd find her, the girl of my dreams. The one who wouldn't think it didn't mean anything, okay? The one who'd realize that being loved meant everything. It meant everything to me.

Beyond Xanadu, there was a girl out there I could love, one who could love me back. And when I found her, I'd bring her to Coalton.

I'd show her this town, these people. We'd build a life here. Because Coalton was a good place to make a life, raise a family. This town was a family. It'd raised me.

Jamie'd been right about Xanadu. She'd played me. She'd used me. I didn't hate her for what she'd done; I could never hate her. But I didn't think I'd be finding her a job at The Merc. I wouldn't be calling her later.

I watched until the sun slipped under the horizon and put itself to bed. Bed sounded good. I needed sleep. Dreams too. Big dreams. My dreams. I thought of Dad. Where he was. What he was doing. Rest in peace, Pops.

I stood and took one last look around. I'd never get enough of this, the beauty of Coalton. I raised my eyes to the sky. "Good night, Dad," I said. Just in case he was up there, painting me a dawn.

PRETEND YOU LOVE ME
Questions for Discussion

1. Growing up in small-town Coalton, Kansas, gives Mike, the main character in this story, a distinct sense of place. How would you describe your sense of place in the world?

2. Discuss the differences between growing up gay in a small town versus an urban setting. What might make it challenging no matter where you live?

3. What roles do your family and community play when you're finding or creating your own identity?

4. How do Mike and Jamie deal with their homosexuality differently? How do they comfort and support each other?

5. Why do you think Mike falls so hard for Xanadu?

6. Do you think Xanadu "played" Mike? Why or why not?

7. Do you see Mike's brother, Darryl, as a heroic figure? Why or why not?

8. How did Mike's relationship with her father guide her life? Did his death change her view of him?

9. Who gained the most in this story? Who lost the most?

10. What do you predict for Mike's future? What do you hope for her? What about Jamie? Xanadu?

TURN THE PAGE FOR A SNEAK PEEK
AT THE COMPELLING NEW LOVE STORY
FROM JULIE ANNE PETERS!

she
loves
you,

she
loves
you
not...

JULIE ANNE PETERS

NATIONAL BOOK AWARD FINALIST

Prologue

The night Sarah and Ben showed up out of the blue. You should've known or suspected something was wrong. The vibe was weird, but then it had been for a while, and Sarah was … Sarah. Up in your room even, when she kissed you and you lost yourself in her. The moment it all came crashing down.

On the plane ride here, to the vast unknown that is Carly, the stupidest thing kept running through your brain. That toy in Dad's office. You learned at some point it wasn't a toy, that it had a name: Newton's swing. Steel balls in a row suspended on a frame. When you pulled balls back on one end and let them go, the same number of balls swung out from the opposite end. The harder you let go of the balls, the farther out the balls on the other side flew. You even remembered the principle, that for every action there's an equal and opposite reaction. How many hours did you spend in Dad's office playing with those balls? He'd say, "Cut it out, Alyssa. You're driving me nuts."

The physics law works not only on objects but on people. Because of Sarah's action, her force and thrust on your life, you went flying into space and spinning out of control.

Chapter

1

What does a stripper keep in her closet? The left side is packed with low-cut tops, short skirts, and dresses. No real skankwear. The clothes don't reek of smoke or booze. Carly has this silk kimono with an embroidered lotus on the back that's very cool. I take out the robe to hold it up to me in the mirror, and then I hear the front door open. Quickly, I stuff the kimono back in the closet and slither out of Carly's room.

"Alyssa. You're up," she says as I casually saunter down the stairs from the loft. Does she think I sleep all day? She sets her workbag on a chair in the dining room and digs into the front pocket for her cell.

"You got a lot of calls," I tell her.

"Here?" She peers over her shoulder at the cordless in the kitchen.

"I didn't answer them," I say. "I only saw a couple of IDs. Someone named Geena?"

"Did I forget to charge my cell again? I keep doing that. Spacey." She knuckles her head.

"And Mitchell."

Carly sighs. "Did the phone keep you up?"

"No. I wasn't asleep." I wish I could sleep, but every time I close my eyes, I think of Sarah.

Carly slips off her high heels and pads across the dining room to listen to her messages, checking to see how many johns have called. I'm just guessing. She fishes through her purse, finds her cell, and plugs it in. "You're welcome to have people call you here," she says. "I can get you a separate number or switch over your cell service so it's free."

"That's okay." I don't want to tell her no one would call me; no one wants to talk to me ever again. Besides, I won't be here that long.

At the wet bar she pours herself a glass of wine. "Why don't you give me your cell number, and I'll give you mine."

"I don't have a cell," I tell her.

She arches her eyebrows as she sips. Swallowing, she says, "Why not?"

I hesitate. "Dad took it away."

She lowers her wineglass. "Why?"

I don't want to tell her.

She shakes her head. "He's such a prick."

I'd like to agree, but Dad was right to take my phone. I have no control over my impulses.

"Have you eaten?" Carly asks. "I don't even know what you like to eat. What do you like?"

"I'm not hungry."

She cocks her head at me like, *I know you're lying.* With her long fake fingernails, she presses the telephone number pad. I wander over to the French doors, my back to her, watching her reflection in the glass. She removes a hoop earring and sets it on the counter.

"Geena, hi," she says into the phone. "I just got in, so I want to eat and shower before tonight. Go ahead without me. I'll see you at Willy's." She listens and then laughs. "Hey, girl. It's a living."

I take in the view — the bare side of a mountain. If I remember right, Carly called it Caribou Mountain. I feel her eyes on the back of my head, so I twist around and force a weak smile. She pulls the scrunchie from her ponytail and, shaking out her hair, says, "You have my eyes. You should let me give you eyelash extensions."

I stifle a gag.

Her phone rings again, distracting her from me. Her business card says she's a massage therapist and personal trainer. I know it's a cover for how she spends her days. She doesn't even try to hide that she's a stripper by night.

She ignores the caller and turns back around. "You need your brows shaped too." From her bag, she retrieves a leather case. She unzips it, and inside are fake eyelashes and glue and makeup. She pulls a chair out at the dining room table and motions me to sit.

When I don't obey, she juts out a hip and fists it.

I want to say, *Don't tell me what to do. You're not my mother.* Except — she is.

She pats the back of the chair. "Come on. It'll be fun."

"No, thanks." It comes out kind of snotty. As I pass in front of her, I resist the urge to check out her eyes.

The only time we've spent together before now was an occasional Saturday when she was passing through town on her way to New York or Miami or wherever she was working at the time. She'd drop by out of the blue to take me for the day. It always pissed Dad off. He hates Carly.

And now his hate extends to me.

"I'm going to work out for a while before dinner," she says, stretching her arms over her head, interlocking her fingers. "You could join me. We could talk." She smiles.

Does she think I'm fat? I'm not as tall and thin as she is, although I've probably lost fifteen pounds in the last month, with being sick and the trauma around Sarah.

"Would it be okay if I watched TV?" I ask.

"Of course. You can do whatever you want, Alyssa. Consider this your home." She opens her arms to me, like *Come get a hug*. I won't go running to her just because she's here now and I need her. A lump rises in my throat, and I don't want to lose it in front of her.

The plasma TV is in the formal living room, so I veer off that way. Carly says, "Not in there."

The sharpness of her voice stops me cold.

"There's a high def in the family room and one downstairs in my exercise room." The trilling of her cell snags her attention again. As she slides it open, she hustles up the stairs to the loft.

I watch TV for, like, ten minutes and get bored. Up in my room, which is actually a *guest* room, not *my* room, I plug in my nano earbuds to listen to my music. I must fall asleep, because when I open my eyes, it's dark out. Goose bumps prickle my skin.

She keeps the air-conditioning on Siberia. In stocking feet, I make my way to the panel in the downstairs hallway, the electronics control center, and punch off the fan. There's a note on the dining room table, propped up against a bowl of floating daisies.

ALYSSA
OFF TO WORK. SORRY WE HAVEN'T HAD A CHANCE FOR A
REAL GIRL-TO-GIRL. IF YOU GET HUNGRY, THERE'S SALAD
OR YOU CAN ORDER OUT.
XO CARLY

She left me her American Express card.

I feel weird spending her money, eating her food. Just... being here.

This grip of loneliness begins in my stomach and crawls up my chest and lungs and throat. I pick a daisy out of the bowl and hold it to my nose, closing my eyes, and the bitter odor reminds me of Sarah and home and... everything.

I pluck a petal. "She loves you." I drop it in the bowl and pluck another. "She loves you not...."

A volcano of hurt erupts inside, and I burst into tears.

Virginia Beach
Last September, first day of junior year

You saw Sarah in the hallway. You didn't know her name then; you'd never seen her before. She glanced right, then left. She turned in a circle. You recognized that first-day panic. You told M'Chelle and Ben to go ahead and you'd catch up. "Um, can I help you?" you asked.

"Yes!" she cried. "I'm so lost. I thought I knew where my next class was, but it's not here. It should be right here." She pointed to a wall where a *GO WILDCATS* banner was taped. "Is this like a tricked-out school or something, where doors appear and disappear?"

"That would actually be interesting," you said.

She laughed. You took her class schedule and immediately determined the problem. "You want 104B, not C. I don't know why they numbered the rooms exactly the same in every wing. It's confusing."

"I'll say."

You handed back her schedule, and she smiled into your eyes.

At the time you thought she looked young, with her braces and ponytail, her too-new jeans and brand-new layered tops right off the back-to-school rack. You remember how terrified you were the first day of freshman year. You said, "I'm going that way if you want me to show you."

"Would you? God, I'd love you forever."

The gauge on your gaydar jumped a few notches. Down, girl, you chided yourself.

She was cute. Too much to hope she might be a lesbian. Too young for you, anyway.

As you walked down the corridor, she said, "I'm Sarah."

"Alyssa." The late buzzer sounded, and you had to hustle to find her class and then get to yours in the adjoining wing. The next time you saw her was in the gym during club week. You and M'Chelle volunteered to man (make that woman) the Gay/Straight Alliance table. You were supposed to talk to people about what the GSA was, the goals and mission, hand out information and permission slips. Was Ben there? He might've had to man (make that girly man) the Gaming Club table.

"Ooh, I love to recruit," M'Chelle said, checking out the freshmen who were trickling in. She rubbed her hands together. "Fresh meat."

"Stop." You elbowed her.

She slapped a rainbow sticker on your forehead, and you immediately removed it.

Almost everyone made a wide berth around your table. Except her. She headed straight for you.

"Hi, Alyssa," she said.

She remembered your name. "Um, hi." You didn't remember hers.

"Hi," she said to M'Chelle, "I'm Sarah."

Sarah. That was it.

"I was hoping there'd be a GSA here. We had one in my middle school."

"Cool," M'Chelle said. "Where'd you go to school?"

"Bethel."

You'd never heard of it. Having a GSA in a middle school was pretty progressive, especially in Virginia.

She took the information sheet M'Chelle handed her. "You don't have to identify as queer — LGBTQ — to join," M'Chelle told her. "That's why it's called Gay/Straight Alliance?" M'Chelle tilted her head to emphasize the inclusiveness.

"Oh, I know." Sarah smiled at M'Chelle and then at you. She had this turquoise shade of blue eyes with flecks of silver. You have a weakness for blue eyes. Alyssa, you admonished yourself. Jailbait.

Still, if she was lesbian.

"It's basically a social group, but this year we're going to do more with diversity issues and tolerance. And we always do Day of Silence." M'Chelle was our newly elected president of GSA, acting all presidential.

Sarah said, "I can't believe we need our parents' permission." She rolled those baby blues at you.

"It's so stupid," M'Chelle said.

To M'Chelle you went, "On three. One, two..." In unison, you chanted, "Forge the sig!"

All three of you laughed. M'Chelle said to her, "Are you interested?"

Her eyes held yours, and you felt that hitch in your lower belly.

"Oh, yeah," Sarah said. "Definitely interested." She flattened the info sheet, with permission slip, to her chest and then wandered off, eyeing you over her shoulder.

M'Chelle about died laughing.

"What?" You blushed. "Quit it."

M'Chelle wheezed. "Fire up the barbie. We got us a smokin'-hot rack of baby back ribs."

I rip the daisy to shreds. If I could only go back and erase every moment, every memory of Sarah's existence. If I could only figure out what went wrong.

Carly's makeup kit is sitting next to a freestanding mirror on the table. I press the button on the base of the mirror and it lights up, illuminating my face. I'm someone I don't know anymore. A reject. A throwaway person. Little girl lost. Sure, Sarah. I should never have helped that little girl lost find her way.

Provocative, heart-wrenching, hopeful . . .

Read all of Julie Anne Peters's inspiring novels

Available wherever books are sold.
www.lb-teens.com